I0817664

FINAL FANTASY XIV Chronicles of Light II

FINAL FANTASY XIV
Chronicles of Light, Volume II

Planning & Production
Square Enix Co., Ltd.
Editor-in-Chief: Kazuhiro Oya
Editors: Tomoko Hatakeyama, Ayako Watanabe
Production: Toru Karasawa, Toshihiro Ohoka, Tsutomu Sakai, Kyohei Date

Writers
Square Enix Co., Ltd.
Natsuko Ishikawa, Banri Oda, Tomohiro Kawasaki, Daichi Hiroi, Yuki Kimura, Koji Yoshida, Shoko Miyagawa, Megumi Onozuka

Cover and Interior Illustrations
Square Enix Co., Ltd.
Toshiyuki Itahana

English Translation
Square Enix Co., Ltd.
Paul Chandler, Phillip Bright, John Crow, Kathryn Cwynar, Joshua Duran-Carlson, Thomas Mills, N. Nasir, Paul Palmer, Kenneth Pinyopusarerk, Lori Snyder, John Townsend

English Editors
Morgan Morris Rushton, John Crow

Special Thanks
Square Enix Co., Ltd.
Nao Matsuda, Kosuke Yamaguchi, Ricardo Antonio Vilaró
The Entire FINAL FANTASY XIV Development Team

Book Design & DTP
TOKYO TEXT Co., Ltd.

Supervision
FINAL FANTASY XIV Producer & Director Naoki Yoshida

With the exception of the four written for this compilation, these stories were first published on the official FINAL FANTASY XIV website, The Lodestone. They have been further edited and reformatted for print.

ISBN (print): 978-1-64609-419-6
ISBN (ebook): 978-1-64609-881-1

Library of Congress Cataloging-in-Publication data is on file with the publisher.

Manufactured in the U.S.A.
First Edition: December 2025
1st Printing

Published by Square Enix Manga & Books, a division of SQUARE ENIX, INC.
999 N. Pacific Coast Highway, 3rd Floor
El Segundo, CA 90245, USA

SQUARE ENIX
MANGA & BOOKS
square-enix-books.com

CONTENTS

To you who have made the journey to the iridescent waters of the aetherial sea, I bid you welcome. Speak softly, my passing neighbor, for here abide we who have shed our mortal burden and attained a measure of peace.

Even were that not so, the coming performance shall feature no actors to deliver dialogue, nor musicians to provide accompaniment. Instead, you shall bear witness to memories unraveling. The works of the living—motes of passion dancing amidst endless tides. Of this spectacle at the threshold of mortal existence, we make a gift. A gift to you, who are part of the unending cycle.

And so, without further ado, let the show begin. There is no bell to ring, I fear, nor curtain to rise. Your eyelids, drawn shut at the brink, I pray you now open once more . . .

Act I

Shards of a Shattered Star

A World Forsaken

Objective: To record and analyze events surrounding the Eighth Umbral Calamity, based on information extrapolated from statements and reports made by Cid Garlond.

Following a series of decisive victories, the former imperial colonies of Doma and Ala Mhigo overthrew their provincial rulers and secured independence from Garlemald. This prompted other occupied territories to rise up against their oppressors and join forces with the Eorzean and Eastern alliances.

The Garleans responded by marching the bulk of their troops to Ghimlyt on the Ala Mhigan border, where the Allied armies gathered to repel them. Though peace negotiations were attempted, the differences between the opposing sides proved to be irreconcilable, with open warfare the only viable recourse.

Against expectation, the well-equipped and highly organized imperial legions failed to capitalize on their early advantage, allowing the Alliance to stage a counterattack. One possible cause for such an ineffectual display on the part of the Garlean troops is the high proportion of conscripted soldiers, who—in the words of Master Cid—lack the "conviction" required to maximize their combat capabilities. Unfortunately, I am not programmed to assess such unquantifiable variables, and this theory must therefore be dismissed as mere conjecture. I can, however, state with some degree of certainty that the arrival of the ones known as the Scions of the Seventh Dawn was a critical factor in the Garleans' defeat.

After the Empire's withdrawal, Cid Garlond and his Ironworks colleagues—including the elusive Nero Scaeva—traveled to the Burn on the Othardian subcontinent to bolster the field generators at Seiryu's Wall in preparation for the Garleans' next offensive. They set about their work unaware of the events unfolding elsewhere that would change the course of history, until they received the first report, which, according to Master Cid, was unusually brief:

"The Garleans have deployed a powerful new weapon on the Eorzean front. We tried to contact our comrades at Rhalgr's Reach, but received no reply."

Despite lacking several essential details, the message was entirely accurate. The reason the sender had been unable to communicate with said comrades was simple: they had been annihilated by Black Rose, a poisonous gas developed by the Garleans. This ingenious weapon halts the flow of aether within organic beings, causing near immediate cessation of respiratory functions. Being highly potent and capable of rapid dispersal across a wide area, the majority of settlements in nearby Ala Mhigo were almost entirely depopulated in the aftermath. Contemporary reports state that the damage extended far beyond Alliance-held regions such as the Black Shroud and Thanalan to several imperial territories, resulting in significant loss of life.

As my present configuration is only equipped with basic audiovisual receptors, I must draw my conclusions from limited and—I am compelled to admit—unreliable sources of information. At the time of Black Rose's deployment, I was otherwise engaged deep within O'Ghomoro and was unable to make detailed observations of the weapon's effects. The yellow-plumed creature that was accompanying me appeared to sense something at the approximate moment that the gas was released, gazing into empty space with an expression that mortals describe as "perturbed."

A World Forsaken

Objective: To record and analyze events surrounding the Eighth Umbral Calamity, based on information acquired from Cid Garlond.

Master Garlond has made numerous attempts to initiate conversation with me, despite my current vessel being no more than a simplistic automaton conceived as a plaything, lacking any oratory mechanisms with which to respond. These utterances, though made in a state of obvious intoxication, provided me with invaluable data. While the individual recordings contain a wide range of observations, many are superfluous to my investigation, so I have compiled only those I deem relevant.

Black Rose wrought immeasurable destruction to organic lifeforms, resulting in widespread environmental upheaval. The ambient aether ceased to flow along its normal channels and stagnated, rendering the land barren and uninhabitable. Inevitably, the wild imbalance of natural energies affected neighboring regions and, in some cases, led to sudden and unpredictable alterations in flora and fauna. Overnight, the crops on which man relied for sustenance became toxic, further increasing the death toll. In the aftermath of these unprecedented disasters, the communities formed by sentient beings fell into disarray, and all forms of societal organization, from small settlements to entire nations, were abandoned as individuals struggled desperately to avoid annihilation.

It did not take long for the cascading environmental repercussions to be felt in Garlean territory. Due to the aftereffects of Black Rose, the ceruleum that once supported daily life in the Empire and powered its magitek armies failed to combust. The machines duly fell silent, bereft of the energy required to set them in motion.

The creatures that escaped the initial devastation were thrust into a battle for survival. Among them, those belonging to supposedly civilized races were particularly quick to turn on their brethren in a bid to seize control of land and resources. While they attempted to justify these wanton acts of violence with a range of superficially logical explanations, it is my assessment that greed and desperation were the primary motivating factors behind their actions.

Master Cid and his colleagues frequently referred to this situation as a "quagmire," though in a figurative rather than a literal sense. Much like an actual quagmire, it threatened to pull mankind into an inescapable predicament. Correct interpretation of the audio data recorded at the time is dependent on accurate comprehension of this metaphorical expression.

The mortals who found themselves in this "quagmire" were no longer governed or protected by social conventions or societal norms, instead reverting to a more primitive way of life, closer to those referred to as "beastkin." However, certain groups of sentient beings were reluctant to accept this descent into savagery, with Garlond Ironworks being one such example.

Its members expended considerable time and effort in largely unsuccessful attempts to bring an end to the numerous conflicts that had erupted. In addition, they hunted down and reprimanded those who sought to profit from the desperation of their fellow survivors, and offered a safe haven to the exploited. While their deeds earned them the support of many like-minded individuals, the number of comrades gained paled in comparison to those lost in the days which followed.

I recorded one particular incident in which a Lalafellin engineer was carried back to headquarters after being mauled by a carnivorous beast while overseeing the digging of a well. Despite the treatments administered by trained chirurgeons, his wounds were beyond healing, and his vital signs began to fade. As he lay dying, one Ironworks member in particular—a Roegadyn male considered to be the stricken Lalafell's closest friend—refused to leave his bedside. Gripping the patient's limp hand and whispering words of encouragement appeared to revive him for a few brief moments. Drawing on his final reserves of stamina, the diminutive engineer demanded that his counterpart live on and produce offspring to continue his legacy. To this, the larger man responded with a trembling voice, "It's high time you started a family yourself," though that was, regrettably, not a realistic prospect.

Smiling, the Lalafell replied, "Sorry, but no one will ever compare to her . . ."

These were his final words.

The Lalafell's death prompted an emotional response from my feathered associate, who pressed his tearstained cheek against the lifeless body. Some time later, once Master Cid and his colleagues had finally exhausted their supply of tears, they gathered for a lengthy discussion, their expressions growing ever more despondent as the talks continued. They eventually arrived at the conclusion that they lacked the means to restore their shattered world, with their only viable option being to entrust future generations with the knowledge that they had accumulated, in the hope that their successors may one day find a solution. This was met with some resistance, however, as many expressed disapproval at the idea of forsaking those in the present day in order to save a world they would never live to see. Unable to deny this, Master Cid simply nodded and said:

"Even so, our sacrifice will not be for naught."

With that, Garlond Ironworks found what I believe to be its true purpose.

Objective: To continue recording and analyzing events surrounding the Eighth Umbral Calamity.

The researchers of Garlond Ironworks continued to investigate the process by which Black Rose—possessed of a destructive power far exceeding its creators' expectations—triggered the Eighth Umbral Calamity. They believed that understanding the nature of this catastrophe could reveal a means by which it might be averted entirely. Their aim was to change the past to create an alternate reality in which the Calamity never occurred—a feat rendered conceivable by their knowledge of the advanced technologies of fallen civilizations. However, many of those who would bear the burden of continued existence in a world ravaged by Black Rose failed to see this as a viable stratagem. Such responses were consistent with my projections, as it is generally the primary objective of all life-forms to secure their own survival in the here and now.

Many of Master Cid's followers either refused to cooperate or expressed a desire to leave the Ironworks altogether. Certain former employees went as far as to appropriate equipment and supplies by force before heading into the wilderness to fend for themselves.

Although the vast majority opposed Master Cid's radical proposition, a select few remained to lend their assistance. Research into the Eighth Umbral Calamity continued, aided by experts in the fields of magic and aetherial science. During this period, one loyal scholar noted that while preventing the disaster may not solve all of the problems that had afflicted the world of the past, the one dubbed the "Warrior of Light" would still be alive. The various members of the team each had their own personal connection with the deceased, and the notion of creating an alternative past in which their hero survived the Calamity met with unanimous approval.

It is impossible to discern the manner in which this theory affected the motivation of the Ironworks staff and their associates, or whether some other external factor triggered a sudden increase in their mental faculties, but the fact that they eventually succeeded in unravelling the mysteries surrounding the Eighth Umbral Calamity is a matter of record.

In addition, by presenting their plan as an attempt to save the Warrior of Light rather than a bid to rewrite history, they were able to gain the support from survivors of many different species and subgroups. Representatives from various settlements came to donate resources and foodstuffs to Garlond Ironworks, despite possessing barely enough to sustain themselves. Many of them were also acquainted with the Warrior of Light, some even claiming to have been beneficiaries of the late hero's acts of philanthropy.

A semiaquatic creature known as a "Namazu," who had arrived bearing donations, imparted information apparently gleaned from premonitory dreams. The following is an extract of his recorded testimony:

"The world was never in such a ruinous state in the visions sent to me by the Big One, no, no. Seigetsu the Enlightened said that the future I witnessed was part of another history, a different chain of events with no Eighth Umbral Calamity at all! Whatever that means . . ."

It remains to be seen whether this is anything more than the nonsensical ramblings of an anthropomorphic catfish. But I shall store it in my data banks for future analysis.

Over time, support for the Ironworks continued to grow, their cause finding allies in the most unexpected of quarters. Memorably, during a routine mission transporting research materials, one of their vessels was ambushed by bandits, only to be rescued by an immense airship captained by a golden-haired Hyuran female claiming to be a sky pirate. She is reported to have made the following declaration:

"My mother was once snatched from the jaws of death by this champion of yours. As her successor as queen of the skies, I mean to see that debt repaid in full!"

Instances of Ironworks representatives being extricated from perilous situations were abnormally frequent, their apparent saviors including multiple non-humanoid entities. In one such example, an emissary who was attacked and thrown overboard while crossing the Ruby Sea reported waking upon the shore of a nearby island with a vague recollection of having been borne to safety by a large beast, possibly chelonian or serpentine in nature.

In a similar incident, an ill-equipped messenger would have fallen to his death while traversing the peaks of Sohm Al, were it not for the intervention of a colossal white-winged creature, later identified as a dragon. According to the official report, there was a brief exchange in which the Dravanian rescuer expressed its disinterest in the affairs of man, particularly his insatiable thirst for conflict, before disappearing into the clouds. It must be noted that due to the lack of independent eyewitnesses or material evidence, this account remains unverified.

Objective: To continue recording and analyzing events surrounding the Eighth Umbral Calamity.

With admirable dedication for a mortal, Master Cid continued to labor until the end of his natural lifespan. The years of painstaking research clearly took their toll, however. One day, as he penned the final words of his grand theory, I observed his hand quiver as if the weight of his quill had at last defeated him. Breathing a weary sigh, he turned to Master Nero, who made the same shrugging gesture that I have observed on many occasions before saying:

"Well, it certainly took you long enough."

Previous analysis of Master Nero's behavioral patterns indicates that this was meant as a compliment, though Master Cid's exasperated expression appeared to suggest it was not received as such. Be that as it may, the brief smile which subsequently crossed his lips led me to believe that he understood his counterpart's intent. Slowly rising to his feet, he then shuffled towards a well-worn device referred to as a "Boilmaster" and poured coffee into two metallic containers, passing one to Master Nero. They duly raised the receptacles, and brought them together in a percussive "toasting" motion—a ritual I have seldom witnessed, there having been little cause for celebration. The pair sipped their drinks and, for once, Master Nero refrained from expressing his distaste for the brew; a noteworthy anomaly. Master Cid then turned his gaze to the stack of papers on the desk and initiated the following exchange:

"So, do you think this mad scheme of ours will ever come to fruition?"

"Only time will tell, Garlond. Lest you forget: the road to ruin is lined with good intentions—which your young protégés have in abundance. We can but hope they do a better job of saving the world than we did."

"Indeed. It's in their hands now."

No further words were exchanged, and my sensors yielded no indication as to the thoughts which occupied the pair's minds.

So, as they stood in silence, I attempted to form my own answer to Cid's question. I could by this time emulate the cognitive processes of organic beings, as I had done on one particular occasion many years ago, in the moments immediately prior to the irreversible dissolution of my previous vessel.

With what might be termed "wakeful eyes," I reviewed the reports made by Ironworks members following their investigations into the Crystal Tower, the mechanical primal known as Alexander, and the interdimensional rift, the findings of which were instrumental in formulating the plan to alter the past. Thus did I discover that each of these missions had one common element: they ended with a key figure entering a form of self-imposed exile, not unlike a deep slumber. At times such as these, when one is to be separated from one's companions, whether it be by sleep or by death, there is a phrase which I have found to be particularly fitting:

"Good night."

And after the night comes the morning, as the sun rises to greet the new day. While it may already be too late to mend this dying world, there are those who would strive to create a place where the sun will shine again, not for their own sake, but for those in a past that may yet be saved.

I think this must be what mortals call "hope."

It is . . . beautiful.

An Unpromised Tomorrow

When one looks upon the chronicles of history, those immovable tomes of ages past, one is certain to find the mark of a great many notable figures. Conquerors, pioneers, heroes—men and women whose lives serve to punctuate the endless passage of time.

I am not one of them. No builder of nations, me, nor less a savior of the oppressed. I am but a humble engineer who had the good fortune to become the eighteenth president of Garlond Ironworks. For two hundred years now, we have kept alive the dream of "Freedom through Technology," passing on the legacy of our predecessors to the next incumbent upon our retirement—save for one poor fellow, who died after three days in the role.

In the end, however, the only name history will remember is that of Cid Garlond, our own appearing as mere footnotes to his legend.

A legend we are only too happy to preserve.

Garlond Ironworks' first home was a workshop in Revenant's Toll, and I am told there was a time when people would flock from every corner of the realm to gaze upon its wonders. A stark contrast to our present operation. Our base now sits nestled in what remains of the Keeper of the Lake, a monument which both time and necessity have done much to diminish, a legion of scavengers having taken their pick of what the elements saw fit to spare.

Indeed, the site is in utter shambles. And yet I can think of no better place for us to have set up shop. The surrounding lake serves as a natural obstacle to intruders, and the dragon whose sinuous frame still holds the whole hulking heap together is said to have shared a storied history with an old friend of the founder. In short, a site as apt as it is inaccessible.

It was there that our engineers and some few volunteers were enjoying a hard-earned rest. After several sleepless nights, work in the Crystal Tower was at last complete, and on the morrow it would be transported across time and space to another world—the First. Meager though our resources were, we had laid on a veritable feast to commemorate the occasion, and one and all had enjoyed the much-needed respite to the fullest. Indeed, many had reveled to exhaustion, choosing to sleep where they fell on the meeting hall floor.

Though I, too, should have been counting sheep, my mind was busy enumerating reasons to stay awake—which were, it assured me, many. And so I sat there, staring into the fire. Thankfully, I was not without company.

"I've always wondered," I began, turning to regard my fellow insomniac.

His crimson eyes seemed to glow in the firelight. A gift from the blood of Allagan royalty, he called them. A gift by which the Crystal Tower had borne him to us. In the morning, he would make another journey, this time bearing all our hopes and dreams for a better tomorrow with him. And though he had assured us it was a mission he gladly accepted, I could scarcely imagine the weight of that burden.

There was so much I wished to tell him, but I put it aside to first ask a question that had long been burning in the back of my mind.

"Why did you do it? Why did you stay behind in the Crystal Tower?"

He blinked at me in disbelief before letting out a curt sigh.

"You would ask me this now?"

"Would you rather I asked you on the morrow?" I replied with a rather forced grin. "I understand you were the only one who could have done it, and hindsight has shown it to be the right choice. Were it not for you, our dreams would be just that. But you couldn't have known that at the time. Not for sure. What if we had never opened the tower?"

What a relief it was to finally speak the words aloud. I feared he would take them as little more than idle banter, but the thoughtful swishing of his tail suggested otherwise, as he returned his gaze to the fire.

An age seemed to pass as we sat there in silence, but I knew my wait for an answer was over when a faint smile tugged at the corner of his mouth. It occurred to me then that he hadn't been gazing into the fire, but *through* it, at something far brighter.

"I would have slept for all eternity," he laughed. "Which would, if nothing else, have been ironic. For it was only as the gates of the tower were closing behind me that I realized what it meant to awaken to one's true purpose."

"Go on . . ."

"In those days, I could but dream of being counted with the likes of Cid, Nero, Biggs, and Wedge—indeed, I would *still* give my right arm to achieve half of what they achieved . . ."

He proceeded to paint a picture of our forebears as paragons of invention, able to race from concept to product in the time it would take him to put on his boots. And then he spoke of his mentor, Rammbroes, head of the Sons of Saint Coinach, and of his pride at having been chosen to take part in the expedition to the Crystal Tower.

He told me that the mission had taken a most unexpected turn when their party was joined by a pair of scholars named Doga and Unei—whom they later discovered to be clones born of Allagan technology which had lain dormant within the tower for millennia. Apparently, when the structure was unearthed in the chaos of the

Seventh Umbral Calamity, the horrors within had awoken, prompting the pair to seek the aid of G'raha Tia and his companions in thwarting the dark designs of the tower's creator, one Emperor Xande. What began as a simple quest for knowledge thus became a grueling climb to the top of the tower, culminating in a battle with darkness itself. Yet far from laying claim to these feats, he was careful at every stage to recall the pivotal role played by the greatest hero of the age. One immortalized in song and script, and remembered to this very day.

"Before me stood the very embodiment of heroism, the fables of my childhood made flesh. And in the light of so shining an example, I saw at last the part I had to play. How could I do aught *but* remain in the tower?"

"Quite easily," I chuckled, "were you and your exemplar not cut from the same cloth. Being of a rather less heroic disposition, however, I can tell you that *my* first act, having endured such an ordeal, would have been to go home to bed. But tell me . . . were you not scared?"

"Of course I was. But courage is not the absence of fear." He leaned back then, to stare up at the ceiling. "It is the triumph over it."

The roof, I should probably mention, was in the process of being repaired, and not without the odd gap. Clear nights offered small glimpses of the stars twinkling in the sky, and G'raha Tia seemed entranced by them as he continued to regale me with memories of days long past.

"So long as we were together, whatever foe stood against us, whatever twist of fate conspired to undermine us, I believed with all my heart that there was nothing we could not do."

I went to speak, but when I glimpsed him gazing up at the heavens, his eyes full of steely resolve, I could only smile and wonder at what a fascinating life he had led. At how a single individual could affect the fates of so many. G'raha Tia, Cid, my grandfather, and the countless others who had given their all to see our plan come to fruition. Would the Warrior of Light have believed that so many lives could be changed? Or what inspiration others could take from so tragically foreshortened a tale? Whatever the answer, the hopes and dreams we had labored so long to keep alive would soon be realized. Even to think about it made my heart skip a beat. I cleared my throat.

"And we have to keep believing. For a brighter future."

I proffered my hand in our customary manner, and G'raha Tia returned the gesture.

"That we do, my friend. That we do."

The following morning, the hour of his departure came at last. We stood upon the precipice of an unknown future, contemplating the promise of a tomorrow we would never see. Yet still we prayed. That our sacrifices had indeed sown the seeds of a better tomorrow. That at journey's end, our departing friend might reap that joyous harvest too. We prayed as the Crystal Tower stirred to life, and vanished in a blinding flash of light.

I can't say for how long we stood there at the shore of Silvertear Lake. It wasn't until the sun broke the horizon that I noted the passing of time—and the deafening silence.

We could only assume G'raha Tia's mission would carry on across the rift, and that we had played our part to its completion. Yet with our duty done, I couldn't help but feel a part of me was missing, much like the Crystal Tower from the skyline of Mor Dhona. I told myself that the void would soon be filled by a sense of accomplishment . . . but I wasn't sure I believed it. For two hundred years we had toiled and struggled, and our efforts had been met, not with thunderous applause, but the languid lapping of the lake.

In the end, it was one of my companions who gave voice to the question on all of our minds.

"Will we be disappearing too, then?"

I would be lying if I said we understood the ramifications of altering history. In the selfsame instant the tower had disappeared, it was quite possible we could have been erased from existence. Yet there we remained. And while that came as something of a relief, it brought with it the unwelcome suspicion that G'raha Tia had failed in his mission . . .

Conscious that others were watching, I shook my head. Causality be damned. I refused to believe our friend would allow our travails to be for naught. The Eighth Umbral Calamity *had* been averted, if not for us then in a divergent timeline.

Unbeknownst to me, the others were busy reaching the same conclusion, and a laugh escaped the lips of someone in the crowd. Though the world yet remained in ruin, it was ours. A comforting—even comical—thought, considering what very well could have come to pass.

Expunction from the pages of history no longer seeming to be in prospect, we enjoyed a moment of solace. Our forebears had overcome a great many trials that we might live to see that day, gaining control of the Crystal Tower, taming the wings of time, even harnessing the forces of the rift, and we were not about to let the event pass unmarked.

Our moment of solace lasted exactly as long as it took the earth to begin shaking. Plucked from our reverie, we frantically scanned our surroundings hoping to find the source of the tremors even as someone cried, "Over there!" We followed his gaze towards the Keeper of the Lake, and what we saw there left us speechless.

The wreckage we dared to call home was collapsing. Steel plating creaked and groaned in protest as it broke apart before disappearing beneath the water. Unbidden, the image of the rickety roof came guiltily to mind, and I wondered if we had been too lax in our renovations. Then the whole pile began to move. The serpentine frame wrapped around the ship was breathing, writhing, breaking free of its resting place.

"By the gods!" a voice shrieked from the crowd. "Midgardsormr lives!"

Our panic was soon drowned out by a deafening roar that all but shattered the heavens.

My ears still ringing, I looked up to see that Midgardsormr had taken to the sky. After circling the lake, he bent his course towards us.

No one dared move, nor even speak. We could only watch in horror as he made his approach. The engineer in me demanded to know why the great wyrm had chosen that moment to awaken, and I dully recalled the Crystal Tower–shaped gap on the horizon. Its departure had doubtless disturbed his rest . . . My blood ran cold at the thought of what might happen next. But my doom-laden musings were soon interrupted by a low, rumbling voice.

"The tower . . . Is this your doing, children of man?"

"A thousand apologies," I croaked. "We didn't mean . . . to wake you."

An agonizing silence followed. Before I knew it, my clenched fists were slippery with sweat. I tried telling myself I had nothing to fear, that the dragon had been a friend to Cid Garlond and the others once upon a time, but try as I might, I could not escape the feeling that I was about to be incinerated. The wyrm grunted.

"Long have I waited. Watched as the world was shaped by your hand. Through war and calamity have I seen you struggle, devoting your fleeting lives to a dream you will never see."

For an instant, I contemplated pleading our case, but he spared me that embarrassment.

"Such constancy in creatures so inconstant is impressive."

Midgardsormr loomed closer then, his eyes fixed on a young girl and the plaything in her hands. I felt my stomach drop as I recognized it as my grandfather's Omega replica. Old as it was, my colleagues jokingly referred to it as a senior member of the Ironworks, and its age was certainly beginning to show. It randomly shut off, however often we replaced its power core, and faulty sensors ensured it haphazardly bumped into everyone and everything, including Midgardsormr himself, when his body still served as one of the walls of our workshop.

In all honesty, building a new replica would have been less troublesome than fixing it. Yet we had agreed that such niceties should wait until after work on the Crystal Tower was finished. I cursed myself for not having stripped the infernal thing for scrap.

Tilting his head down further to regard the faltering automaton, Midgardsormr made a most unusual sound. And though I knew nothing of dragons, I was almost certain it was a laugh.

Recognizing the wyrm's amusement, the trepidation I had felt but moments before vanished in an instant. My blood was racing, and I could feel an unfamiliar heat welling up within me. Suddenly, I remembered G'raha Tia's words from the previous night.

"Courage is not the absence of fear. It is the triumph over it."

Gathering my wits, I began to realize that Midgardsormr's presence was not frightening, but exciting; that his choice to appear before us at that of all moments was an omen of much-needed change. His eyes shifted to regard me, then, and I found the courage to return his unblinking gaze.

"Tell me, child of man. What dost thou see at dream's end?"

"I see . . ."

In my mind's eye, I glimpsed a world where the Eighth Umbral Calamity had never come to pass, where Eorzea's champion bestrode the realm, unbroken. But just as suddenly, I saw that this was G'raha Tia's future, and not ours. Yet the skills we had honed to make that dream a reality were still ours to employ . . . Another image flashed before me.

"I see a world pulled back from the brink."

This time, Midgardsormr's booming laughter was unmistakable.

"Very well. Under my protection shalt thou and thine rebuild, gaining newfound knowledge and the wisdom to wield it. Thus shall the children of man usher in a new Astral Era."

And so our journey began anew. Would that G'raha Tia could see all that we will accomplish. Though we shall remain forever on different pages of history—and different *books*, besides—I take comfort in knowing we strive for a future of the selfsame brightness.

A Dream Partnership

Amaro in whom the old blood has quickened have a lifespan far exceeding that of their unawakened kin. Yet even these long-lived specimens are not spared the ravages of time. Eyes become clouded, wings grow feeble and frail . . . And in the case of the hulking Seto, leader of the Wolekdorf amaro, old age has brought with it an ever-growing desire to doze, as if the combined weight of more than a hundred winters were bearing down upon his eyelids. This day is no different. The venerable creature surrenders to the siren call of sleep as the sweet scent of flowers fills his nostrils, his mind's eye soon flickering with visions of a warmly remembered past.

A young amaro, emaciated and exhausted, stretched himself flat in a sunbaked corner of the city of Nabaath Areng. One glance at the pitiful creature told a story of protracted abuse, of a body beaten and deprived of anything beyond the bare essentials required for survival. No man nor beast would willingly choose those searing flagstones for a bed, but the bulky wagon to which the amaro was harnessed afforded him little choice in the matter. So here he would lie, conserving his strength until his owner returned to rouse him.

Ah. The master has returned.

A corpulent Hume emerged from a nearby stone-built shopfront and strode purposefully towards the wagon, a cruel-looking whip gripped tightly in his sausage-like fingers. Crafted from the elastic sinews of a lizard, the lash delivered a terrible sting, which the amaro knew only too well. Even if fatigued to the point of collapse, when the whip spoke, he somehow found the will to answer.

It comes . . .

Would it be the neck or the shoulder? The back or the rump? The amaro hoped it would miss his snout, scrunching his eyes shut in anticipation of that agonizing snap which preceded every journey. But it never came.

Confused, the amaro opened his eyes to see a young man standing directly between him and the scourge of his days. The stranger seemed scarcely out of boyhood, yet he balanced an oversized greataxe upon one shoulder with apparent ease.

"Surrender yourself, Lamunth! The 'Jade Fox' has been unmasked."

Thus did the amaro first meet Ardbert, the man who would later name him "Seto." It was an encounter which would, in the fullness of time, blossom into a true and lasting friendship.

The seed for this roadside confrontation had, in fact, been sown several moons earlier, with the discovery of fake gemstones in the markets of Nabaath Areng. Of such cunning artifice were the jewels that even the most practiced appraisers had been taken in by their seeming perfection. Pride stung and reputations in tatters, the members of the Jewelers' Guild had offered a bounty of staggering riches for the capture of the "Jade Fox," as the mystery counterfeiter had come to be known.

Word soon spread, and would-be bounty hunters from across the land had converged upon the city in a mad scramble to claim the reward. Yet despite their best efforts to sniff out the Fox, they succeeded only in uncovering still more of the counterfeiter's fabrications.

It was a pair of novice adventurers—Ardbert and Lamitt—who finally brought the Jade Fox to justice. They had enlisted the aid of Branden, once a knight of Voeburt, and with his help, pierced the intricate veil of illusory magick placed upon the forgeries. Thus laid bare, the baubles' origins could begin to be deduced, the evidence leading them at last to a man by the name of Lamunth.

Upon collecting the bounty from the grateful jewelers, the three agreed to split the lavish purse equally. Yet recalling Branden's not inconsiderable thirst for revelry, the other two had expressed reservations about awarding him his share all at once. They knew as well as he did that the whole lot might be drunk in the space of a night. And so he had grudgingly accepted Lamitt's proposal to spread the spoils over a period of moons, even if it *did* mean joining them on the road for a while . . .

Ardbert, for his part, had his own plans for this newfound fortune. Learning that the authorities had taken possession of Lamunth's maltreated amaro, he wasted no time in negotiating a price for the creature.

The amaro meekly tottered along behind his liberator until they reached the party's lodgings, whereupon he immediately collapsed into a listless heap.

"What were you thinking, boy?" Branden quipped. "The beast's all skin and bones. I doubt he could survive a turn around the city, let alone a trip across the desert. Why, there's not enough meat on him for a bowlful of stew!"

The amaro snorted loudly, as if taking umbrage at the insult.

"Don't listen to that lout, Seto," Ardbert said warmly, scratching the underside of the amaro's jaw. "I'd sooner see *him* in the pot than you. And we'll show him your true value soon enough!"

In fairness to the knight, the city officials had shared Branden's low opinion of "Seto." They deemed the weakened creature a worthless investment, and would, Ardbert knew, have soon put him out of his misery. Unable to bear the thought, the young man had been moved to act. It was simple compassion which drove him, yet there was also curiosity—for in the piteous creature's demeanor, he swore he had glimpsed a spark of something more.

Born on a small isle in the seas of Kholusia, Ardbert had spent his childhood amongst the birds and the beasts, there being no others of his age to play with in the mountain village he called home. It was there that his grandfather, the boy's only living relative, had instructed him in the care of all manner of livestock. This education included the habits of the noble amaro, and thus Seto's unusual behavior had instantly piqued Ardbert's interest. He had watched the poor creature bide his time, waiting until his cruel master had departed before sinking down to rest, in what appeared to be a deliberate bid to escape further punishment. And such rare intelligence was a thing to be nurtured.

"Time to earn your keep, Seto!"

At a whistle from Ardbert, the amaro trotted further out into the Fields of Amber and flopped heavily to the ground. Ardbert, meanwhile, quickly ducked behind a boulder, taking his place alongside the crouching figures of Branden and Lamitt. Local merchants had hired them to slay a vicious pack of coyotes that threatened the caravan route, and a bewildered Seto was playing the role of bait.

"Still not much of a meal, is he?" Branden muttered, his bulky frame folded double in an awkward effort to remain unseen. "I hope those beasts are hungry . . ."

Dimly aware of the larger man's grumbling, Seto mused over his recent change in circumstances. Unlike his old master, Ardbert never struck or beat him. And he always made certain Seto had plenty to eat and drink. He had even brushed the filth from his feathers. Ardbert's touch was kind, and when he scratched that spot beneath Seto's jaw, the amaro almost felt like purring. It was an unfamiliar feeling.

Then there were the "tricks." Seto was mystified as to their purpose, but not wanting to anger his new owner and risk everything he'd gained, he did his best to perform as Ardbert directed. And now it seemed he was to be sacrificed.

I should have known. Men are all the same.

As he lay there despondent, resigned to his fate, Seto spotted the pack of coyotes approaching at an easy lope, and realized why he had been fed so well.

"Seto—to me!"

Greataxe raised, Ardbert came charging in his direction. Seto tilted his head in momentary confusion, then sprang to his feet. Concluding that he had *not* been left to die after all, he set off towards his new master as fast as his legs would carry him. And though he was unable to take flight, his body having yet to recover from years of malnourishment, he flapped his wings with frantic strength all the same.

The predators duly took up the chase, and the sight of the earth-bound amaro scrambling along in a blind panic had Branden in tears of laughter.

"Hah! The scrawny rascal can move when it suits him!"

Bridling at the knight's mocking tone, Seto changed course. A dozen yalms short of his onrushing master, the amaro hopped high into the air and glided straight over Branden's head. Moments later, the coyotes, which had been snapping at the amaro's tail, were now snarling in the big man's face.

"Wha—? Argh!" Branden yelped, his smirk evaporating as he brought his shield up just in time.

Thus did the adventurers draw in their quarry and put them to the sword. They would go on to complete many such tasks, with the mark's nature dictating how Seto would play his part: a feeble cry for the ravenous; a mighty roar for the territorial.

The true range of the amaro's acting skills would only become apparent much later, however, during the hunt for the "Amber Terror"—a predatory bird of nightmarish size known to haunt the Hills of Amber. Even Ardbert was astonished to hear Seto mimic the mating call of a female phorusrhacos, his near-perfect cries serving to lure out their otherwise elusive prey.

Wounded in the initial exchange, the Terror chose to flee, and the adventurers were compelled to give chase, eventually cornering the monster in its nest and bringing it down amidst a frenzy of scything talons.

"Would you look at that!" exclaimed a panting Lamitt, who, even in the fierce heat of the fields, refused to doff her dwarven helm. "It had its very own treasure trove."

True enough, atop the bed of dried grass sat a haphazard pile of glinting trinkets.

"Well, well, well! I'd heard these birds had a fondness for shiny things!"

Branden's eyes sparkled as he reached down and plucked a saucer-sized medallion from the heap. He held it aloft, and the heavy disc flashed like a second sun at midday.

"Now *this* is a find," he crowed. "Nabaath royalty would award such tokens to victorious generals. It must be over two hundred years old . . . which means the Terror must have taken it from a descendant. Or dug up a grave." The knight grinned hugely. "Either way, it will fetch a handsome price from the right collector."

As he moved to tuck the prize into his pouch, Ardbert shot out a hand and snatched the medallion away.

"No so fast," the younger man snapped, with a grin of his own. "This medal should go to the one who earned it."

"Is that so?" Branden replied, unabashed. "Then you'd best give it back. Who shielded you all from that axe of a beak? Who delivered the killing blow to that monster's neck?"

"Why you, old friend—and fine deeds they were. But you wouldn't have had the chance to do either had Seto not lured the Terror out of hiding in the first place."

Ardbert rummaged through his pack for a moment, then produced a narrow leather strap. This he threaded through the medallion's eye before hanging the trophy around Seto's neck.

"For a comrade, brave and true!"

The amaro snorted loudly and held his head high.

"You'll hear no argument from me," chuckled Lamitt. "I'd rather see Seto get his due than watch Branden drink another tavern dry."

"Bah, have it your way!" Branden exclaimed, throwing his hands up in surrender. "Three cheers for Seto! The wiliest amaro that ever lived!"

Light-hearted though it was, Ardbert's gesture that day served to recognize Seto as an equal—a full partner in the band's growing list of accomplishments.

Such was their success, in fact, that they were approached soon after by one Renda-Rae, a seasoned hunter who wished to join the party renowned throughout Amh Araeng as the bane of beasts.

Later, in Lakeland, they would enlist the sword of the silver-haired Cylva, while delving into the mystery of a missing daughter of noble lineage. And back in Amh Araeng, their ranks would swell once more with the addition of the redoubtable mage Nyelbert, who had, until then, been their rival.

Together they traveled. Together they fought. Together they suffered. Plentiful were their hardships, yet for Seto, the joys of their journey far outweighed the sorrows.

Awakening from his nap, the elderly amaro breathes a small, contented sigh at the weight of the medallion around his neck. It had been lost to him, once. He had been defending the settlement from stray sin eaters when the leather strap, stretched taut by a neck grown twice as broad, suddenly snapped, sending the golden disc tumbling into the black depths of the lake. How kind of the traveler to retrieve it for him.

It was at his request that the pixies of Lydha Lran had crafted the strap from which the medallion now swings—imbuing it with a dreamer's charm in so doing, if he is any judge. How else could one account for the remarkable clarity and frequency of these slumbering sojourns to the sun-dappled past?

Suddenly, he is seized by the urge to travel. To *soar.* Perhaps he cannot traverse the realm as once he did—not with these aging bones—but a jaunt to the far shore of the lake should not be beyond him.

He would visit the one they call the Weaver, and thank them for this gift; for these blessed dreams.

The amaro stands and unfurls his wings, stretching them out to catch the breeze. Old though he may be, he would remember how it feels to fly again.

Small Mercies

This is a tale of days long past—before the infernal Light burned unrelentingly in the skies over Norvrandt. In a chamber deep within the castle of Gruenes Licht, a young Nu Mou peered intently into a flask, its contents illuminated by the moonlight that cascaded from the clerestory above. Beq Lugg was one of very few of their kind here in Voeburt, a nation dominated by the Drahn and Galdjent—by whose grudging alliance the kingdom had been formed. The youngster's aptitude for all things arcane, however, was undeniable, and so it was that they were awarded the post of court mage, along with the use of this chamber, where they toiled day and night to unravel the mysteries of the soul.

Though it was closer to dawn than dusk, Beq Lugg gave no thought to sleep. It was at this late hour that Princess Pauldia always came calling. The cheery Drahn girl with the curious glint in her eye was fond of Beq Lugg, whose retiring, reclusive nature could not have been more different from the fawning courtiers among whom she had grown up. And so she would come, time and again, to speak of every trifling thing that had caught her interest that day.

This night, however, the princess offered no word of greeting, nor any other word for that matter. Sensing something was amiss, Beq Lugg set down the flask and turned to see their guest's brow uncharacteristically furrowed.

"Dear Pia, whatever is the matter?"

Only the princess's closest acquaintances used the nickname, and she had always been pleased for Beq Lugg to do so, yet she gave no sign of having heard her friend.

"Don't tell me—it's that Sauldia has inherited the three treasures, is it not? Yes, I, too, would be jealous were I in your place."

The royal treasures of Voeburt—three relics emblazoned with the mark of the two-headed wolf—had been passed down for generations from ruler to anointed heir. The bequeathal ceremony, which had taken place a few days prior, officially recognized Pauldia's elder sister as the next queen of the land. And while Beq Lugg was not particularly well versed in the affairs of mortals, even they could imagine how this might affect the girl.

"Jealous? No—that's not it at all! I *love* my sister, and no one could be wiser, or kinder, or worthier of the throne than her! I want nothing more than to stay here and support her as I always have! But Father . . . Father now talks of *marriage*!"

Looking at the poor child, her shoulders shaking and tears welling in her eyes, Beq Lugg chided themself inwardly. They had assumed from the tales of their brethren that all mortals, however unconsciously, coveted power and position, but they should have known that this one was different. Why else would she visit *them* of all people. Yet how were they to comfort her? Beq Lugg had scarcely begun to ponder this conundrum when another visitor—a tall and slender Drahn draped in lavish white robes—strode airily into the chamber. Barely acknowledging Beq Lugg, let alone begging leave to enter, the court mage Tadric made straight for the girl.

"Oh, my poorest Princess Pauldia," the mage began, dripping with affected sympathy, "no one feels your pain more than I. Yet you must understand His Grace's position. Only once you have been married into another family will the people come to accept your dear sister as the one and true queen."

Though visibly taken aback at the sudden intrusion, the girl nonetheless answered quickly.

"I know this, of course! And that Father only wants the best for his kingdom and his subjects. But what of his daughter—?!"

"Oh, I *quite* agree, Your Highness," the mage oozed. "Fortunately, King Roaldric is a wise and compassionate man. Could he but see the depths of your dismay, I have no doubt he would conclude that an unsought marriage will bring happiness to no one." Here he paused before adding, "*As I should be only too glad to tell him*—with your permission, of course."

The princess blinked disbelievingly.

"You would do that? For me? Thank you, Tadric! Thank you with all my heart!"

Her eyes brightening again, she gave Beq Lugg a sideways glance and whispered, "Nice to see that *someone* understands me."

Shoulders sagging, the Nu Mou let out a weary sigh and returned to their solitary labors.

Some days later, the princess came once more to Beq Lugg's chamber to report that the matter had been settled. After hearing Tadric's plea on her behalf, the king had agreed to abandon plans for her betrothal. There was, however, one condition—that Pauldia renounce her status as princess, and serve instead as a court mage.

"It is a position I would be only too glad to accept," she declared with a hint of longing, "had I any aptitude at all for magic. And so I come to you. You told me that you were studying the secrets of the soul, yes? That you believed there was a means by which the hidden talents that slumber within us might be unlocked?"

Averting their eyes so as to avoid the princess's pleading gaze, Beq Lugg shook their head.

"My research is far from complete, Pia. While it is true that I have developed an elixir which can safely stimulate one's dormant physical capabilities, awakening arcane talents is another matter entirely. The procedure would entail making irrevocable alterations to the subject's soul—which I could not in good conscience attempt without exhaustive and *lengthy* testing."

Beq Lugg did their best to explain the dangers. The soul was a complex and delicate thing, they said, and even the slightest misstep could do untold harm to her mortal body—or worse. But Princess Pauldia would not relent.

"I don't care! All I want is to stay here with my family! If I cannot meet Father's conditions, I will be sent far away. We . . . we may never see each other again!" The girl's tone grew ever more impassioned as she continued, "*Please*, Beq Lugg—you are the only one who can save me!"

Though they would not admit it, the young Nu Mou shared her feelings. They had no desire to lose their best friend in that lonely castle—their *only* friend beyond their flasks and tomes. Besides, after all the kindness the princess had shown them in their time there, did they not owe her that much?

After staring at the floor for a while and finding no help there, Beq Lugg grudgingly nodded.

The next day, Pauldia's newfound powers were recognized by the king, and she proudly took her place among the finest mages of the court.

Though her status had changed, Pauldia's visits remained as frequent as ever. Listening to the girl breathlessly sharing the minutiae of her days, Beq Lugg's lingering doubts about the powers they had bequeathed to her were gradually eased. And yet their heart was not entirely free of worry.

"Word has it that strange beasts have been appearing near Longmirror Lake of late. Promise me you'll take care of yourself, Pia."

In the decades since King Roaldric I had ascended to the throne, the Kingdom of Voeburt and its people had enjoyed a period of nigh-uninterrupted peace. Yet this only served to make the news that a shepherd boy had been found butchered more shocking. The youth had reportedly fallen prey to a fearsome beast which had appeared as if from nowhere. Though the fiend was quickly dispatched by the royal knights, a similarly grisly incident followed some few days later, casting a pall over the city that would not be lifted.

While it was initially assumed that the beasts had wandered into the kingdom from parts unknown, further investigation uncovered a more disturbing truth. The "beasts" had, in fact, been sons and daughters of Voeburt whose bodies had undergone a ghastly transformation through the influence of some unholy power. This revelation plunged the kingdom into chaos, no one knowing when their neighbors or even their loved ones might metamorphose into bloodthirsty abominations.

In the dark days that followed, it was Princess Sauldia who arrived like a comet to pierce the nation's gloom.

"I told you no one was worthier of the throne!" Pauldia beamed as she raced into the room. "Sauldia now fights at the vanguard in our battle against the monsters!"

The girl had every reason to be proud of her sister. Relations between Voeburt's knights and its court mages had always been strained at best and outright hostile at worst. And yet, Crown Princess Sauldia had managed to unite them under her leadership, assembling a fighting force blessed with enough might and magic to put down each threat as soon as it arose. Though the cause of the ghastly phenomenon remained a mystery, the crisis had at the very least been contained.

Back at the castle, however, the matter weighed heavy on Beq Lugg's heart, privy as they were to a terrible secret: that the methods they had revealed to Pauldia in her hour of need might, in theory at least, turn mortals into monsters. But could she stoop so low? No. The Nu Mou shook their head, comforting themself that it would never so much as occur to the pure-hearted girl to use the knowledge they had shared in such a way. And so they returned to their studies, hopeful that the worst was past.

Alas, it was not long before news arrived to give the lie to that hope. Crown Princess Sauldia had been wounded on the front lines—failed, it was said, by one of her knights, who had since been expelled from the guard in disgrace. Faced with such distressing tidings, Beq Lugg could only seek solace in their research, engrossing themself ever more deeply in their work. Whatever was behind all this, it was none of their concern. Sooner or later, the culprit would be found, and forced to answer for these odious acts. The world had a way of balancing itself out, and this time would be no exception. Everything would be all right in the end.

How many moons had passed since then? Their every waking hour consumed by their studies, Beq Lugg could scarcely say. That night, too, they were peering intently into a flask when the door to their study flew open and someone raced into the room. Turning around with a start, their gaze was met by none other than Sul Oul, a fellow Nu Mou who served as a steward to the king.

"Beq Lugg! At last, we have unmasked the villain behind these infernal transformations!"

Beq Lugg suppressed a gasp. This was the moment they had been waiting for, but also the one they had dreaded. They did their best to appear impassive as Sul Oul continued.

"It was that fiend Tadric! A band of adventurers as good as caught him in the act!"

Beq Lugg breathed a sigh of relief, knowing now beyond a shadow of a doubt that their dear Pauldia was innocent.

"I will be joining the adventurers to hunt the traitor down and bring him to justice. But monsters swarm the grounds even as we speak. You must lock yourself in here until the danger has passed!"

Their warning delivered, Sul Oul made to leave, but Beq Lugg called after them.

"Wait! Where is Pia—where is Pauldia?!"

"Rest easy," the older Nu Mou replied firmly. "She is safe in her chambers, and I have arranged for one of the adventurers to keep watch over her. And with that, I must go!"

Yet Beq Lugg could not rest easy. They had met with the adventurers of whom Sul Oul had spoken, and while they seemed an eminently capable bunch—one Beq Lugg had been happy to assist—they were, nonetheless, strangers to the land. And Pauldia's life was at stake. Panic gripping their heart, they dashed out of their study, hells-bent on preventing their best and only friend from coming to harm.

But Beq Lugg was a scholar, not a fighter, and with monsters lurking around every corner, they could do little save scuttle between the shadows. Despite their best efforts, however, they soon found themself face-to-face with a slavering beast.

"M-Mercy!" they croaked, aghast.

"Out of the way, you stupid mutt!"

The silver-haired swordswoman was in front of them before Beq Lugg knew she was there, plunging her blade into the hideous creature, which seemed every bit as shocked as its prey. After watching it slump lifeless to the ground, the elf cast a cold glance at the cowering figure at her feet, then raced down the hall without so much as another word. If Beq Lugg was not mistaken, she was one of Ardbert's companions—which meant she may be the selfsame adventurer to whom Sul Oul had entrusted Pauldia's care!

Instantly forgetting the umbrage they had taken at being likened to a dog, they set off after the woman as fast as their legs could carry them, coming upon her just as she was kicking down the door to Pauldia's private chambers.

"How *dare* you?!" Beq Lugg screamed, barging past the adventurer in search of their friend.

And there she was. Beq Lugg stood frozen. From behind them, the swordswoman advanced, her blade drawn.

"Too late, it would seem. All we can do now is put her out of her misery . . ."

The sight of the elf's bloodstained blade was enough to shake Beq Lugg from their reverie.

"No! Have mercy on the girl, I beseech you!"

"Are you mad?!" the woman spat back. "Look at her arm! It's already begun!"

Beq Lugg knew in their heart that the adventurer was right, yet they did not yield. They could not stand idly by and let their best friend—however hopeless her plight—be slaughtered before their eyes.

"Please, I—I have studied the secrets of the soul! I may very well be able to save her. You must spare her life! You *must*!"

It was a lie, of course. The process, once begun, was quite irreversible. Yet they had to try.

The adventurer gave the Nu Mou fairly clinging to her leg a searching look, then let out a sigh.

"This castle has a gaol, yes?"

Cursing all the while, the silver-haired swordswoman knocked Pauldia unconscious and carried her down to the dungeons, with Beq Lugg muttering directions. No sooner had she locked the door than she took to her heels, doubtless eager to join her companions in their search for the traitorous Tadric.

Beq Lugg, for their part, sat still as a stone in front of the cell, waiting for their friend to awaken. And when at last she did, it was with words unlike any they had heard her speak before.

"Hells take you, Tadric!" the girl seethed, her voice a feral snarl. "You promised me you would bury my sister and make me queen! I tricked that dog into divulging the secrets you craved—and you *betrayed* me!"

It was as if the girl could not see the friend of whom she spoke sitting there right before her eyes. Clawing at her skin, she began to daub the dungeon walls with glyphs in her own blood.

"Wretched sssister! Were it not for you, I could have lived in happiness with my family forever! Curse you, Sauldia! Curse your rotten soul!"

Beq Lugg had sat agog throughout the whole tirade, but at this they found their voice once more.

"Enough, Pia! Is your sister not part of the family you hold so dear?! How many times did you tell me how much you loved and admired her?!"

Slowly, the girl turned. Peering into her widened eyes, Beq Lugg could see a dawning realization, as if she were only now remembering things long forgotten.

"You . . . you are right . . . I . . . I love Father . . . and Mother . . . and my sister, too . . . Why . . . ? Why did I . . . ? What have I done . . . ?"

As the words left her lips, she slumped forward, a shadowy mist beginning to seep from her body before dissipating into the air. In that moment, Beq Lugg saw the truth—that Tadric had bound the poor girl's heart with dark magicks and forced her to do his bidding.

"Forgive me . . . Beq Lugg. My . . . friend . . ."

A tear tumbled from her cheek and struck the dank stone floor. When at length she raised her head, Beq Lugg saw that the curious glint in her eye had been extinguished. Only despair remained there, her stare a wordless cry for mercy.

Before the vesper bell tolled that day, Beq Lugg left the castle, never to return. And though Ardbert and his fellows succeeded in apprehending the architect of these tragedies, they could not save Sauldia from one final act of spite. Thus was the proud kingdom of Voeburt robbed of its heir and condemned to an age of decline. When the Flood came, it was a shadow of its former glory, all but powerless to defend itself against the sin eater hordes—and so did the kingdom fall, and fall for good.

It is claimed that poorest Pauldia was still in her cell on the day Gruenes Licht was finally abandoned. As for what became of the ill-starred princess after that, neither Beq Lugg—nor anyone—can say.

In the Beginning, Beyond the End

A pile of milky white bones.

Nestled in the crook of an ancient tree's gnarled roots, the bones glowed dully in the sunlight. *Those are mine.* A baseless conclusion—their life was as fresh as the large flower blossoming around them.

They uncurled, indulging in a leisurely stretch of limbs and wings, and gazed up at the massive, fluted tree that embraced their remains. A mess of round red arils and jagged green fronds. Beyond, a golden sky.

Before long, a gaggle of similarly shaped figures came flitting towards them crying, "Madbloom! Madbloom!" A curious word, but one amongst the crowd came forward to silence the fervor.

"Enough, enough! First, a name—nothings have no place in our world. Once they have a name, their mind will clear."

So began a second discourse, ending with a triumphant outburst. This time, a different one lifted their voice, speaking slowly and with purpose.

"Yours is the color of forgotten dusk, smothered by unending Light. From east to west shall you fly, coveting the treasures of Darkness. Let it be thus, now and ever after, *Feo Ul.*"

A beautiful name. Somehow, they knew those bones longed only for beauty.

They accepted this gift, taking flight with their newfound fellows away, away from the ancient tree. Yet they glanced back. The bones lay mute, offering no words of parting. Well, something must be said to commemorate this beginning—or ending, as it were.

"What a happy ever after!"

Those were Feo Ul's first memories.

After learning some rhyme and reason from their compatriots, Feo Ul's insatiable curiosity sent them flying off to explore. Even the wonders of Il Mheg soon grew tiresome, so they began venturing abroad, which only invigorated calls of "Madbloom!" amongst the others. *Let the idle gossip.*

One day, in high spirits, Feo Ul was bound for their favorite destination of late: the Crystarium. Mankind's bastion against the Light, marked by the enigmatic tower at its heart. The static brightness of the sky above was defied by the bustle of the city's people below. Not an idle hand nor an ill-tempered soul among them. All were busy, all were merry. So vibrant and full of life—to Feo Ul's considerable delight.

But as mischief is in a pixie's nature, so too did Feo Ul desire to see some small misfortune befall these earnest people. Setting minor things awry each visit fed their ravenous hunger.

They started with unlatching the gate to the livestock pen. Dashing past the legs of a grazing amaro was enough to spur the birds from their confines to their keeper's dismay. Leaving a cacophony behind them, Feo Ul next made for the gardens. Apples hung heavy on the trees, and a well-placed charm ballooned them to the size of a Hume's head, exploding as they struck the ground one by one. Then to the barkeeper's cask that sprung a magnificent leak, then to the shopkeeper's wares that danced in midair . . .

The city seethed like an agitated beehive.

"It's that pixie!" They had been spotted, but too lithe and agile were they to be caught, cavorting just beyond the reach of grasping fingers. After many a game of hide-and-seek, a hooded figure was led into the fray. Feo Ul understood people's rules and behavior well enough to deduce that this was their leader.

"Then I'm your mouse, sweet kitten! Catch me if you can!" They flipped once in challenge before darting off.

A pause—then a roaring cheer. "Get 'em, Exarch!"

Glancing over their wings, they spied the hooded figure in mid-dash, robes aflutter with surprising speed.

What greater amusement could Feo Ul ask for?

Their contest would not be easily settled. Time and again, Feo Ul was driven to near capture, only to escape a swiping hand by a hairsbreadth. Restraining magicks were countered by pixie charms as all throughout the city they ran, pursuer and pursued. At long, long last, the former came to a halt in some quiet corner, shoulders heaving with exertion. *Too slow!* Buoyant with victory, the pixie circled around and tugged at the cowl that had refused to fall back—a final taunt.

The heavy fabric gave way to brilliant red. Whirling about, the man met Feo Ul's gaze. Both eyes were also a rich and vibrant ruby.

"How lovely! We're the same shade, you and I! You must be Feo Ul as well!"

". . . What?"

"Am I wrong? What's your name, then? You're the leader of this place, no? But just look at your arm—it's made entirely of crystal! Why is that?"

Feo Ul peppered the intriguing man with query after query, and his lips twisted with consternation as he carefully considered his every answer. *Clever, this one.* Not everyone exercised due caution when conversing with pixies.

"I know," they declared. "Let us be friends. If we are, I shall work no further mischief upon your city, nor will I attempt to befuddle and bewitch you with wordplay. But you must promise the same—we must be as flowers and bees."

They hovered before him, excited and impatient. At length, he nodded.

"Very well."

So it was that Feo Ul learned the man's name. The Crystal

Exarch—or so he was called by his people. His body was an extension of the tower, and he sought salvation for this world plagued by Light. Ensuring Feo Ul's silence on the matter, he also divulged that his true home lay beyond a nigh-impenetrable rift. But while his secrets did not end there, to lay all bare would imbalance the scales, for Feo Ul had not nearly enough secrets of their own.

The rest must remain a mystery, they decided. Mysterious things were far more interesting anyway.

Though it was a place where they could no longer engage in prankish pursuits, Feo Ul came to frequent the Crystarium more than any other. Over years they watched the city grow more robust, more intricate, more elegant. Oh, how curating beauty was essential to survival—who was the bricklayer who had spoken thus?

Scraping mortar, the artisan had explained that while the people of the Crystarium would never give up, acts of creation served to reaffirm their commitment. Pride and hope required constant reinforcement. So Feo Ul watched mankind persevere, brick by charming brick . . .

Of course, Feo Ul also saw how bricks come tumbling down.

That day, the city was unusually grave. A Lakeland hamlet had been attacked, and the contingent sent to defend it suffered heavy casualties. Following the flow of pedestrians, Feo Ul arrived at Spagyrics. Blankets lined the floor in place of beds, upon which more than twenty men and women lay in varying states of distress. Some had sustained lighter injuries, but most were still fighting for their lives, their pain a gruesome chorus. Chirurgeons worked tirelessly, clothes and faces flecked with blood.

In a corner of the room knelt the Crystal Exarch, weaving magicks to tend a wounded guard. When Feo Ul drew close, they nearly cried out in shock. They knew the invalid: Liruna, a Viis old enough to have seen the world before the Flood, and who had been one of the first to seek shelter at the Crystarium's tower. She had joined the nascent city guard and used her woodland hunting skills to protect others, alongside her partner, Guecelo. Just last year, the couple had been blessed with a child.

"Don't steal her away," Liruna had chuckled when Feo Ul came across the mother feeding her babe. She allowed them to touch the child's cheek, soft and round, as she snuggled against her mother's breast.

A breast now soaked with blood as Liruna lay prone, her face sallow and stomach torn.

The Exarch's feverish efforts produced little result; Liruna had gone too long without treatment. After binding her wounds and administering medicine, all that remained was to pray her spirit would return from the brink. Yet so weak was her rattling breath that Feo Ul thought it might fail should the flow of magicks cease.

Through the strained breathing came faint, broken words. The Exarch bent his head close. "Guecelo turned . . . sin eater . . . I killed him . . ."

Feo Ul understood now—the twenty-strong guards gathered here were the only ones who had retained their natural forms.

"I failed . . ."

Tears welled in Liruna's lavender eyes and spilled down her face. "Exarch," she rasped. "The others . . . my Lyna . . . look after them . . ." Her eyes slid shut, freeing more rivulets of mourning.

It took not half a day before she passed.

Another day the Crystal Exarch spent assisting chirurgeons, taking stock of the situation, and consulting with the Settlement council. Another day without rest.

Feo Ul trailed behind him as he at last returned to the tower, trudging up the stairs to the Ocular. His weary feet carried him deeper, into the Umbilicus. After a moment's hesitation, Feo Ul slipped through the gap of the closing door, before it shut with a dull thud. At once, their friend slumped against the door. He sighed, bowed head swallowed by his hood. A crisp silence settled over the room.

Then, the smallest of sounds. Something like an unworn pebble had clattered across the floor. Then another, and another. Feo Ul soon discovered its source.

The Exarch's crystal arm was falling apart.

The tower's immense power rendered him immune to the ravages of age, but the transformation had taken its toll. "It pained me so much at first that I was bedridden for weeks." He laughed, testing his afflicted arm. "But now I hardly mind it. Granted, imbuing the crystal with the requisite flexibility was a challenge indeed."

This "challenge" had involved smashing the solid crystal to bits before painstakingly stitching it back together with magick. Stony beasts might employ such methods to become animate, but the dumbstruck Feo Ul had met neither person nor pixie foolish enough to do anything of the sort to themselves. That said, the simulacrum was as functional as flesh. The enchantment had become part of him, preserving its form even while he slept.

So he had once confided in them long ago. And yet, the Crystal Exarch's arm continued to crumble. He made no move to recover the pieces, simply leaving them where they lay. Feo Ul could not see his face, but they knew his eyes were dry. His arm was weeping for him.

The crystals bounced and scattered pell-mell under shelves and strewn books. *Should even one be lost . . .* "If they are of no value to you, give them to me," they said, recovering a glimmering stone. He did not reply. "These shards of your will—of mankind's determination. They are beautiful beyond compare."

They piled the precious stones before their friend, and as they placed the final piece, they heard his voice, soft but firm.

"I yet have need of them."

Time passed, but never again did the Crystal Exarch allow the enchantment to falter. He was the picture of strength as he labored to save the world from Light's devastation. *Coveting Darkness so.* They watched him from afar. *A true Feo Ul, you are.*

Beside the Exarch walked a Viis, just ten summers old—the daughter of Liruna and Guecelo.

Beneath the golden sky, the people carried on. Rustling leaves brought Feo Ul back to a memory of awakening. To milky white bones that slumbered in a cradle of ancient roots. *Does he have one as well? A pile of bones he left beyond the rift? Or will he return there someday and leave bones of crystal behind?*

No secret of theirs could ever match the weight of *those* answers.

So mysteries they remained. Regardless, when all was said and done, Feo Ul hoped to speak the same words to commemorate his ending—or beginning, as it were.

One Name, One Promise

"In this den of pirates and thieves, those who cast the darkest shadows are wont to wear white. Helps them blend in . . . disappear into the streetscape. In that sense, I reckon ye were born for this line of work . . ."

So the man mused indifferently as he grabbed at the small boy's silver locks. They were not father and son, nor blood relatives of any sort. Just a child who knew no life but that on the streets and a merchant of ill repute who was all too eager to employ the urchin in one shady scheme after the next. Business partners, and nothing more.

It was a different time, back in the days before Admiral Merlwyb forbade piracy and brought a measure of order to Limsa. In that lawless place, a street rat could do worse for allies than a black marketeer of questionable moral fiber.

Needless to say, some patrons were bad, while others were worse. Allow yourself to be lured in by the promise of easy coin, and you might find yourself with a cutlass to your chin. There was but one constant—once the job was done, both parties moved on, sometimes without so much as a fare-thee-well. And thus Thancred spent his formative years. For better or for worse, he was an apt pupil, agile of body and sharp of mind. He could take care of himself and gave the dangers that lurked at every turn a suitably wide berth.

At one point, he even managed to ingratiate himself with the

Dutiful Sisters—keepers of the Code, feared even by the most fearsome buccaneers. And yet, in the end, he chose to move on. There was something about them—the quiet passion, the pride they took in their work—that never sat right with the boy.

It was by no means a glamorous life—nor less an easy one—but it was the only life he knew. That is, until the day he took it into his head to ply his trade on the piers. Word had it that a trader was arriving from across the seas, and coinpurses would be flush with gil and ripe for the taking.

The elderly Elezen whom he chose as his mark had other ideas, however. No sooner had the boy lifted a hand than he found himself flat on his back, his limbs bound by powerful magicks. A short life in gaol beckoned, or perhaps a quick death.

And then the strangest thing happened. The man took him by the hand, led him to a quiet corner away from the bustling crowds, looked him straight in the eye and said, "My name is Louisoix Leveilleur. I am a scholar from across the seas. What is your name, child?"

"Thancred," the boy mumbled, still in disbelief.

"Thancred . . . what? Have you any family?" the old man continued, with a sympathetic smile.

"Just Thancred," the boy shrugged. "And I don't have a family—at least, none that I know of."

The man who had called himself Louisoix paused for a moment, stroking his beard, before appearing to come to a conclusion.

"You are quick and able beyond your years. Were you only in a place where you could learn to use these gifts for the good of all, rather than merely as tools for your own survival—why, there is no telling what life you might lead . . ."

Thancred listened in silence, his frown speaking volumes. *It's not as if I chose this, you know.* But Louisoix responded with a sad-yet-knowing smile, and the words that would change the boy's life forever.

"Come with me to Sharlayan. You are a gifted child, and there is much that I would teach you . . ."

And so it was that Thancred's new life began.

To commemorate the occasion, Thancred was to claim the surname of "Waters." Such flourishes had been unnecessary on the Lominsan streets, but would be indispensable in more respectable locales. Thancred chafed at first, not keen to declare his lowly heritage to all and sundry, but Master Louisoix would brook no opposition. "Thaliak, guardian of rushing rivers and purveyor of knowledge," the sage mused. "A lad such as yourself could do far worse for a protector." And so Thancred grudgingly accepted the name he would come to wear with pride.

Louisoix also found a suitable mentor for the child—an old hand in covert operations who would train Thancred to follow in his printless footsteps. Sharlayan was a society that valued knowledge and expertise in all forms, and shadowy agents were not shunned as disreputable rogues, but respected as key contributors to the nation. It was in such a capacity that Louisoix hoped the boy might excel and find his true calling.

Stunned as he was at this turn of events, Thancred was no fool. He understood the future Louisoix envisioned for him, and endeavored to do all he could to meet his patron's expectations. He honed his body that he might infiltrate the most impregnable of strongholds in the harshest of environments, and his mind that he might charm the wariest merchants and socialites in the most critical of circumstances.

Before he knew it, the streetwise child of the Lominsan alleyway was no more. In his place stood a confident youth who could pose as anyone's friend and confidant long enough to procure the knowledge his client demanded.

A short while later, Thancred's surpassing skills were recognized, and upon his skin was inscribed the sigil of an Archon. When

Louisoix gazed upon this mark, he could scarce contain his joy. The boy he had personally led out of penury and taken under his wing had realized his potential.

It was at about this time that Thancred first met the child he knew only as Ascilia. One of the first recruits to Master Louisoix's Circle of Knowing, he was on a top-secret mission in Ul'dah, tasked with doing what he could to quell the flames of war that threatened to engulf Eorzea.

To his acquaintances, he was simply a traveling bard hoping to hone his skills and study swordplay in this land of gladiators and mercenaries. In truth, his mission was to use his knowledge of the primals as a bargaining chip, that he might gain the trust of the Syndicate, the Sultana, and any others who wielded influence in this land overflowing with wealth and intrigue—in the hope that he might stave off, however briefly, the threat of warlike Garlemald.

But the best laid plans of men oft go awry, and it was not long until tragedy reared its ugly head, and the child Thancred had only just befriended was consigned to a crueler fate than even he had known. As the dust settled, the young girl clung to her father, pleading with the gods for him to remain a moment longer.

A part of him was keenly aware that the child was all alone now, as he had once been. This part pitied her, knowing what she would be forced to sacrifice to survive in this cruel and unfeeling world. Yet another part of him—a more selfish part, he would admit—seethed with pain and regret. As much as he had grown—as strong as he had become—in the end he was powerless. *I failed her when she needed me most.*

Fortunately, the child was not without friends in the world. The songstress F'lhaminn soon resolved to serve as her guardian and protector. And so Thancred's role in the child's story came to an end—or seemed as if it might. But, for reasons he struggled to explain, he could not let go so easily. Perhaps it was the knowledge that the child's father had betrayed his Garlean spymasters before his death, and that danger might still follow in his wake. Or perhaps it was something far simpler—though the former made for a convenient excuse.

Needless to say, he had many more important responsibilities. Nevertheless, whenever his duties brought him to Ul'dah, he would make sure to look in on Ascilia lest she get caught up in anything unsavory. Dispatching common louts was easy enough, but on those occasions he found himself face-to-face with an undercover Garlean operative—no doubt one who had followed her father's trail—shivers would run down his spine.

When it became clear that it would be nigh impossible to shake their trail, Thancred decided to step forth from the shadows and make a proposition.

"You should take on a new name and assume a new life. Only then might you free yourself of your father's legacy. Trust me, it is for your own good."

Ascilia looked into his eyes and considered the implication of his words without prejudice. After a moment, she nodded in agreement. ". . . Very well. But what name shall I take?"

Thancred closed his eyes, thought briefly for a moment, then spoke.

"Minfilia," he said with quiet conviction. "Minfilia Warde."

It was nearly as inspired a name as the one Louisoix had convinced him to embrace so many years ago. A common enough name for a Highlander girl—yet not one so overused as to draw unnecessary attention. A name that would keep her safe in Thancred's absence.

"Minfilia . . ." she said with a smile. "Yes, I rather like the sound of it."

One night, after seeing to some reconnaissance task or other, Thancred found himself aimlessly wandering the streets of Ul'dah, as he was wont to do. It was then he spotted Minfilia sporting a pickaxe and other assorted gear. *The girl is nothing if not devoted to the cause.*

"Is something the matter?" he asked. "Surely your tasks didn't require you to stay out quite so late?"

"Oh, Thancred . . ." Minfilia responded calmly. "It's nothing, really. I simply . . . got distracted."

For all her outward projection of strength, something was clearly weighing on the girl's mind. And so Thancred flashed an understanding smile and offered to escort her home. It was not far to the humble abode where she lived with F'lhaminn, and he hoped that he might learn more of her troubles. The conversation quickly turned from that topic to the rumors of the day, and several inconsequential laughs later, they arrived at their destination.

"Thank you, Thancred," Minfilia offered, before fixing him with a look. "Do take care not to overdo it at the tavern. You are too quick to forget yourself, especially in the company of women . . ."

"I will heed your sage advice as if my very life depended on it," Thancred replied in a tone that made it clear he had no intention of doing anything of the sort.

Minfilia sighed as she pushed the wooden door open. For a moment, the warm, orange-hued glow of the lanterns within bathed the alley and Thancred in light. With a farewell wave, the girl stepped inside, and as the door closed behind her with a creak, that fleeting glimpse of warmth and tranquility vanished along with her.

From beyond the threshold a thousand malms away came a gentle voice.

"Welcome home, my dear . . ."

Alone in the alley, Thancred took a deep breath. *It is not for you.* He had seen the girl safely home, and though it had been a simple task, he felt prouder than he had in a long, long time.

How many years has it been . . . ? Thancred had long since lost count. He pondered the memory as he delved deeper into the tunnels beneath the city of Eulmore in the First—quite literally a world away from home. Just as he had been many times in his younger days, he was here on a mission: a mission to rescue a young girl.

The streets of Eulmore were lined with soaring, majestic buildings carved from pristine white marble. Though there were many differences, of course, Thancred could not help but be reminded of Limsa Lominsa. *In this den of pirates and thieves, those who cast the darkest shadows are wont to wear white.*

He had shed the Eulmoran soldier's garb he had worn to gain entry, donning in its stead his own coat of purest white. The garments were light and flowing, befitting a man who had traded two daggers for a gunblade—a man resolved to serve as guardian and protector. The white, too, was Thancred's choice—a color that would allow him to travel unmarked in this world flooded with Light. Were he an honorable knight burning with a sense of duty, no doubt he would have chosen to clad himself in black, raising high the villain's flag in a land where despots draped themselves in the mantle of virtue. But such indulgences would have to wait until after. After he had saved her.

The reef from which the city of Eulmore was carved extended far below the surface of the ocean. The massive subterranean chamber in which Thancred found himself was said to have been used as a storehouse in one age, and as a safe haven to shelter the people from sin eaters in another. Under the rule of Lord Vauthry, it had been converted into a makeshift gaol and pantry for meol—the substance that served to provide sustenance to the citizens of Eulmore and to secure their loyalty.

It was the deepest chamber of those cavernous halls that Thancred sought, a location he had identified only after months of reconnaissance. He evaded the eyes of the watchmen, painlessly and effortlessly dispatching those whom he deemed might interfere with their escape. Were he on his own, infiltrating the most heavily guarded areas of Eulmore would be a simple task. But to spirit away a prisoner—a child who knew nothing of the battlefield, no less—he would need to take every precaution.

After disposing of yet another guard, Thancred arrived at his destination. Though his allies in the First called her "Minfilia," the Exarch had cautioned him not to expect a reunion. Even so, Thancred felt a connection with this girl he had yet to meet. He knew in his heart of hearts what he must do. Exhaling softly, he turned the key and unlocked the door.

The chamber was unnervingly *ordinary*. Where Thancred had expected a dank cell, he found instead a simple yet all-too-comfortable-looking bed and a smallish chest of drawers. A desk and matching chair suitable for study, equipped with parchment and a quill. The centerpiece of the room was a mighty bookshelf, lined from top to bottom and end to end with impressive tomes. Aside from the lack of windows, one would scarcely have cause to complain. Yet that made this makeshift cell all the more unsettling. There was no despair, but nor was there any hope to be found. It was simply a place for the god-king of Eulmore to keep the Oracle of Light as his prisoner and pet until the end of days.

Sitting atop the bed in the center of the chamber, the young child turned to her unexpected visitor and stared at him with eyes of crystal. "You . . . you are?" The girl's voice was at once reminiscent of and entirely different from young Ascilia's.

Another life had been waiting beyond that door. A life of love and hope. Of family.

"Minfilia. It's time to go."

As Thancred spoke the name, he saw her smile in the dark. Her silhouette against the blinding light. He extended a hand. After a moment's hesitation, the girl took it.

This time. This time, I will make it right.

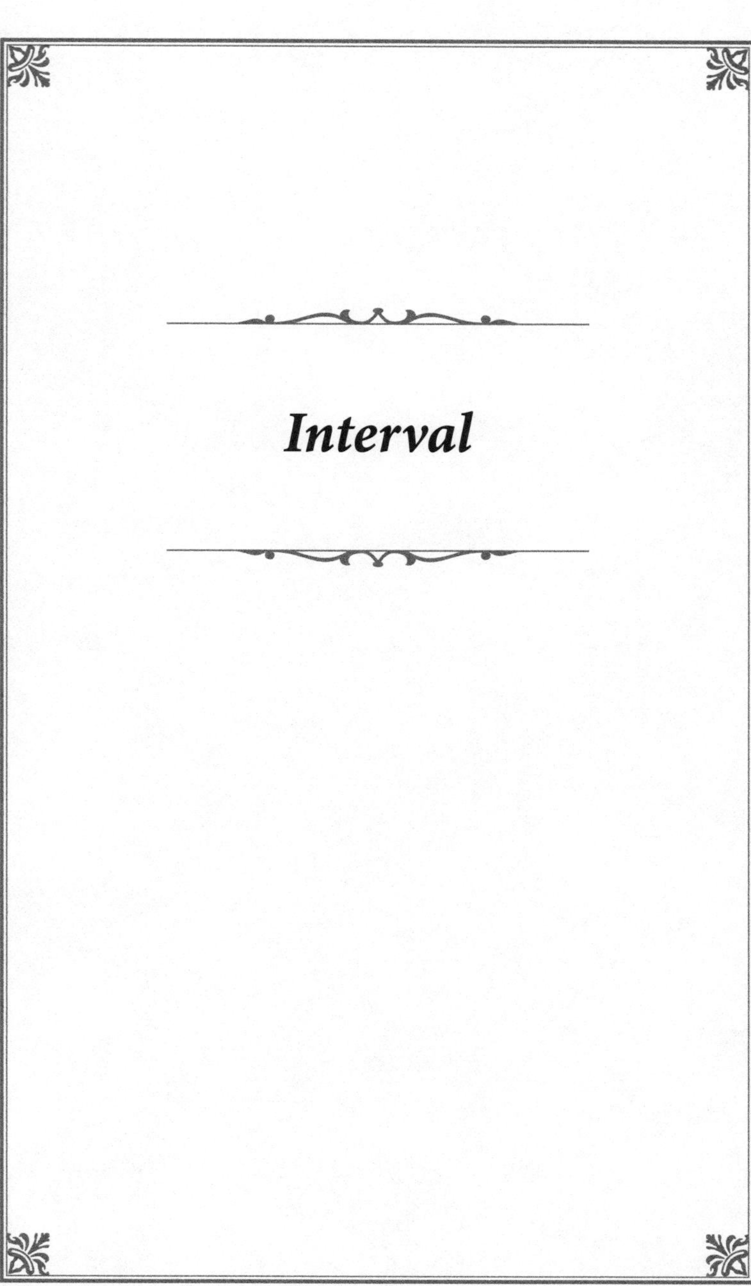

Interval

Through His Eyes

In a time long forgotten, men and gods were one and the same. And upon the star that was their home, men ruled supreme over the corporeal world, within and without which existed an aetherial realm.

Throughout the ages, this realm has been called many names, but in the beginning it was known as the Underworld—the place to which departed souls returned. As water flows to the sea and rises to the sky before raining upon the land once more, the Underworld was a fundamental part of the circle of life. And for this reason, it was regarded at once with familiarity and reverence by men, who, despite their godlike powers, could not claim dominion over it. Wise though they were, they could catch only fleeting glimpses of the realm, channel but a sliver of its power, and do naught to control its ceaseless flow.

However, among those who abided in that age, there were a chosen few who possessed an affinity with the Underworld. And among their number, one stood tall . . .

Another idyllic evening had descended upon Amaurot. Citizens strolled carelessly along the streets of the gleaming capital, identical black-robed figures bathed in gentle torchlight. Some would while the night away in agreeable company, others retire early to their beds—the illumination served equally well for both.

But he had chosen to spend the time alone at a park, reclining upon the manicured lawn. The cowl of his robe had fallen back to reveal locks of white hair, which framed the unique red mask covering the upper half of his face—the sole item among his apparel that was his and his alone. To see him lazing there, most would have assumed he was simply gazing up at the stars, or perhaps the glittering towers that seemed to reach for them. The sights that were reflected in his eyes, however, were a far cry from any seen by most men.

What he beheld was the aether that comprised all things, radiating life. From the depths of the land to the heights of the firmament, its light shone bright. Here and there, lives that had served their purpose drifted upon the current before suddenly plunging down unto the Underworld.

That he could behold these wonders was not a wonder in itself. Many were blessed with the sight. Yet very few indeed were as strong in the gift as he. As a man focuses his gaze upon the object of his interest, he needed but to direct his attention towards the aether to behold all the lives borne upon the currents. So acute was his vision, he could make out not only the soul—the heart of life—but also discern subtle differences in the hue of each, telling individual lives apart. And by virtue of this transcendent skill, he had often been likened to a denizen of the Underworld.

For a while he continued gazing up at the sky, watching the dance of aether alone with his thoughts, until the soft rustling of grass announced the approach of another. Noticing this, he shut his eyes tight as if to will away the din, but the steps only drew nearer, growing louder and louder, before finally becoming a voice overhead.

"I heard the tidings. Congratulations, Hades . . . or should I say the honorable Emet-Selch of the Convocation of Fourteen?"

If I pretend not to notice, perhaps he will leave me in peace, he thought without much hope. And, as expected, but no less to his disappointment, the owner of the voice did not make to leave. Resigned, he grudgingly rolled over and heaved himself to his feet. Having repositioned his cowl, he addressed the grinning visitor with unconcealed displeasure.

"There is naught to congratulate—I merely filled a void. One which, I would remind you, only existed because you refused the honor."

"Come now, it went to the candidate best suited to the office. You find practical use for that which you see, while I enjoy the seeing for its own sake."

"And what does that say about your suitability for your own office? Perhaps I shall raise the subject at the Hall of Rhetoric."

As he said these words, he glared daggers through his mask, but the threat—idle, as they both knew—served only to elicit a snort of amusement from the Chief of the Bureau of the Architect, his close friend Hythlodaeus. Attired in a black robe and a white mask, the man looked entirely unremarkable. Yet, like Hades, he was eminently gifted in the ability to behold the Underworld. As a matter of fact, were it purely a question of vision, his was the keener of the two. Precious little escaped his eyes, which could discern essence and appearance as plainly as night and day. This made him amply qualified for the highest office of the Bureau of the Architect, the institution which oversaw the creation of concepts. *And incurably smug.*

Irked by Hythlodaeus's unshakable good cheer, he snapped, "Was there something else?" And immediately regretted it when he saw the man's grin broaden.

"As a matter of fact, yes. Have you informed a certain someone of your appointment?"

"Hardly necessary. The memorandum will see to it, if the gossips in the street haven't already. News pertaining to the Fourteen is wont to spread quickly."

"Were you to ask my opinion, I would tell you such a momentous message warrants a personal delivery. Shall I ascertain our friend's whereabouts? It will take but a moment."

"I did not ask for your opinion, nor less your help. I understand you have pressing tasks and would not keep you from them."

For the first time since Hythlodaeus arrived, the grin faded from his lips, the tilt of the man's head all but asking how Hades could have known. And though he was certain he would regret answering the unspoken question, in the end he found himself yielding to the interminable silence. With a sigh, he continued.

"A short while ago, you received a visitor from the Words of Lahabrea. This invariably means you have been tasked with an inspection of considerable import, and by rights should not have time to spend in idleness. That you should seek me out at such a juncture suggests you have a consultation or—the mind boggles—a request."

For a moment, Hythlodaeus said nothing, as if mulling over the words. Then his shoulders began to shake with laughter.

"You wound me, old friend! I merely chanced to notice you lying here and wished to offer my congratulations." As he continued, his voice took on an impish tone. "And I daresay, given your new responsibilities, you've even less time than me to spend in idleness. Of course, you were never one to rouse yourself, save when you deemed a matter worthy of your attention."

Though said in jest, the uninvited observation did not improve his mood. "You have offered your congratulations," he said testily. "If there is naught else, I shall be on my way."

Seeing him turn to leave, Hythlodaeus hastily changed his tone. "Wait. As you say, I have a consultation for you . . . and a request. Will you not hear me out, most eminent Emet-Selch?"

"An immortal bird?" Hades repeated as they made their way through the restricted area of the Bureau of the Architect.

Hythlodaeus nodded. "To be precise, it is not a living being, but magick woven in the likeness of a bird. One possessed of puissant healing powers. And, as befits a masterwork of the Words of Lahabrea, it is a thing of beauty."

"I don't doubt it. So what, then, is the problem?"

"As I said, it is not a living being. The concept proposed was a magick in avian guise. With this in mind . . ."

Hythlodaeus stretched out a hand to the enormous gate that stood before them. Soundlessly, the towering doors swung open . . . and Hades found himself wincing at the ear-rending cry that emanated from within. Furrowing his brow, he stepped across the threshold to be greeted with the sight of a magnificent bird, its plumes fairly afire, circling high in the vaulted hall. Having marked the creature's undeniable beauty, it took him but another moment to identify the problem—an unmistakable light shining in its heart. His breath caught in his throat.

"A *soul* . . . How?"

Through their mastery of creation magicks, men could weave anything into existence. Anything they could imagine, they could bring forth—anything, that is, except a soul. As Hades well knew, souls spontaneously manifested within creatures that were born in accordance with the laws of nature. It was a gift from the star itself, long held to be impossible to recreate. No artificial being, no matter how subtly sculpted in the image of nature, could come to possess a soul. Such creations occupied a separate classification known as arcane entities.

"There was an accident," Hythlodaeus began. "During the concept's examination, a drifting soul merged with it—a soul burdened with regret, judging by the being's behavior. It rages against the pull of the Underworld."

As he listened, Hades kept his gaze fixed on the creature, which flew about in a frenzy. No sooner would it dash itself against the wall in an explosion of broken feathers than it would heal itself and repeat the grisly feat. This self-destructive dance unfolded again and again, with the creature occasionally giving vent to its overflowing magical reserves—or fury, as it seemed to him—as fiery breath.

Witnessing the excruciating display, his thoughts poured forth unbidden from his lips. "Consumed by the fear of death, it thrashes blindly about. It will know only pain and suffering and inflict the same upon others. A pitiful existence."

"Such moving empathy. It's as if you wore the feathers yourself."

Hades waved a dismissive hand. "Yes, yes. But what do you intend to do with it? Masterwork or no, we cannot well leave it as it is."

There, Hythlodaeus turned to face him, that irritating smile having returned, and again he knew a pang of regret. "As it is immortal after a fashion, we here have not the ability to return it to the Underworld—our efforts would only cause it pain. Nay, we require the services of a powerful mage, and I know of none more powerful than you."

Once more he found himself glaring daggers at his friend, whose grin had become broader than ever. But rather than give him the satisfaction of a complaint, he decided that he would make a debt of it. Without another word, he focused his mind, and as he did, his silhouette wavered and danced. Then, all of a sudden, like a shadow lengthening, his form began to swell.

Through the thrum of gathering aether, he heard Hythlodaeus remark, "Never ceases to impress me . . ."

He knew well what his friend beheld—the unbridled power of the Underworld, pouring forth into his being. In such moments, he felt as if he was one with its flow. Though mages were plentiful, not even among the rest of the Fourteen could one find another capable of wielding such power.

Ere long, his transformation was complete, and Hythlodaeus was left to crane his neck up at him. "Indeed, there is no better candidate. Allow me to congratulate you again, Emet-Selch."

He let out a quiet breath, a sigh mingled with laughter. Then he faced the bird and set about his task.

". . . Your Radiance? Your *Radiance.*"

The voice rumbled from a distance, impatient and insistent.

Drowsily, he opened his eyes, and through the haze of sleep, inadvertently focused upon the flow of aether—the habit of eons. Unlike eons ago, however, there was no brilliant shine to greet his sight, but a wan, sickly glow. A guttering candle where once a signal flame blazed. His face reflexively contorted in disgust. Gathering his scattered thoughts, he finally remembered where he was. *Dozed off in the chair again. Ah, the joys of old age.*

"Your Radiance. It is the appointed hour."

The voice rumbled from right before him. He cast a bleary gaze towards the sound to see a young man, tall and strapping and golden haired, regarding him anxiously. Though he was still well shy of his twentieth nameday, the crease which adorned his forehead added years to his grandson's appearance. *This body's grandson*, he corrected himself. Then he remembered—the boy, Varis, had been eager to report on his recent suppression of unrest in some forsaken province or other. *Scarcely a matter warranting a formal audience, let alone rousing me for.* Perhaps the boy had finally scraped together the courage to crow about his accomplishments. Perhaps he was put up to it by ambitious courtiers. Regardless, it was naught but the feeble plotting of malformed creatures. Wearily, he hauled himself to his feet and shuffled past the youth towards the door. He had barely taken half a dozen steps, however, when Varis found his tongue.

"What is it about me that displeases you so?"

He stopped at the unexpected address. Casting a glance over his shoulder, he saw the boy wearing an expression of pure anguish, and, in that moment, he looked every bit as young as he was. To let this question spill forth, his frustration towards his grandsire must be great indeed. After a moment's pause, he replied under his breath.

"Your body."

"What . . . ?" The boy's face was a picture of confusion, but he offered him not a word more, turning away and slowly taking his leave of the room.

As he made his way to the audience chamber, a self-deprecating smile rose to his lips. Though Garleans are known for their large frames, the body he wore was by no means exceptional in that regard, nor was that of the woman he took for his wife. Yet their firstborn son was a prodigiously tall and robust specimen, unprecedented even among his kind. As the boy grew, his physique was held in awe and admiration by all, though to him it was a source of great vexation.

In the end, they were all just malformed creatures. Feeble, frail, and foolish. Thrashing blindly about in their fleeting, fragmented lives, repeating the same mistakes over and over again. Never could they replace his brethren. Yet in spite of himself, when he cradled the newborn in his arms and stroked that downy hair, he could not help but hope. For what, he could not be certain, but he hoped nonetheless. It made little difference in the end, for his son had succumbed to some absurd illness and returned to the Underworld long before his time. Not without leaving behind a legacy, however—a living, breathing, and ever-present reminder of that momentary lapse.

At length, his frail body brought him to his destination. He paused before the door, took a deep breath, and shut his eyes tight—as if to will away the din.

Whispers from the Dark

Proud Ala Mhigo, squirming under the Empire's heel. Castrum Oriens, poised atop its western border with Gridania . . .

Concealed as he was by the shroud of the rift, the slight upturn of Lahabrea's lips could hardly be thought indecorous.

He waited as the black-plated figure traversed the castrum in the moonless black. Gaius van Baelsar, legatus of the XIVth Legion, was far from his comfortable chambers now. No guards watched as he took up an unassuming position in the corner of a lonely storage sector.

It was conduct far beneath a legatus's station—veritably cloak-and-dagger—but then, what choice did he have? *Poor fellow.* Lahabrea's smile widened quite against his volition. He feared he might laugh at any moment.

"This will do. Show yourself," Gaius ordered into the night.

The legatus had been hand-selected for the task ahead. It would not do to keep him waiting. Lahabrea called upon a trifling bit of magick to reposition himself behind the man.

"How kind of you to arrange for this reunion. I presume my gift was to your liking?"

Their first conversation had taken place only a few days prior.

Doubtless planning decisive action to turn the unfolding turmoil to his advantage, Gaius had taken to solitary rumination upon his return from Carteneau. He was not the sort of fool to take his safety inside the walls of the castrum for granted, however. Even deep in thought, he was quick to notice the uninvited presence at his back, and as swift to draw steel. A mortal intruder would have been dead in an instant.

Lahabrea, on the other hand, had merely drifted like a shadow from the blade's path, unperturbed.

"Black Wolf," he acknowledged. "I am Lahabrea of the Ascians. I come to offer you the power to conquer eikons."

That power had lain dormant beneath Gyr Abania for five millennia, lost to history with its Allagan makers. "He who unearthed it," the Ascian whispered, "would no longer need to cower behind steel walls . . ."

Gaius had given no indication that he believed the shadowy figure's tale. Yet neither did he interrupt its telling. If nothing else, the intruder's presence confirmed to him that the Frumentarium's reports of the "Paragons" were accurate. And thus did he see fit to dispatch his most trusted tribunus to excavate the site and ascertain the truth.

All had unfolded as promised. The legatus had acquired his proof, and now he found himself inclined to hear more.

"You will soon order a new conquest of Eorzea. For one such as you, there can be no finer prize than the Ultima Weapon . . . Or am I mistaken?"

"You are well-informed as to the inner workings of the Empire." The deepening crease in Gaius's brow was evident despite the concealment of his helmet. "But what of those of your so-called weapon? It will not serve."

". . . Oh?"

"It was where you said it would be. A machina of immense proportions. Yet it is little more than a fossilized relic."

Though Lahabrea had left closer inspection of the Weapon to his inferiors, he was well aware it was inert. There was no need to divulge this just yet, however.

Amongst the countless mortal lifetimes the Ascian had witnessed, Gaius van Baelsar's was exceptional. This was a man who had subjugated five city-states and still hungered for more. Who executed orders without compromise, never hesitating to strike his enemy at the first opportunity. Such a pragmatist would not have slunk his way into this shadowy corner merely to express his displeasure. He wanted something.

Lahabrea waited.

"Given its age, its condition was not unexpected. Nor is it a problem in itself."

The Black Wolf hid his consternation admirably. His words were carefully chosen.

"The Empire has some experience with Allagan technology. Analysis of comparable relics should yield a means to restore the Weapon," he went on, his tone almost conversational. And then he stopped. "Yet it would all be for naught without its core."

Lahabrea smiled. He had been correct to judge this matter worthy of his personal attention.

"I see you grasp the predicament." Spreading his arms for dramatic effect, he continued, "The slaying of gods requires energy beyond measure. Thus were the vaunted technologists of Allag compelled to employ a source of power even *they* did not fully understand . . ."

"Spare me the theatrics," Gaius interjected. "That you thought to tempt me with the Weapon is proof enough of your knowledge. The nature and whereabouts of the core are no mystery to you."

"Indeed." Lahabrea paused before resuming his tale, "Though they knew little beyond the fact that it worked, what the Allagans employed as a source of energy was itself a storied relic." Lahabrea flicked the fingers of one outstretched hand to reveal a stygian crystal: the very power that the legatus desired. "I entrust it to you, and no other. That this star might know the peace it once enjoyed . . ."

"Your hopes for the star do not concern me, Ascian. If this stone can grant me the power to end the succession of feeble rulers and false gods—to free this land and its people from their enervating influence—then that is the use to which it shall be put."

"Of course. Wield it as your own hopes decree, or in the name of those you would protect. I shall not obstruct you."

Gaius made no move to accept the crystal. Perhaps he yet harbored reservations about aligning himself with one whose true nature was beyond his comprehension.

But not for long. To a man who dreamed of bringing the world to heel—*in the name of His Radiance*—the call of power would be irresistible.

"'Go forth. Conquer. Rule.' Those were the words of your emperor, were they not?"

The legatus's silence remained pleasingly steeped in suspicion.

"Yet you alone see the greater cause. You alone see how unconquered lands cry out for a strong hand . . ."

It had taken some time to find a suitable candidate for this endeavor. Naturally, Lahabrea's agents had furnished him with considerable background information in the course of their search.

That Gaius was a formidable martialist and an ironfisted ruler weighed in his favor, but it was his fair-mindedness that had been the most compelling factor. He welcomed talented recruits of any origin, and was so diligent in his care for freezing orphans that, had he belonged to a more religious nation, he would surely have been destined for sainthood. Such virtuous zeal made it a near inevitability that he would seek to make use of the Ultima Weapon's power, never believing it could beget the chaos that Darkness demanded.

"You may have been watching me, Ascian, but do not presume to know my mind." Though his words were defiant, they rang faintly of defeat.

Gaius stepped forward, his hand outstretched to take the proffered stone, but he paused at the last.

"Tell me: how did you come to possess the core?"

As he searched for an appropriate response, an image drifted up from the recesses of his mind, and he glimpsed faces of which he had no memory. Why should they appear to him now? Lahabrea forced back the unease before it could overtake him, though the resulting pause did not escape his interrogator's attention.

". . . We retrieved it, lest it be discovered by the ignorant. Not a soul alive understands the crystal's true power—nor have any ever . . ."

The unease resurfaced, given new life by the thought of a distant past. When did he himself learn of the Heart of Sabik?

And from whom?

It was of no moment. Naught mattered beyond the Rejoining, which would return the star to its rightful state. He had labored to that noble end for over twelve thousand years without rest, abandoning countless bodies as they became too frail to sow the seeds of chaos. Even as the years whittled, and the centuries gouged, and the millennia ground his once-bright passion to grey and lifeless dust.

Even as time scoured his heart of the faces of those he had once loved.

He could no longer recall his family, nor even the face that had first been his own. Yet his purpose remained, along with Zodiark and those who would see Him restored. That was sufficient. There was no cause for this . . . discomfit.

"Nor have any ever . . . ?" Gaius prompted.

Lahabrea assumed an impassive expression. He had said all he intended to say. He only needed to place the crystal in the Garlean's open palm.

Why won't those damnable faces disappear?

A smiling woman with a spark of curiosity in her eyes. A man with flaming-red hair and a determined brow.

Who were they?

No. Victory was close at hand. Gaius would use the Ultima Weapon to sow Darkness in Eorzea, and even should servants of

Light attempt to thwart the Rejoining, the auracite's magick would lay them low. If only he could surrender the accursed thing . . .

Why do they stay my hand?

They should have been a long-forgotten memory. Cast aside in pursuit of his duty like countless others.

Why do they remain to plague me, when so much else was lost?

Vexed, he thrust the Heart of Sabik into Gaius's hand, and the faces were gone.

He would not explain himself to the legatus. Set once more upon his long-decided course, he turned away from the crystal.

Away from the voices that called to his heart still.

Ere Our Curtain Falls

"Emet-Selch!"

My name rang out in the Capitol, the caller's voice resounding around the foyer.

I could hardly pretend not to have heard (alas), and thus turned to face my pursuer. I had been *so close* to escaping . . .

The voice belonged, as I knew it would, to a white-robed youth of small stature, who was hastening across the hall. His red mask marked him out as one of the Convocation of Fourteen. Elidibus.

I fixed him with an inquiring look as he recovered his breath. When at last he spoke, it was (as ever) in earnest.

"Do you know of the volcano we'll be discussing at the next session?"

"I know that we are due for some pyrotechnics . . ."

According to reports circulated among the Convocation, there had been unusual aetherial activity on an isolated volcanic isle—which is to say, an eruption was forthcoming.

The island had one village upon it, and a wealth of fertile farmland—all of which would soon be lost. But that was simply the way of the world. As in many such cases, our role was merely to acknowledge the fact. The islanders would do the same, and those who deemed it prudent had likely already begun to move elsewhere. While it was true that the Convocation intended to discuss the matter, the conclusion would be no less inevitable.

But then why had Elidibus approached me?

"Well . . . Azem went there and is resolved to stop the eruption."

Naturally. I felt my brow furrowing, and fought to suppress a scowl that threatened to pull my forehead down over my eyes.

"How?" I eventually managed.

"You have heard of Ifrita, yes? The fire spirit?"

"Lahabrea's masterwork. An impressive concept, even for him."

"It truly is incredible," the youth said with quiet fervency, the determined line of his lips curving into a grin. Generally, I found his ardent admiration for the rest of the Council endearing—if embarrassing—but at that moment, I was rather preoccupied with the implications of his suggestion. It's a wonder my brow ever recovered.

Ifrita. A manifestation of concentrated fire aether. I could see what Azem was planning: transform the volcano's aether into Ifrita, draw her away, and then destroy her elsewhere. This would safely disperse the excess aether. Of course, the plan required someone to procure the concept of Ifrita for Azem. But if that someone was not Lahabrea himself, who else could it be?

As everyone knew, concepts were stored in the Bureau of the Architect, and not all could be readily removed for personal use. The chief of the bureau, however, could grant access as he pleased.

Who else indeed. I pictured my friend cheerfully sending Azem off to battle without a second thought. Forgetting my mask, I clapped my palm to my forehead in exasperation—which Elidibus duly took as a sign that I understood.

"If things get out of hand, Azem could be censured again," and here the youth paused. "But I'm sure that won't happen. Not with your help."

My brow resumed its descent.

". . . Very well. But are you certain it is wise for the emissary to ally himself with so divisive a figure?"

"Oh, I'm not," he replied with practiced deftness. "I'm simply giving Azem's opinion on the matter equal weight. The rest of the Fourteen have yet to reach a verdict, after all."

On this point, I could not argue—though I wasn't particularly inclined to agree. And so I shrugged, musing inwardly that Azem was lucky the current emissary was such a kindly soul. Before we parted ways, however, I couldn't resist asking one more question.

"Did you happen to find out *why* Azem is so keen on preventing this eruption?"

The youth frowned, inevitably striving to recall his conversation with Azem as accurately as possible. It wouldn't do for the emissary to speak unadvisedly, after all. I waited politely.

"If I recall correctly," he began at length, with the air of one about to reveal a grave truth, "the grapes grown on that isle are particularly delicious. Or so Azem said. They must be truly remarkable."

"Indeed." I couldn't bring myself to shatter his faith. I did, however, vow to treat my "friends" to a lecture on priorities.

Blissfully ignorant of my misgivings, the young man smiled to himself again and bade me farewell. As he wandered away, I swore I heard him murmur something about Azem's "ever-refreshing perspective."

That's the sort of person Elidibus was; eager to fulfill his duty, he also respected and admired the Convocation more than any other. To many of us, he was as a younger brother of sorts. And when it became clear that he was the most suitable candidate for Zodiark's heart, it mattered not how strong our resolve . . . There was none among us who did not waver.

Could there have been any greater shock, then, than our subsequent reunion?

This was soon after Zodiark became the will of the star, and our Final Days were averted. The people were divided, unable to decide what to do with the future that now stretched out before them. Many wished to trade the new life which had sprung forth to reclaim those lost in sacrifice to Zodiark. No small number, however, insisted that the fate of our world should be entrusted to those selfsame freshly minted souls. All were at their wits' end.

At once, we saw it, shimmering. It poured out of Zodiark's breast, and resolved into the shape of a man. As he looked us over—mouths agape, no doubt—he gave what passed for an earnest smile.

"Fear . . . not . . . You will make . . . the right choice. And I will see it through."

How long had passed since then I did not care to remember. In any case, my role as Solus zos Galvus, founder of an empire, had concluded, and I was drifting. I thought I might settle down for a nice, peaceful nap in the rift for a century or so. It would serve to rinse away the cloying residue of Solus, whose body I had left back in the Source. One should not remain perpetually in character.

Not that there was much point in me retaining my sense of self. I had thought more than once that it would be easier simply to have done with it and discard my "real" form altogether. Yet given the state of the other two unsundered, some part of me was convinced that if I remained stubborn, a reason more compelling than hollow sentiment would come along eventually.

"Emet-Selch."

My name rang out in the darkness, tugging me back to consciousness.

Again? I elected to ignore the disturbance, but the voice was persistent. Once more it called, closer now.

Though the voice was the same as the one which had ambushed me in the Capitol so long ago, it sounded as if it belonged to another person entirely. Perhaps it did.

"Lahabrea is gone," the voice said softly.

I could hardly continue to feign slumber at that, so I righted myself and turned to face Elidibus. The silence that stretched between us then only affirmed the truth that had gone unspoken.

For us, death was not the end. But "gone" . . .

"We knew this day would come."

I closed my eyes, letting out a measured breath, or what passed for one in the emptiness of the rift. He was right, of course. Lahabrea's boldness had only grown with the passing of ages—segueing inevitably into recklessness. Across many vessels and many worlds he blazed his trail, each mad leap forward leaving him that much more broken. Not satisfied with having brought about the Seventh Umbral Calamity, he labored needlessly to prolong it.

Was it his affinity for concepts of flame that made him so like the fire itself? From peerless Ifrita to that hopelessly immortal bird, his creations had burned bright and beautiful—as did he.

He should have known what becomes of the flame once all else is ash.

I opened my eyes to take in my brother's face, but the lips visible below his mask bore no expression. Would he never again show what he felt for us, as he once had so readily? Were those very sentiments long lost?

"What is it, Emet-Selch?"

"Nothing. I was only thinking how similar Lahabrea was to his creations."

"His creations?"

I had little difficulty reading Elidibus's uncertainty this time. He couldn't remember. If his clenched fists were any indication, he shared my conclusion: yet another part of him had been lost. Ever since the day he had reappeared to us as the embodiment of "hope," time's tides had conspired to wash away what bits and pieces remained of the person he once was.

"Will you not look at your crystal?" I asked.

When Elidibus was still Elidibus and Lahabrea still Lahabrea, we had collected all of our memories of the Fourteen and committed them to crystal, that those who would take our seats one day might learn. Elidibus would, I was sure, find much within to help him remember—yet he shook his head.

"I am Elidibus. So long as I remember my duty, that is enough. Aught else I would only lose again in the course of this timeless struggle . . . and if these memories are truly so precious, pray do not ask that I forget them twice."

On this point, too, I couldn't argue—though, again, I could hardly agree. As he was now, however, I doubted that Elidibus could tell my shrug was affected.

"I make for the Source, to put an end to the one who laid Lahabrea low," he said, as teleportation magicks began to roil around him.

"Sounds like a real hero. No match for you, in other words."

"We must always prepare for the worst. If we are to succeed, you must resume your efforts as well."

I was half inclined to tell him I preferred to sleep, but of course he was already gone, leaving me alone in the darkness.

That was the last time I ever saw Elidibus.

And now . . . ?

Now my charms are all o'erthrown,
And what strength I have's mine own,
Which is most faint, as is my breath
That quavers here at brink of death.
'Twas e'er my fate to wager all
For that which wrought my brothers' fall,
And thus the aether beckons me
To depths of black eternity,
To dream of things long lost and gone,
And futures which might yet be won—
Though not by me, lest you mistake,
For others wait, the stage to take,
And while their worth is far from sure,
I bid the falling curtain—pause.
Let "encore" be my final word,
Their epilogue to death preferred.

Act II

Defining Moments and Memories

Behind Every Manderville Man

The man crossed the wilds bearing a chocobo. But that couldn't be right . . . could it? Julyan blinked, and found that it was. The chocobo did not bear the figure who trotted up to greet her, but was instead borne serenely upon his back.

"I find the practice most beneficial in promoting the development of the lower body," he offered by way of cheerful explanation.

Though Julyan had marked him down as an eccentric sort, even her wildest imaginings had not prepared her for this. *If ye want strong legs, stuff lead in yer boots like the rest of us.* She sighed. The man had scarcely arrived and already she felt a twinge of regret at ever having humored his romantic invitation.

The chocobo-bearing individual in question was, of course, Godbert Manderville. The man who would, in time, become Eorzea's greatest goldsmith, and go on to earn an obscenely large fortune from his jewelry business before joining the exclusive ranks of the Syndicate. As of this moment, however, he was but another unheralded artisan with little to his name—beyond his name itself, which identified him as a scion of the illustrious House Manderville. Lineage aside, his present assets amounted to youth, passion, and the shiny black locks which would one day fade to their trademark white.

As for the young and fresh-faced Julyan—who would later join Godbert as an equal partner in Manderville & Manderville—she was already a celebrated culinarian in Ul'dah. She did not manage her own restaurant but had instead gained widespread repute by cooking at the homes of the well-to-do. Her popularity was such that her services were booked several years in advance—an impressive achievement, even given the many hours of preparation required for her signature dishes, and her strict policy of attending to but a single reservation at a time.

One fateful day, Julyan was out in eastern Thanalan in search of goat meat for a stew. She had inspected the cuts on offer at the Sapphire Avenue Exchange and, finding them wanting, concluded that the best option for procuring a fresh, high-quality sirloin was to hunt down a myotragus herself.

After locating a herd of the wild mountain goats, Julyan crouched low in the long grass, and ilmed her way forwards, appraising the bigger billies as she went. The meat of the nannies was considered juicier, and its marbling more desirable, but her dish demanded a gamier flavor. *There. That's the one.* Having singled out a suitable specimen, Julyan took her beloved skillet in hand. Though she knew some frowned upon this unorthodox use of a cooking utensil, as far as Julyan was concerned, it was all part of the culinary process.

She gauged the distance to her unsuspecting quarry, then broke cover with a powerful leap. At that very same moment, there was a blur of motion from behind the outcrop directly opposite—a blur which resolved itself into a muscular man wearing naught but shaded spectacles and a pair of form-fitting smallclothes.

"Ye bloody pervert!"

Believing herself the target of an opportunistic deviant, Julyan shifted her posture mid-flight, extending a foot to spring from the back of the myotragus and deliver a crushing, downward blow upon her would-be assailant's skull. Instead of the satisfying crunch of bone, however, her ears were greeted with the earsplitting clang of metal upon metal.

Godbert—for it was indeed none other—had produced a goldsmithing hammer seemingly from thin air to arrest the descent of the deadly frying pan.

"Stay your hand, good lady!"

His gentlemanly plea fell upon deaf ears, however. For, once lit, the fire of Julyan's rage was not so easily extinguished. Face twisted into a wrathful mask, she brought her skillet down again with tremendous force, only for the frantic goldsmith to once more block the strike.

Who in the seven fiery hells is this bastard?! Never before had she met a man who could fend off one of her blows, let alone two. Yet shocked as she was, Julyan remained focused on the battle at hand, determined to bury her opponent beneath an avalanche of unrelenting fury. A thousand skillet strokes later, he fell to his knees in defeat, their contest decided not by strength of arm, but by implacable force of will.

"Give up," Julyan growled, leveling a fierce gaze at her bested foe. "Yer comin' with me. The Brass Blades'll know what to do with ye."

"B-But this is all a misunderstanding! If you would only allow me to explain . . ."

Godbert spoke swiftly, outlining his plan to acquire myotragus horns for a jewelry project, and how his choice of prey had—wholly coincidentally—overlapped with Julyan's own. The truth of events thus made clear, rage gave way to remorse, and she found herself stammering out an apology.

"Forgive me. Mayhap I . . . judged ye too quick."

"Oh ho ho, no harm done!"

Godbert brushed off the incident with a good-natured laugh, his magnanimity persuading her to forgo the many questions which came to mind—such as why anyone with any sense would go out hunting in their undergarments.

Thus unfolded the famous couple's fateful—and near-fatal—first encounter.

As for the almost-forgotten goat, being trapped in the center of that raging melee had proven *actually* fatal. Fortunately, the two hunters were content to split the spoils, with both taking the particular prize of horn or meat which they had set forth to claim. When the time came to part ways, Godbert, perhaps emboldened by the success of their unplanned cooperative endeavor, ventured a gentlemanly proposition.

"Might I have the pleasure of your company again, my lady?"

The invitation was as unexpected as it was sudden. Julyan gave it due consideration, impressed by this stranger who had been the first to hold his own against her. Differing professions aside, she also admired the commitment they shared in gathering their own materials. Yes, she would accept, she decided . . . even if the man himself did seem decidedly odd.

As it transpired, their next meeting was a surprisingly conventional affair. Godbert took her on a tour of Thanalan's notable landmarks, and in the evening treated her to a meal at an Ul'dahn restaurant. It was over dinner that he laid out his grand ambitions.

"The jewelers of this city are too fixated on following trends," he said, his eyes glittering. "Every display in every store is strewn with the same tired designs. And so, finding naught here to inspire me, I set forth on a journey. Everywhere I went, I would hunt fiends and mine ores, and using every material from bone to gemstone, I've fashioned a collection of pieces unlike anything Ul'dah has ever seen. All that remains is to establish a store, and let my unique works enchant the hearts of all who cross the threshold . . ."

At this, anyone familiar with the Godbert Manderville of the present might well nod sagely, recognizing his bold assertion as the first rung on his storied ladder to success. Lacking any such knowledge of future events, however, Julyan heard only the unworldly wafflings of a dewy-eyed dreamer.

As well she might. Julyan had taken great pains to maintain a realistic outlook as she methodically carved out her place in Ul'dah's cutthroat culinarian society. Improving her cooking skills had been the bare minimum. What dishes were most in demand? How was she to distinguish herself from other talented chefs? To secure the reputation and status she currently enjoyed, her research into the industry and potential clientele had been thorough indeed.

From her hard-won perspective, Godbert's plans seemed hopelessly naive. While she did not know much about the jewelry business, she knew Ul'dah only too well and saw at once that he was clearly underestimating the complexities of the market.

"Aye, ye might make a few gil to begin with," she admitted, briefly regarding the food on her fork before looking him squarely in the eye. "But what happens when the novelty wears off?"

"Well . . ." the bespectacled goldsmith began, his expression only slightly less enthusiastic than it had been, "I am confident that maintaining a ready supply of quality pieces will ensure a steady stream of custom."

Julyan stifled a snort. *If only it were that bloody easy . . .* Yet even as she picked apart his ideas with clinical detachment, she became aware of a growing pang of disappointment. Had she been expecting something else from this peculiar gentleman? Something more? While she contemplated these questions, she noticed him very deliberately removing his glasses to regard her with a bare and earnest countenance.

"Lady Julyan," he began. "Aside from mine own dear parents, only you have ever bested me in martial combat. And with your skillet-wielding grace, you have enthralled me, heart and soul. Be mine, I pray, and I swear that I shall fill your days with joy."

Julyan sat for a moment in bemused silence, her estimation of Godbert's character falling another few notches. *We've barely met, ye daft sod . . .*

"I'm flattered, truly I am," she eventually offered, "but I fear my heart belongs to another."

It was a convenient falsehood, and not *entirely* untrue. After all, a client of hers *had* recently asked for her hand in marriage, and while she had as yet declined to give him an answer, the union itself was not a *wholly* unappealing prospect . . .

Her suitor was heir to a merchant house operating under the auspices of the East Aldenard Trading Company. Marrying into such a family would guarantee financial security, and her would-be husband, being a good and wholesome man, was a fine catch by any measure. But was she truly ready to close off all other paths forward in favor of this one? Mired in indecision, she had thought Godbert's outing preferable to agonizing over her reply.

With the alternative seated in front of her, however, Julyan was ready to make a choice. If she was to be married, it would be to a respectable man of stable means.

". . . Is that so?" Godbert interrupted her introspection with unconcealed disappointment. "Be that as it may, I hope you will accept a gift."

So saying, he produced a small box and held it out.

"I crafted this piece especially for you. Keep it or discard it, it is yours to do with as you wish."

Julyan hesitated for the briefest instant, before politely accepting the token, not wishing to hurt his pride any further. And on that muted note, their evening together came to an end.

The following night saw Julyan visit the abode of her preferred suitor, who greeted her arrival with ill-contained excitement—quite rightly, given she had come with the express intention of accepting his proposal.

Ready at last to give her answer, she took a deep breath and stared into the eyes of her future husband. *It's for the best.* At that moment, an image of Godbert wielding his goldsmithing hammer flashed across her mind. *Then why am I still thinking about* him? And suddenly, fresh doubts assailed her.

The grating sound of shouting tore her free of her spiraling thoughts. Dragging her focus back to the present, Julyan realized that the sumptuous drawing room in which she stood had been invaded by a gang of mask-wearing, sword-wielding brigands. She had heard news of a spate of burglaries targeting Ul'dahn estates, and it seemed the thieves had chosen this mansion as their next target. Leveling cruel blades at her would-be fiancé, they were now demanding access to his treasure vault.

Well, someone's *got to sort this lot out . . .*

Julyan unhooked her trusty skillet and exploded into action. Untrained ruffians that they were, their numbers counted for nothing against the cast-iron whirlwind which swept into their midst. Once the interlopers were rendered comatose—a deed accomplished with quite astonishing swiftness—Julyan bent down to check on the well-being of her not-quite betrothed. Cowering in the corner of the room, he looked up at her wide-eyed, his face a picture of horror.

"Wh-What kind of monster are you?"

Oh bugger. Julyan chided herself for her foolishness. She should have known this man and his well-bred sensibilities could never accept a woman of her fiery disposition. His offer of marriage duly rescinded, she left the premises a free agent. Yet rather than regret, she felt only relief.

Later, as she wended her way home with unhurried steps, she remembered Godbert's gift with a start. Occupied as she was with matrimonial matters, she hadn't even thought to open it.

Taking the box from her pocket, she flipped the lid to reveal a piece of cameo jewelry. It was an exquisite agate carving set into a base of sculpted horn.

"Bloody hells . . ." Julyan whispered, her voice hoarse. There, etched into the surface of the stone, she saw the figure of a leaping maiden brandishing a skillet. The same maiden who had been scorned as a monster scant moments before, captured here in loving detail, as if she were the Fury Herself . . .

Distractedly brushing a tear from her cheek, she began to understand Godbert's confidence in the enchanting nature of his work.

She was less sure, however, that the "steady stream of custom" he envisaged would not eventually slow to a trickle.

"Talent like his can't be left to fade into obscurity," she swore to herself. "That man's got somethin' special about him, an' if anyone can help him achieve his dreams, it's me!"

Barely having given voice to this thought, she broke into a run, her feet guiding her unerringly to Godbert's lodgings.

In the days that followed, Julyan and Godbert became partners in both life and business, eventually co-founding the hugely lucrative enterprise of Manderville & Manderville. As Godbert himself later admitted, his skills alone would never have yielded him more than a modest profit, let alone a seat on the Syndicate. He had Julyan's shrewd eye for business to thank for his great success.

Godbert might be the craftsman, but I'm *the one who carved that rough diamond into the greatest goldsmith Eorzea has ever seen.*

Julyan smiled fondly as her fingers traced the cameo she kept ever at her bedside.

Echoes of Delusion

The evening found them at their usual table at the Shiokaze Hostelry. Though he and his traveling companion had by now become a familiar sight in Kugane, few there had any inkling just how odd a pair they made—a dragonslayer, albeit retired, and a dragonet.

"It's well you had me to get us out of our predicament," Orn Khai observed in that insufferably smug tone of his—and not for the first time. But this, Estinien decided, was one time too many. Face darkening, he snatched a piece of sun-dried squid, known to the locals as surume, from the plate between them, making the diminutive dragon blink.

"A predicament of *your* making. *Your* false lead that caused us needless toil." Tearing off some chewy squid with his teeth, he let out an irritated sigh. *Gods, how did it come to this?* But the answer he knew all too well.

It had begun amidst smoke and ash at the Ghimlyt Dark, when he had plucked the Warrior of Light from the jaws of death. Having borne his stricken comrade to the Ishgardian encampment, Estinien had promptly taken his leave, reasoning that his skill with a lance would be of more use on the battlefield than in the infirmary. And so he had turned his steps back towards the fighting, minded to lend the Alliance his strength . . . only to learn that it was no longer needed. For Zenos had withdrawn from the front lines, leaving the imperial forces defanged and in disarray.

Thus had Estinien found himself aimlessly wandering the snow-swept fields of Coerthas, which is where he had heard a familiar draconic voice calling out to him—Orn Khai. In the past, he had aided the dragonet in his quest to find his sire's long-lost consort; a journey to the Far East which had, it would seem, given the creature a taste for adventure. And now he wanted Estinien to accompany him on another.

"I've no interest in playing nursemaid," Estinien had replied in a tone that brooked no discussion.

But Orn Khai was not to be discouraged. Having inquired as to the Elezen's age, he retorted with a smirk, "I've lived tenfold your years. It would seem *I* am the one who must play nursemaid."

In such a manner did their conversation unfold, and a pain began to manifest in Estinien's temples, first niggling then raging, until—driven to the limits of his patience—he had declared with a snarl, "I had forsworn the slaying of dragons, but for you mayhap I shall make an exception!"

This said, he had drawn his lance and made as if to thrust it at his interlocutor—who duly cheered.

"Yes, that's the spirit!" Orn Khai gleefully exclaimed before proceeding to apprise Estinien of his plans. He had previously heard tell, he explained, of an intriguing legend—that of Seiryu, a dragon worshipped in the Far East as a benevolent guardian, but feared in certain corners as a man-eating fiend. "I wish to ascertain the truth of the tales. If this dragon devours man-flesh as some believe, it falls to us to end its reign of terror!"

So it was that the Azure Dragoon had set forth once more to the Far East, a none-too-willing traveling companion to an all-too-willful dragonet. And through painstaking effort, trudging hither and yon gathering information, they had learned the truth of the legend . . . to their mutual disappointment. For the dragon known as Seiryu was no dragon at all—at least, not of the kind they knew—but something more akin to a serpent. And to compound their chagrin, their quest having dragged on far longer than intended, they had found themselves at the limits of their funds. For some days they were forced to endure empty bellies, but their luck had turned when Orn Khai came to the attention of the proprietor of Kugane's most famous hostelry. Like many a Hingan, the woman believed dragons to be bringers of good fortune, and she had offered them board and lodging in exchange for attracting customers.

And here we are. A spectacle for drunkards.

"How ungrateful!" Orn Khai said with mock indignance. "I find myself less and less inclined to sear your squid!"

As little as Estinien cared for the dragon's pertness, at that moment he cared less for the dry rice wine without a savory accompaniment. "Fine. I'm grateful," he managed, resisting the urge to roll his eyes. "Now sear me another one, will you?"

Seemingly placated, Orn Khai breathed fire upon the surume, which released a mouthwatering aroma as it crackled and charred. Estinien allowed it a moment to cool before helping himself to another bite of this strangely addictive snack. Even as he savored the flavor and texture, footsteps rang out from the direction of the tavern's entrance.

"Welcome to the Shiokaze Hostelry!" Orn Khai cheerily called out to the newly arrived patrons.

With a brief shake of his head, Estinien drew breath to offer his own half-hearted greeting, only for the words to die on his lips when he turned around and saw the two Lalafellin maidens standing upon the threshold.

"There you are!" shrilled the one in the pink kimono. Though she had adopted the local attire, there was no mistaking Tataru Taru, the Scions' indomitable receptionist. And beside her, even less mistakable in her distinctive robe, was Krile Baldesion, staring wide-eyed at him. Whatever it was that the Archon saw, it clearly amused her, for she was suddenly racked by paroxysms of poorly stifled laughter.

"Forgive me," she said tearily, struggling for breath. "I had heard that the Azure Dragoon had hung up his lance. But I did not expect that he would take up the serving tray in its stead."

To that assessment, Estinien could offer no retort. And as much as her amusement irked him, above all he was troubled by the creeping sense that he was about to be drawn into yet another bothersome affair.

He turned to Orn Khai. "'Tis time we went our separate ways, little one. But so long as you remain here, you shan't want for comfort. Fare you well."

Sparing the visitors no further glance, Estinien picked up his travel sack with the tip of his lance, swung it over his shoulder . . . and leapt. He shot up to the hostelry's upper level, landing gracefully amidst startled revelers, who broke out in rapturous applause at what they assumed must be a performance. Disregarding the ovation, he dashed through the door and out into the night.

He knew at once where to bend his steps—Kugane Ohashi. For across this bridge, there lay the rest of Shishu, entry to which was forbidden to all ijin save a privileged few. Surely it would be the last place they would think to look for him. But he had scarcely settled into his spot against the bridge balustrade to let the haze of the wine clear from his head when, from among the passing traffic, the Lalafells appeared again.

"You do know they won't let you pass without one of these?" Tataru waved a parchment in front of him, bearing Far Eastern script and a crimson seal. *An entry permit . . . Why am I not surprised?* But what *was* surprising was how quickly they had managed to track him down. At that moment, a boat plying the channel below chanced to draw near. He did not stop to think, and sprung onto its mast.

A few moments and several leaps later, Estinien was taking in the city from the roof of Kugane Castle, a self-satisfied grin upon his face. *Let them try and find me here . . .* Absent-mindedly, he withdrew what was left of his surume from the pocket where he had secreted it, raised it to his mouth, and . . . stared. On a nearby walkway, two Lalafells were emerging, led by a Sekiseigumi blade bearing a lantern. *What sorcery is this?*

In that instant, it occurred to Estinien that they may well have a good reason to seek him out. The thought quickly faded, however. Perhaps it was the wine—a potent variety sourced from the main island—or perhaps it was simply his nature, but the more they pursued him, the more determined he became to elude them. *Just need to steer clear until morning.* Thus resolved, he stepped off the rooftop and dropped down, down, down to the ground.

After what seemed an eternity, the night sky began to take on the grey of dawn. A little longer, and the *Kuroboro Maru* would leave port and bear Estinien away, beyond the reach of Scion troubles. But even as he allowed himself to hope, the selfsame cheery voice that had haunted him all night rang out.

"Anyone would think you were trying to avoid us!"

You cannot be serious . . . Groaning inwardly, he turned to face his unrelenting pursuers, his mind racing as he considered his options. It was then that the Baldesion woman fell to one knee, cradling her head.

"A-Are you all right?!" Tataru crouched down beside her companion in a state of alarm. The Archon had plainly overexerted herself during their night-long game of cat and mouse. Unable to stop himself from feeling a measure of culpability, he was about to proffer a hand when Krile's shoulders began to shake with laughter, as poorly stifled as before.

"Oh, Estinien . . . Never would I have imagined . . ." She made an effort to look at him, but the sight of his face seemed only to add to her amusement, sending her into further paroxysms.

"What's this, now? Did you see something from his past?" Tataru asked, her voice dripping with curiosity. Though it was already well on the way to being a warm day, Estinien felt a chill to rival a

Coerthan night. He knew that, like the Warrior of Light and Ysayle, Krile was blessed with the Echo, and could peer into the past through another's eyes. He could not begin to guess which mortifying episode in his life she had just witnessed. There were simply too many.

Finally composing herself, Krile stood upright and regarded Estinien with a look of pity. "Be at ease. I am not so heartless as to reveal what I saw. Not here and now, at any rate."

Damn you to the bottom of the seventh hell.

"But enough about that," she continued sweetly. "We were hoping to speak with you—if you have a moment?"

Estinien's shoulders rose and fell as he sighed in resignation. The chase was over.

Later that morning, Estinien stood upon the deck of a merchant vessel bound for Radz-at-Han, on his way to the Empire. He had been charged with finding—and if possible destroying—an alchemical weapon by the name of Black Rose. Left unchecked, the Garleans would inevitably bring the deadly gas to bear against their enemies, Ishgard among them. The method of his recruitment apart, he could not well stand idly by while his comrades were thus threatened, nor could he deny that he was well suited to the task.

As he gazed out at the Ruby Sea, he rested a hand upon the reassuring weight hanging at his waist—a leather pouch heavy with coin. The spoils of some lucrative venture pertaining to Far Eastern legends, according to Tataru.

Yet another bothersome journey. But at least I shan't want for funds.

Reaching into his travel sack, he pulled out a piece of freshly seared surume, a parting gift from Orn Khai. He took a bite, making sure to chew it slowly. There was no telling when he would see any more.

At around the same time, Tataru and Krile were sitting at the Shiokaze Hostelry, taking refreshments with their new friend Orn Khai.

"So, tell us, Krile . . ." Tataru began, her cheeks flushed from the rice wine, "what scandalous event from Estinien's past did you see?"

Like the morning sun peering out over the horizon, a coy smile slowly broke on Krile's lips. "I'm sorry? Whatever gave you the impression I saw such a thing?"

Their boisterous laughter could be heard as far away as the water's edge. But thankfully not beyond.

The Burden of Duty

Birdsong and laughter drifted on the afternoon breeze as the Doman Enclave enjoyed yet another beautiful day. Yugiri was returning from Rissai-juku, enjoying the rare pleasure of a leisurely stroll, when the children's commotion brought her to a halt.

"You're wrong! He got them fighting an imperial general!"

"Nuh-uh, it was a tiger! It caught him off guard and clawed at his head!"

Another argument over the origin of the scars on Lord Hien's forehead. *And every assertion straying further and further from the truth.*

"You're both wrong! He got them in a duel with the monkey king!"

Pitched battle with an auspice was more imaginative than most rumors she had heard. *And closest to the truth besides.* Still, it was but another flight of fancy. Yugiri could say this with confidence, for she was there that fateful day when Lord Hien received his most distinguishing marks.

When she was a child still living beneath the waves of the Ruby Sea, Yugiri and the other youths of Sui-no-Sato were forbidden from venturing beyond the safety of the village. Nevertheless, time and again the adventurous among them would sneak past their elders to behold the wonders of the surface world. They journeyed unto Doma, but what they found was not the proud kingdom of ancient legend. The city proper was a ruin, and black-clad imperial soldiers marched through her streets.

The sight of such misery and destruction was more than the children could bear, and so they ran, over root and under branch, as fast as their legs would carry them. So determined were they to return home that no one noticed when Yugiri fell behind. Soon she was lost and alone in the dense bamboo groves of Yanxia. But not for long.

She entered into a clearing where stood a young boy, who gripped firmly in his hands a wooden sword ill-suited to his small frame. Steady and rhythmic were his swings, and his sweat-soaked garments led her to wonder how long he had been at his task. Yugiri's fear at her unfamiliar surroundings gave way to curiosity as she mustered the courage to speak.

"What are you doing?"

His sword did not waver as he carried on swinging and replied.

"Training. If I am to fight, to protect the ones I love, I must become stronger!"

"But . . . you're only a child. It's not your place to fight, much less protect anyone."

The boy stopped at that, and at last regarded the unexpected spectator.

"I am not a child," he declared. "I am Shun Rijin, a samurai of Doma. A samurai's duty is to protect their people. And to do that," he said, as he assumed his stance, "I must train."

One day the young boy would fulfill his duty and bring freedom to his homeland, and though she did not know it then, Yugiri would be at his side. But today was not that day, and as the skies began to darken, she was reminded of her pressing need to return to her village. With young Shun to guide her, she found her way back to the eastern shore, and shortly thereafter Sui-no-Sato. Safe at last. *But for how long . . .*

It was only a matter of time before the Empire plumbed the depths of the Ruby Sea, and the people of Sui-no-Sato would have no hope of withstanding an imperial assault. *Not unless I am prepared to do my part.* The very next day, she returned to the surface to join Shun in the bamboo grove, and tried her best to match his movements with a wooden sword of her own.

Every day she would sneak away to train with him, and every day the two grew closer. Shun had found a much-needed friend with whom he could share anything, and, through their friendship, a measure of the childhood that war had denied him. The simple game of ishikeri she taught him was enough for Shun to forget the worries of the world, if only for a short while, and when Yugiri explained that the children of Sui-no-Sato played such games all the time, she was struck by the awe and envy in his wide eyes. *So much has been taken from them. So much have I taken for granted.*

The skies were clear and the sun was shining when Yugiri arrived at the bamboo grove for another bout of training, only to find Shun sitting quietly, arms folded, brow furrowed. Doma Castle had suffered terrible damage when the Empire invaded and laid siege to it, and having decided to repair and repurpose it, the Garleans had begun conscripting villagers en masse. For a fortnight the people had been forced to labor without cease, rest afforded only to those who collapsed from exhaustion. Unable to ignore their plight, Shun had gone to his father, Lord Kaien, the former king of the imperial province, and begged him to put an end to the suffering. To stand and fight.

"You know not what you ask of me, my son. What you ask of Doma." His father ruled in name only—a puppet of the Empire—and knew well the cost of disobedience. "You may think it cowardice or heartlessness to accept this treatment, but I do so that my people endure. That they survive . . ."

Shun had managed to bite back the anger and keep silent before his father. But there, in the grove with Yugiri, he could no longer contain the rising fury, nor the bitter tears.

"I have to help them! I *have* to!" He looked away, trying in vain to hide his face. "I am a samurai of Doma, I *must* fulfill my duty!" But Yugiri had no words to comfort him—only her company. And so they sat together in silence and watched the clouds drifting by overhead.

After a time, Shun rose to his feet. "I'm sorry, Yugiri, but I have to return home." She saw how he trembled still, fists clenched, and refused to meet her gaze. *Don't lie to me.*

Yugiri followed him, keeping to the shadows, and as she suspected, he did not return to the family estate, but instead traveled along the One River, until he reached his true destination—the Swallow's Compass. Built in tribute to Ganen, his forefather and the legendary hero who united Doma, the once-great mausoleum now sat in disrepair, and the imperials turned away all who would make pilgrimage there. But few knew the mausoleum grounds better than Shun and his family, and Yugiri watched from a distance as the young samurai stole past the guards and disappeared through a hidden passage in the wall.

As she crept through the dark, moldy corridors, eyes fixed on Shun, the silence was broken by the grinding of metal on metal. The boy scurried into the shadow of a pillar as Yugiri scrambled to hide behind a nearby gong. No sooner had they concealed themselves than a gargantuan, steel-clad figure emerged from the darkness, a shining jewel signifying its heart—a kiyofusa.

The soulless sentry, Shun well knew, was charged with safeguarding the tomb's treasures from would-be robbers. He also knew it did not distinguish between friend or foe, and so he held his breath, hoping to remain undiscovered. Eventually, the kiyofusa receded back into the dark of the mausoleum, prompting Shun to make his move. Yugiri leapt from her hiding place to pursue him, but, in her haste, set the gong in motion, and before she had made it even five steps, a thunderous clang filled the air. The ringing of the gong was answered by the rattling of steel as the kiyofusa made its return, intent on dispatching the intruder.

The guardian was upon her in an instant, its monstrous blade held high. *You fool* . . . As it came crashing down, she fell to the ground and shut her eyes to brace for the end. Yugiri winced at the sharp screech of sword locking with sword, and when she opened her eyes, she saw Shun standing over her, struggling to keep the sentry at bay.

"Get back! Quickly!"

Though she was very nearly frozen with terror, Yugiri managed to crawl to safety as Shun parried the kiyofusa's strike, driving its blade to the side. The construct would not be deterred, however, and dealt a rising stroke that sent Shun tumbling backwards. He managed to deflect the blow at the last moment, and though bruised, believed himself otherwise unharmed . . . until he felt the warmth flowing from his brow.

"Kami give me strength," he muttered. The guardian would overpower him ere long, but there was a certain regularity—a predictable pattern to its movements. Shun grinned—there was hope yet, provided he could force it to miss a second time.

The steel behemoth swung its sword in a wide arc once more, and though the boy thought himself prepared, with its deceptive speed the sentry nearly took his head again. But Shun would not let another cut slow him. The kiyofusa shifted as before to recover from the momentum of its own attack, and seizing the opportunity, he stepped as close as he dared, and with all his strength, drove his blade into its crystalline heart. The jewel shattered, and at once the mountain of metal crashed to the floor, a lifeless heap. A hard-won victory, to be sure, but one he dared not waste time savoring, for the kiyofusa was but one of the mausoleum's many protectors.

"We have to get out of here. Now!" Shun whispered as he helped Yugiri up, and together they retraced their steps quickly and quietly, never stopping until fresh air once more filled their lungs. Whatever Shun had hoped to achieve was forgotten now, a crisscross of fresh scars the only reward for his efforts.

"I . . . I owe you my life," Yugiri began, but their respite was short-lived, for they were soon spotted by an imperial guard making his rounds.

"Younglings? Here?" The guard cocked his head, then smiled . . . though there was no kindness in his eyes. "Well, I hope it was worth it," he said as he reached for the sword at his hip.

"Please!" Shun pleaded. "She's only here because of me. Spare her, I beg you!" The boy got down on his hands and knees and pressed his bloody forehead against the dirt.

"Noble for one so young, I'll grant you that. Still . . ." Yugiri was frozen with fear as the guard drew his blade. *Did we escape one death only to meet with another?*

"My, what a piteous scene."

The trio turned and saw Gosetsu—honored general, renowned samurai, and faithful retainer of House Rijin, standing some distance away. "Lord Kaien will be inconsolable when he learns of his son's execution." The guard looked again to the children, squinting at Shun in particular. The blade in the man's hands was shaking.

"I-I have my orders. Anyone caught trespassing in the mausoleum is to be executed." He tightened his grip. "No exceptions."

"A man of duty, I see . . . But how, pray tell, do you intend to explain that mere children were able to sneak past you undetected? I shudder to think what punishment the viceroy might impose for such negligence."

Yugiri saw the blood drain from the soldier's face. Slowly he lowered his sword, then sheathed it. ". . . Away with you, then. And let no one else see you," he said, before resuming his patrol.

"Such recklessness does not become Doma's heir, Master Rijin. What if I had not come quickly enough to dissuade the guard?"

Rising from the ground, Shun could not bring himself to look Gosetsu in the eye. "Our people need help. I . . . I thought if I could find the monkey king, he . . ."

"Qitian Dasheng would indeed prove a formidable ally, if the tales of his prowess are true. Let us suppose your plan had succeeded, and with his aid you saved those being forced to rebuild the castle. What then?"

Shun opened his mouth to speak, but they both knew he had no answer.

"I, too, wish to see our people spared imperial cruelty, but a far crueler fate awaits deserters upon recapture. Will you subject them to that risk? Have they even the resolve to bear it?"

Shun was trembling now, and the towering samurai knelt and spoke to him gently.

"Forgive me, Master Rijin, but I mean only to remind you of your father's lesson. That you must understand what you ask of your people. What you ask of Doma."

Yugiri saw Shun grappling with the truth of the grizzled samurai's words.

"He asks too much of himself, too," she said. Yugiri went on to recount Shun's gambit that allowed them to escape the mausoleum relatively unharmed.

"Bravery well beyond your years. Lord Kaien will be proud. And happy to see you delivered home, my lord."

In time, Doma Castle was rebuilt, and the conscripts were allowed to return to their villages. But the bamboo grove where two children had once played would be abandoned, for Shun was preparing to train under Gosetsu's watchful eye. *And we must say our good-byes.*

"My father was right—for now we must endure. We are not ready to oppose the Empire. Myself most of all." To Yugiri's surprise, he allowed himself a wry smile. "Someday, I will make Doma a land like Sui-no-Sato, where children laugh and no one lives in fear—I swear it."

Though there was no telling when that day might come, Yugiri couldn't help but share in his hope.

"And I'll be there when you do!"

"I will hold you to that!"

The sound of skittering rocks roused Yugiri from the memories. The children had ceased their bickering and were engaged in a game of ishikeri. *For they live not in fear. For they are free.*

"Have you room for one more?"

In many ways, he was still a child at heart. Yugiri looked on with a smile as Lord Hien added his voice to the chorus of laughter. *A child at heart . . . and a man of your word.*

Her Father's Daughter

With the peace negotiations at U'Ghamaro a resounding success, the long and bitter conflict between the kobolds and the people of Limsa Lominsa at last drew to a close. It was a joyous occasion that marked what many hoped would be the beginning of a new age of harmony and cooperation.

Her duties done for the day, Admiral Merlwyb Bloefhiswyn retired to the command room and—as was her custom—began polishing the two muskets that were her constant companions. No sooner had she started than she found herself adrift in bittersweet memories . . .

In 1562 of the Sixth Astral Era, Lominsan merchant vessels were regularly raided by the savage Sahagin, who coveted the crystals housed within. Crystals were the foundation upon which the nation's metalworking industry flourished, and should the supply be interrupted, the furnaces would go dim, and smithies forced to set their hammers aside.

Fortunately, one man had a mind to set the situation to rights: Bloefhis Bloefhisyn, former captain of the League of Lost Bastards, and one of the most dangerous pirates in the realm. While he had yielded his command to his daughter Merlwyb some years ago, he still wielded much influence among his fleet.

When he announced a campaign to eliminate the Sahagin threat, all answered the call, and his daughter was no exception. And so it was that Merlwyb would plot a course for the Rhotano Sea, in hopes of doing her father proud.

A chance came one day when her vessel, the *Lively*, received a distress call via linkpearl from a nearby trader. The *Orion* was under attack by a Sahagin raiding party and requested immediate aid. Knowing that time was of the essence, and believing the situation to be within her power to resolve, Merlwyb chose not to alert her father and request reinforcements, and elected instead to hurry to the *Orion*'s aid on her own.

The Sahagin enjoyed a natural advantage in battles at sea, but owing to Merlwyb's masterful tactics and the unerring aim of her first mate and gunner, Lorens, the *Lively* was more than a match for their foes. In no time, the Sahagin threat was quashed—all that remained was to escort the *Orion* to port, and Merlwyb's duty would be done.

Unfortunately, it was not to be.

A lone Sahagin straggler, scarcely breathing after one of Lorens's bullets had torn through his gut, marshalled what remained of his physical strength and spirit and offered a fervent prayer. By the power of the crystals housed in the *Orion*'s hold, his desperate plea was given form, and the Lord of the Whorl emerged from the depths.

Gazing upon the colossal form of Leviathan, far larger than any sea serpent, Merlwyb knew the battle was lost. The first thrash of the primal's tail snapped the *Lively*'s keel like a twig, and it would be but a matter of moments until the once-proud vessel capsized.

Amidst the churning waters, Merlwyb led the fortunate members of crew who had not been cast overboard to the still-afloat *Orion*, where they lay battered and beaten, all but resigned to their fate. Their captain's eye, however, caught sight of a glimmer of hope in the form of several ships headed their way.

Father's flotilla.

Taking aim at the primal's massive tail, Lorens breathed a sigh of relief. Merlwyb, too, was joyed, though she cursed her naivete. *The title you may hold, but he is still the true captain. You have much to learn.*

The battle raged on, the primal and its beastman thralls claiming countless victims, but in the end, Bloefhis and his fleet managed to drive their foe back beneath the depths. It was this day that the Lominsans first grasped the sheer power of Leviathan—a deity that could single-handedly nigh sink Limsa's mightiest pirate fleet, and in defeat, live to fight another day.

Less than a week after the battle, and with nary a word, Bloefhis sailed off into the horizon with a patchwork crew of men from several ships. The Bastards that remained clearly acknowledged Merlwyb's authority as captain—there was no danger of mutiny—but a sense of confusion and unease at her father's unexplained departure permeated the ranks.

In the months that followed, the Sahagin attacks on trade vessels grew more frequent and intense. More troubling, however, were the rumors the survivors brought back to port—that the beastmen fought not alone, but with Lominsan vessels at their side. These pirates named themselves the "Serpent Reavers," and were said to be commanded by none other than the legendary Bloefhis Bloefhisyn himself. The revelation that their own beloved hero now sailed with their hated foes cast a pall over the city and its people, who began to dread what grim tidings would come next.

Under the cover of a moonless night, a single vessel departed from the docks unseen. On its deck stood Merlwyb with a handpicked group of her most trusted sailors, her grave face unflinching as the chill winds bore down upon them. Word of Bloefhis's unholy alliance had seen the Bastards fall out of favor with the other pirate bands, and led many to regard them with distrust and suspicion—Merlwyb most of all. *We will assume the worst.*

Yet despite her precautions, she was soon joined by an unwelcome visitor. Hearing footsteps, she turned and found a veritable mountain of a man standing before her. Though the iron mask obscured his face, it nevertheless spoke to his identity as none other than Mistbeard, notorious pirate and her father's greatest rival. *Come to deliver justice to the turncoat's daughter, I'll wager.*

"You mean to bring him back, do you?"

Though muffled somewhat by the mask, she sensed a measure of sympathy in the booming voice.

"No. I mean to kill him."

For a long moment, the gargantuan pirate regarded her in silence.

"And there I was thinking I'd have to knock some sense into you," he said at last. "Here, take these."

He brought forth two muskets and held them out to Merlwyb.

"Your guns?"

"Yours, now. If you will have them."

"I'd be a fool to refuse. But why?"

"The sun has all but set on the age of us old buccaneers. Bloefhis knew this as well as I—that's why you lead the Bastards now. If you've a mind to do your duty, then let me help you see it done."

Merlwyb had no idea if there was any love lost between Mistbeard and her father. Nevertheless, holding the twin muskets close to her chest as the ship struck out into the black waters, she could not help but feel heartened by his words.

Just before the first rays of dawn broke across the horizon, Merlwyb's ship came ashore on the small island that the Serpent Reavers were said to have claimed as their hideout. And indeed, after she had disembarked with a party of axemen and ventured a ways inland, they were set upon by a motley band of pirates and Sahagin sentries. *The rumors are all true, then . . .*

With muskets firmly in hand and a heart of steel, she shot and killed one after another. Among her adversaries were former companions and childhood friends, though their wild-eyed expressions rendered them nearly unrecognizable. Alas, though she fought bravely, her foe was legion, and one by one her axemen were wounded or worse. *So this is how it ends . . .*

Merlwyb had all but resigned herself to her fate when a shot rang out, and a Sahagin a few feet ahead of her crumpled to the ground. She whirled and came face-to-face with Lorens, her trusted first mate, from whom she had gone to great lengths to conceal her departure. *And failed, clearly.*

"What in the seven hells are *you* doing here?!"

"It'd be a sorry first mate that lets his captain get 'erself killed on a suicide mission, no?" Lorens fired back with a grin.

Merlwyb scoffed. "If you'd taken any longer, that's exactly what would have happened."

"What can I say?" Lorens shrugged. "Ye were gone by the time I climbed out of the hold, and ye didn't have the courtesy to leave a map."

The captain and her mate carried on with their spirited banter as they engaged the Reavers in perfect harmony—Merlwyb taking deadly aim with her muskets as Lorens supported her from a distance. They made short work of their foe and gave her allies a chance to regroup, and when the dust had settled, she sent them back to the ship with the injured. Together with Lorens, Merlwyb forged ahead towards the center of the island, where they came upon the entrance to a cave.

It was deep within the caverns that they finally found Bloefhis—or at least, what remained of him. The once-imposing figure had wasted away. His pale skin clung to his emaciated frame, and his flowing locks and beard were flecked with white and grey. His slack jaw hung open, and spittle pooled on the earth below. Merlwyb and Lorens could only stare in horror as Bloefhis began to speak, his voice a muffled gurgle.

"My daughter . . . Lorens . . . have ye come . . . to join us?"

Lorens glanced at Merlwyb, who stood in silence, before answering in her stead.

"What in the name o' the Navigator happened to you, Cap'n?!"

"It is impossible for mere mortals to stand against the power of a god," Bloefhis intoned as if in a trance. "Swear allegiance to Lord Leviathan, and we may live free beneath the waves . . ."

Had it been years later, when the nature of primals was better understood, they would have known then and there that the former captain had been tempered, and regarded him not with scorn but pity. But on that cold morning in that darkened cave, all Merlwyb knew was that the people would condemn her father as a demented traitor. Still, a part of her believed her father's words were no longer his own.

"'Impossible' is a word coined by the weak! You taught me that! And you know bloody well that freedom isn't gifted by a god, but claimed by our own hand!"

Bloefhis shook his head and sighed.

"My poor, wayward daughter . . . I thought I raised ye better than this . . ."

In her heart of hearts, Merlwyb had known from the start how it would have to end. She had come not to reason with her father, but to hand down his sentence—and treason was a crime punishable by death.

"There are none but us on this island now." she said, her tone measured and firm. "I hereby challenge you to a duel to the death. Should even a shred of a pirate's honor remain in you, you will accept."

The sickly, mocking grin slowly faded as Bloefhis rose to his feet and met her gaze. Though he said nothing, his answer was clear. Lorens would serve as the sole witness, and there would be no seconds for either party. *A sorry excuse for a duel, but it will suffice.*

Father and daughter came together, and then—exchanging no words—turned their backs on one another. Their footsteps echoed hollowly as they walked farther and farther apart. *Malms away now.*

She recalled the day she'd lost him—doomed him to this fate with her arrogance and recklessness. They came to a halt at opposite ends of the cavern and awaited the sign.

Lorens extended his right hand, slowly opening a clenched fist. The gold coin caught the light as it began to tumble through the air.

Orphaned while still a babe, Lorens had known no family but the Bastards, no father but Bloefhis.

It'll be my bullet. My burden. Even so, I'm sorry to make you a part of this.

The clink of the coin striking the ground resounded throughout the cave, and in an instant, father and daughter spun to say farewell.

Merlwyb's bullet flew straight and true and buried itself into her father's left breast. Musket still dangling from his hand, Bloefhis fell to his knees.

"Merlwyb, Lorens . . . I'm sorry I had to put ye through this . . ." he managed between ragged breaths. "Promise me . . . ye'll do me proud . . ."

The smile in his last moments was that of the father Merlwyb knew and loved. Lorens stared down at the motionless body of his former captain.

". . . This ain't over. That godsdamned primal is still out there, and our ragtag band ain't equipped to finish the job."

Clenching a fist, Lorens continued.

"So I'll go on a voyage. Aye, find myself a few good men—more'n a few—and see if we can't build ourselves up into a force to be reckoned with. Least I can do to redeem his memory."

Lorens said no more, and simply looked Merlwyb in the eye, but the question was clear.

You've your plans . . . but what have I?

The barrels of her twin muskets polished to a fine sheen, Merlwyb put them aside, and strode to the window to gaze out upon the sea. This was not the first time the memories of that fateful day came unbidden, and it would not be the last. And each time, she gave thanks to the two men who had seen her through that most terrible of trials. One had since set aside his mask and serves to this day as one of her closest advisors.

The other, alas, disappeared in the days following the Calamity. Yet deep down, Merlwyb knew that he was out there somewhere, waiting to make his return when dire storms again threatened the seas.

After all, if I am my father's daughter, then in all but blood he is my father's son.

Set with the Sun

Her father was dead.

It had only been a few days since the event, and Fordola wanted nothing more than to run far, far away. Her mother had not stopped crying, and she knew that adding her own tears to the deluge would only make matters worse. All the while, the disdain of imperials and Ala Mhigans alike ate away at her. What was the point of living like this—of living at all?

As the sun began to dip towards the horizon, Fordola made for the outer walls, slipping shadowlike through alleyways disregarded by the patrolling imperial soldiers. She squeezed through a crack in the stonework barely larger than herself to reach her sanctuary. Here, she could gaze out upon the easternmost peaks of Abalathia's Spine, and—more importantly—be alone. Relaxing, she squinted into the setting sun, which had painted the sky her favorite shade of fiery red . . .

"How can the sky burn so?" she had once asked her father. And he hadn't tried to palm her off with some convenient myth, admitting frankly that he didn't know. That was her father: honest and kind—and quite earnest when he asked her what *she* thought the answer might be.

A prickle of unease jolted Fordola back to the present. She twisted around to see a pair of glowing gold eyes regarding her from above a wide, froglike maw. The abaddon's bulbous blue form quivered in anticipation of its coming meal. It must have wandered up from the water's edge in search of prey. She blinked as its long tongue flicked out to taste the air, tracing her scent.

She was going to die. Yet where she ought to feel fear, she found nothing but cold certainty.

How strange it was, then, to be proven wrong.

"Hyah!"

The woman's yell reached her first. Then a rush of air, a thud of impact, and . . . the creature was gone. An instant later, another thud drew her gaze some distance to the right, where she noted the now prone abaddon, stumpy legs flailing pathetically in the air. Nonplussed, Fordola stared as the woman—who she could only assume was some kind of martial artist—jogged back to her side.

"Anything broken?" the woman was inquiring cheerily, her hand extended down to where Fordola sat (when had she fallen?). With effort, Fordola eventually mustered the wherewithal to shake her head—after rather too long, judging by the almost comically relieved "Thank goodness!" she received in reply. Though most of her face was obscured by a mask, the woman's smile fairly glowed. It almost reminded Fordola of the fire in the sky.

"I'm Yda," she continued. "Nice to meet you!"

When Fordola made no move to reciprocate, Yda clasped her hand in both of her own, and shook it up and down as one might a small child's.

"Um," Fordola began.

"What's your name?" Yda interjected, heedless.

". . . Fordola."

"Fordola! Did you come here alone? Where are your parents?"

"My mother's at home," she muttered sullenly. "But my father is . . . He's . . ."

"I'm sorry," Yda nodded, and said no more about it.

In fact, she seemed to forget the subject entirely.

"Shall we meet here tomorrow?"

"What?" Fordola managed. "Why?"

Yda tilted her head in confusion. "Because we're *friends!*"

"Since when?" Fordola fired back. This "Yda" may have saved her life, but that didn't make them friends.

"Don't worry! If any more monsters turn up, I'll kick them halfway to Doma," the woman replied, staunchly missing the point.

"So you'll come?" she continued, showing no inclination to let go of the idea or Fordola's hand.

There was nothing for it. Fordola nodded.

Accompanying Yda wherever she happened to be going became a regular occurrence for Fordola in the days that followed. She would never forget the joy of swimming across Loch Seld—or the trial of explaining away her salt-reddened eyes to her worried mother afterwards. She also learned to hunt. Her first kill, which Yda roasted over a campfire, tasted nothing like the meals her mother made, but was delicious nonetheless. And for the first time since her father's death, Fordola found that she could smile again.

Yda spoke often of her younger sister after that. She too had faced their father's death at an early age, and Yda had been desperate to cheer her up, to take her anywhere that might bring a smile to her face.

"You reminded me of her, you know. I couldn't just leave you like that."

She also mentioned that she was staying in Gyr Abania temporarily while she and her comrade did their "work." What they intended to accomplish, however, Yda would not say, waving away her questions with a smile.

Fordola had *some* idea, though. She had heard Yda talking to this partner of hers via linkpearl several times, always about "the refugees," and while she couldn't begin to guess at the details, it was enough to tell her that they were enemies of the Empire.

Yet in spite of this, and to her own surprise, Fordola felt perfectly at ease.

"Why don't you come with me?" There was no hesitation in the offer. Her mission accomplished, Yda would be leaving Ala Mhigo soon—with Fordola, if she so wished. They could live somewhere else, somewhere free, together.

Fordola didn't know what to say. It was all so sudden—and what about her friends and family? Could she bring them too?

"We can only take so many people. One or two we can slip in with the cargo, but no more than that." Yda looked pained. "I'm sorry . . . Maybe it was wrong of me to ask."

She would think about it, she promised, so Yda told her where to meet for their escape, and when. After that, Yda would be gone.

After much fretting on her own, Fordola decided to share her dilemma with her four closest friends. They were silent while she told them everything, and for a good while after. It seemed they didn't know what to say, either.

It was Emelin who spoke up first.

". . . Sorry. I can't just leave my family behind. But I don't want you to leave us either," she managed, before curling in on herself, looking like she might cry.

"My granddad's really old," muttered the thickset boy next to her, apologetically. "I don't think I could go either."

Fordola's shoulders slumped. Of course they'd never agree.

It was Charlet, a little boy who often trailed after her like an adoring younger brother, who spoke next, with tears in his eyes.

"I-I know you want to! You were so sad 'cause . . . 'cause of your dad, but you're happier now, so . . . if you want to . . . I'll miss you, but I think you should go."

At this, Charlet's older brother, Ansfrid, let out an exasperated snort.

"Don't be so stupid! Why does she need an *Ala Mhigan's* help? That's what *we're* here for! Don't you *dare* leave, Fordola." His lip trembled even as he glared at her, fists clenched at his sides.

And then Charlet began to cry.

"I don't," he sniffled, "I don't *want* you to go. I want everyone to be together forever!"

"Don't leave us! We'll always be your friends if you stay!" Emelin wailed.

Though she would rather they hadn't been such crybabies about it, Fordola was happy to hear how much her friends cared. They understood how hard it was to be neither Ala Mhigan nor Garlean, and she couldn't abandon them now—not after everything they had gone through together. She would tell Yda no. She was staying in Ala Mhigo.

Her decision made, Fordola resolved to see Yda off with a smile. She would miss her terribly, but they were certain to meet again someday.

And so she turned for home, oblivious to the figure observing her from the shadows.

The appointed day dawned without fanfare.

When the sun had made its way across the sky, Fordola made hers to the agreed spot to wait, just as she had countless times before. The Yda that came to meet her, however, behaved quite unlike the care-free soul she knew. On every other occasion, she had bounded hap-pily towards Fordola the moment their eyes had met, but today she hesitated, scanning their surroundings warily. Fordola followed her gaze, but noticed nothing out of the ordinary in the ruins.

"Yda?" she called out in a small voice, but the woman was dis-tracted, pressing her linkpearl to her ear.

"It's not looking good here either," she told whoever it was—her partner, Fordola guessed. "Change of plan. Go now. Don't wait for me."

What was she talking about? Distant shouting crackled from the linkpearl. Somebody wasn't happy. Fordola strained to hear.

"I'm sorry, Papalymo! Look after Lyse for me!" Yda said with her customary cheer, silencing the connection. Relieved, Fordola ap-proached, sure that Yda was still herself after all.

It was then that she heard the footsteps. Heart hammering, she spun to see two, three, and then more and more soldiers fanning out around them—at least ten in total.

"Nice trick."

Yda's voice was colder than she had ever heard it—so cold that it took a moment for Fordola to realize who she was speaking to.

"Wh-What?"

"You knew I'd find out if you blabbed to the guards, so instead you made sure you were followed . . . Imperial *rat!*"

She made to protest, but her voice died in her throat when she realized the truth of the situation. Yda was putting on an act—though the soldiers *had* followed her.

"Thought I'd be able to make some decent money off a merchant's daughter, but you had to go and spoil everything . . . You'd better run while you can, or I'll strangle you where you stand!"

All lies to keep the imperials from accusing her of treason, and Fordola had no choice but to go along with them. She bit her tongue, feeling furious and pathetic at the same time.

Run.

Yda mouthed the word as one of the soldiers raised a magitek transceiver to his lips. At nearly the same instant, another soldier, who had been slowly closing the gap between himself and Fordola, reached out to grab her—but Yda's foot hit the earth, propelling her forward in the blink of an eye, and he collapsed from a kick to the gut with a cry. Alarmed, the others rushed to surround Yda, who danced back and forth on the balls of her feet, fists at the ready.

"Feel free to attack all at once, if you're so scared!"

"Cut her down!"

The soldiers brandished their blades with angry cries, and Fordola ran. She'd only make things harder for Yda if she stayed.

She fled through the ruins, weaving around rubble as she went. But nimble as she was, she could not hope to match a soldier's stride, and she found herself swiftly overtaken. Cowering from the wicked flash of the blade that arced towards her, Fordola lost her footing—as did the imperial, who was at that same instant propelled gracelessly into the nearby rubble, courtesy of a bone-crunching kick to the side. He slumped to the ground, unmoving.

Yda turned and met Fordola's eyes. With her usual mask gone, Fordola could see the lines of ink forming a traditional Ala Mhigan design. Her eyes—blue, Fordola now noticed—were so kind. *Please run,* she wanted to say, but she couldn't find her voice. Her body still trembled where she stood, frozen in place, but Yda approached as if nothing was wrong.

"Live, Fordola," she said, laying a soothing hand on her hair. "Find some hope to hold on to."

Fordola could only nod, barely able to contain the sobs that threatened to burst from her chest, as Yda graced her with one final smile. Then she was gone, running hard and fast in the other direction, beckoning their enemies to follow.

With the sky burning red behind her, Yda danced.

Imperials fell one after another to her blows, but even she could not evade every blade, every fist, every bullet that came her way—and soon the salt-white ground turned crimson too. From a distance, Fordola watched as Yda's strength waned.

More and more soldiers were coming to join the fray. She even saw a hulking magitek monstrosity approaching, the grating screech of metal on metal adding to the clamor which now resounded around the ruins.

Fleet of foot as she was, Yda surely could have escaped alone. Yet there she stayed, fighting this impossible battle. She was going to die, and why? For the sake of one child? For her?

Why me?

If she went for help, they might make it in time. But who could she ask? Who would help an enemy of the Empire? No one she knew. She cursed her own uselessness.

Still, she kept moving. One step at a time, though her legs trembled to take them, and repeated Yda's final words to herself until they were a part of her. She would live.

In the end, she faced no inquest for having been present, thanks to Yda's deception. Nevertheless, she knew that if her loyalty to the Empire should ever again be cast into doubt, her mother, and perhaps even her friends would pay the price as well. It would be imprisonment or death for the lot of them.

If these were her choices, then she would prove herself a worthy citizen of the Empire. Though she had yet to find the hope that Yda spoke of, she chose to believe that she would one day.

Until then, she would live.

The tattoo stood out starkly against Fordola's complexion, its ink fresh under her skin. She traced the traditional pattern with her fingers. Today, she and Ansfrid, Emelin, and Hrudolf would join the XIIth Imperial Legion—but it was another day that occupied her thoughts as she set out, one long past, but vivid as a burning red sky.

She carried the memory with her as she took one step, then another, towards her waiting friends.

True of Heart

In the year 1572 of the Sixth Astral Era, the city-state of Gridania was beset by myriad crises. From without, Ala Mhigan refugees flooded into the Black Shroud, fearing invasion and subjugation at the hands of the Garlean Empire. Within the Twelveswood, the Ixal stole past Wailer sentries to fell sacred trees, and in turn made offerings of their hewn trunks to Garuda.

It was in the midst of this turmoil that the Archons of Sharlayan came bearing a monumental request. They beseeched the city-states of Eorzea to look beyond their borders and join with their neighbors in common cause once more: to revive the Eorzean Alliance.

This bold request could not be given full consideration until many questions had first been answered, and so the Seedseer Council was called to order. Made up of the gifted Hearers, who could hearken to the voices of the elementals, the council governed Gridania in accordance with the will of man and elemental alike. However, the spirits of the forest did not speak as people did, for their thoughts were borne on waves of aether. Any effort to translate them into words was, at best, an interpretation of their intent.

Thus were the Hearers forced to infer and embellish—not out of a desire to mislead or manipulate, but out of necessity. Nevertheless, this process invited interpretations of interpretations, which all too often led to disagreement and discord. Matters of great import would become mired in debate, which would subsequently be settled with a vote.

Such were circumstances in the best of times. Now, however, the chaotic fluctuations in the aetherial currents confounded the most seasoned of Hearers. The air was thick with urgency, but they could not discern any meaning in the morass of emotion. All eyes in the Lotus Stand looked to their leader for clarity—the Elder Seedseer, Kan-E-Senna.

Displaying a singular talent for magic, even by Hyuran standards, the Elder Seedseer ever commanded the attention of others. This was in no small part due to the horns which grew from her head and marked her as a Padjal—a Hyur blessed by and possessed of an uncanny ability to communicate with the forest. Her natural gifts and unyielding determination ensured that, before she had seen her twelfth summer, Kan-E-Senna would be chosen as Elder Seedseer by the great one, that she might lead the Seedseer Council.

Although much of her life since had been spent in quiet solitude, she attended every council meeting and served as a mediating voice whenever arguments grew heated. She heard the elementals more keenly than any, and could divine their intentions when no one else could.

And so, on this momentous occasion, the future of a nation and its people would be dictated by her words. *The elementals must needs have a voice, and it falls to me to provide it.*

Kan-E opened herself to the aether of the Twelveswood, and at once she felt the elementals clamor—their dread and terror threatening to engulf her. Holding fast, she concentrated and tried to make sense of the confusion. Yet no sooner would an image begin to form within her mind than it would be swept away by a surge of intense emotion.

For the first time in her life, the thoughts of the elementals were too entangled for even Kan-E to unravel. She dared not share this with the council; the Elder Seedseer was the caretaker of Gridania, and if the people's faith in her was shaken, then all could fall to ruin.

But by the same token, she could not misrepresent the elementals, even if only to beg a brief reprieve. Doing so would be a betrayal of her station and her gift, and would surely invoke the ire of the forest's guardians.

Kan-E stood mute before the council. *I know not what to do.*

Before she could find her bearings, the spirits cried out once more—the aether surged and crashed against her, and when it had receded, all that remained was the quiet murmuring of the troubled Hearers.

The forest has fallen silent. Though none could know her mind, the Elder Seedseer's expression made it plain that something had gone terribly wrong. The Hearers erupted into discussion, talking over one other, speculating as to what the elementals were saying even as Kan-E was deaf to them. With only the faintest hint of a tremor in her voice, she called an abrupt end to the meeting.

Kan-E had been denied. Striving to push the panic from her mind, she began searching for accounts of similar incidents. She scoured the records of past council meetings, studied the chronicles of historians, and made discreet inquiries into the tales of traveling bards and wandering minstrels. Each time she came upon a story bearing even a passing resemblance to hers, she took great pains to reenact the hero's triumph. Ceremonies to appease forgotten gods, esoteric prayers and rituals, obscure meditations of dubious intent—she attempted every method, for the Elder Seedseer would spare no effort. Nevertheless, the elementals remained silent.

At the end of her tether, she turned to the instructional texts for novice conjurers. Compounding her frustration, Kan-E realized that she had yet to internalize some of these most basic lessons, for she had struggled to find time for her studies in the years following her appointment. She resolved to address her deficiencies and to learn all she could about the elementals, and buried herself in the histories of the Fifth Astral Era, which told of a Twelveswood before the rise of Gelmorra. Yet while the breadth of Kan-E's knowledge grew by leaps and bounds, the answers she desperately desired eluded her still.

I cannot lead if I cannot fulfill my most important duty. Absent the judgment of the elementals, all Gridanian affairs would grind to a halt. And so, bereft of other options, Kan-E called upon an old friend and mentor: A-Pitat-Rapa.

The former Elder Seedseer, who was said to be nigh on three centuries old, had been spurred by ailing health to retire to the mountains that he might live out his remaining days unburdened by leadership and its never-ending demands. When his successor came to his doorstep with furrowed brows, however, he beckoned her into his home with a warm smile.

It had been ten years since last they had met—when Kan-E had taken up the mantle from A-Pitat. Some within the Seedseer Council had regarded the young Padjal with skepticism, and did not scruple to let their opinions be known, even in the face of the great one's blessing. It was A-Pitat's endorsement that had put their minds at ease, for if the Elder Seedseer himself vouched for her, what cause had they to gainsay him?

Perhaps they should not have been so quick to withdraw their objections. So great was her shame that, despite having come to confide in her mentor, she could not share the most disgraceful detail: that the elementals had abandoned her. A-Pitat sat and nodded as she related her story, observing how a decade of service had deepened the wrinkles on her otherwise youthful face.

Kan-E had anticipated many reactions to her tale, but his kindly chuckle was not among them.

"How ironic that you cannot hear the elementals, considering how alike you are at present," he said. The young Padjal stood speechless, as she had not so long ago before the Seedseer Council. Fortunately, unlike the elementals, A-Pitat could clarify his intent.

"You speak of troubles, yet give no voice to those darkest within. So long as you keep your own counsel, I can offer you no words of comfort."

Before Kan-E could muster a reply, a shrill cry from outside the window cut through the silence. "Elder Seedseer! Come quickly, kupo! We need your help!" the distressed moogle said, motioning for Kan-E to follow.

With an abrupt farewell, she left A-Pitat's home and ran after the moogle until they reached a small clearing in which lay an ashen A-Ruhn, Kan-E's younger brother. Attending to him was their sister, Raya-O, whose grave expression spoke volumes.

Kan-E joined her at A-Ruhn's side and called his name, only to hear him reply in a strange tongue before being overcome with convulsions and voiding the contents of his stomach onto the verdant grass.

This is my doing. Unable to depend on the Elder Seedseer, the elementals were attempting to speak through A-Ruhn. The sudden tumult of aether was too much to bear, and it burned through his body like a fever. He would not survive much longer.

"A-Ruhn is in such pain! Sister, do something!" Raya-O cried.

As Kan-E raised her hands and began to work her magicks, she was struck by an epiphany. *Ask and they will answer.* A simple thing, to ask for help, yet for the longest time she could not. *My duty. My responsibility. My burden alone.*

But it needn't be so.

Kan-E took A-Ruhn into her arms and carried him to the Guardian Tree. Within this eldest tree of the Twelveswood did the great one reside.

"O great one, I come before you with a confession," she began, but when she listened for a response, she heard naught. Kan-E and Raya-O rested their brother against the ancient trunk, but his suffering did not abate.

Speak and be heard. Kan-E looked up at the mighty boughs and laid bare the truth of her heart.

"I can no longer hear the elementals," she said. Hearing this, Raya-O's eyes went wide with shock.

"But my true failing was that I kept this fact hidden. That I refused to share my plight with those who look to me for guidance, and with my mentor who has put his faith in me. That I said nothing to my own family, whom I treasure most of all."

"I was deaf to the elementals' calls for succor, yet I said naught. You who I am duty-bound to heed, I neglected in your hour of need. Thus did you reach out to A-Ruhn instead of me, so deep was your despair."

There was no wind, and yet the branches of the tree began to sway and shake.

"Though it shames me, I confess this truth, and beseech you to place your trust in me once more. Trust in me and I shall make your voices heard, that together we can shape the future of the Twelveswood."

As Kan-E finished her plea to the great one, A-Ruhn's ragged breathing calmed. Slowly, he began to mouth words, as if taking great pains to choose each one.

In this way did Kan-E address the elementals, A-Ruhn speak their response, and Raya-O listen. The three siblings worked in concert and together gave form to the once-unintelligible message.

"Within the moon doth our doom stir."

With this grave revelation, the lesser troubles of Gridania were eclipsed by what lie on the horizon. The destruction of all Eorzea. A Calamity which would have remained unforeseen if not for the efforts of the three Padjal.

In that moment, Kan-E conceived a plan. A plan which surprised her siblings in its boldness, but which they soon agreed was wise. In spite of the prophesied annihilation itself, the Elder Seedseer had found renewed hope, and as she basked in the shade of the Guardian Tree, the thick branches rustled in the warm wind, until something fell from above and landed at Kan-E's feet. *A gift . . . and a promise.*

Upon returning to Gridania, Kan-E reconvened the Seedseer Council, and when the Hearers arrived at the Lotus Stand, they were greeted by a perplexing sight. The Elder Seedseer was present, as were her brother and sister, who were not officially council members. A-Pitat, who had scarcely been seen since his retirement and convalescence, was in attendance as well. But their surprise at these unexpected guests paled in comparison to their horror when Kan-E spoke and confessed that she had been unable to hear the elementals.

"Thankfully, with the aid of Raya-O and A-Ruhn were the elementals calmed, and their warning finally understood," she said. At once, the Hearers began to whisper amongst themselves, but when Kan-E told them of the coming Calamity, they fell deathly silent.

"The trials ahead will be greater than any we have ever faced, and I do not possess the strength to lead you alone. I confessed this weakness and this doubt—this truth—and after did receive of the Guardian Tree this gift."

Kan-E drew forth and held aloft a staff.

"This is Claustrum, bestowed upon me by the great one. The elementals often speak in riddles, but the great one's intent in this matter is plain: my siblings and I must work as one to see that the elementals are heard." *'Tis a key. A constant reminder that true strength lies in the courage to bare your soul and beg succor.*

"From this day forward, I propose that the duties of Elder Seedseer be carried out not by one, but by three." Her siblings looked to the gathered Hearers with a resolve none would question. Seeing this, A-Pitat stepped forward and spoke.

"Three hearts united in single purpose. Doubtless the elementals are overjoyed at this news, and together with the Seedseers shall lead the peoples of the Twelveswood unto a future most bright."

As their first act, the trio of Seedseers took inspiration from Kan-E's studies of the Fifth Astral Era and proposed the reformation of the Grand Companies and the reestablishment of the Order of the Twin Adder. The Archons of Sharlayan had offered similar counsel, and the emergence of a shared threat provided the impetus needed for Eorzea's city-states to come together in the spirit of cooperation.

Satisfied, A-Pitat returned to his home to live out the rest of his days in peace, though Kan-E would call upon him again many times before he passed. In one of their final conversations, he reflected upon the incident which had spurred her to involve her siblings in governance. "Only when we are true of heart does the path reveal itself," he reminded her with a smile.

Sage wisdom that delivered me and our people when all was nearly lost, and that I shall not soon forget.

An Empty Throne

At the far end of the audience hall in the Holy Vault of Ishgard, set upon a dais spanning its breadth, was the archbishop's throne. From this sacred seat, the church's most powerful men had ruled for centuries, but no longer.

The throne lay empty—a relic of the time before the war's end and the republic's birth. Where once power was hoarded, it was now shared. Where once the privileged conspired in secret, the people's chosen now debated in earnest. Count Artoirel de Fortemps was one such representative, and on this day, like many others before it, he sat in attendance as a member of the House of Lords.

"If there are no further comments, I move that we end the session with a vote," Aymeric declared, his voice echoing across the grey flagstones of the chamber. "Once yours is cast, you are free to take your leave. My apologies for keeping you all until such a late hour, my lords. I know full well you have great demands upon your time."

Says the man with the greatest demands upon his, Artoirel thought wryly. Between scrambling hither and yon on official business and presiding over house sessions, he knew that his friend had precious little time for himself.

At the lord speaker's words, the members rose to their feet and began making their way to the ballot box in the predetermined order. Many were still fumbling their way through the unfamiliar business of republican governance, Artoirel himself not least of all, but he pressed on with dutiful determination. Having cast his vote, he returned to his seat to gather up his belongings when the empty throne chanced to catch his eye. As he beheld it, his vision blurred as the memory of a day seventeen years ago came flooding back. A day from what now felt like another life . . .

The shirt's collar felt stiff as canvas, but Artoirel endured the discomfort. The occasion called for the finest finery, and the outfit his manservant had assisted him into made his dinner garb appear uncouth in comparison. It was not every day, after all, that Ishgard saw a changing of its ordained ruler. Wishing to be part of the historic occasion of Archbishop Thordan VII's coronation, highborn and lowborn alike had gathered before the Vault, the mass of citizenry extending as far as the Hoplon. However, none save a privileged few outside of high-ranking clergy and the archbishop's personal guard were permitted to attend the official proceedings.

In his capacity as the scion of House Fortemps, Artoirel stood beside his father in the audience hall, endeavoring to look as dignified as his thirteen summers would allow. His youngest brother Emmanellain was there too, and, to his credit, was behaving himself despite being too little to appreciate the gravity of the event.

Haurchefant, however, was absent—on account of not bearing the name Fortemps, their lord father had earlier explained. Yet even before this, Artoirel had always sensed that there was something different about his brother, if only through his aloofness and the disdain with which their mother treated him.

Thus the ceremony proceeded with his family short a member, but if anyone else was bothered by it, they did not let it show. And after a series of solemn rites, Thordan VII finally appeared in the sacred vestment of the archbishop. Holding the Fury's Grace, the holy crozier of his office, he strode purposefully and majestically towards the throne as Artoirel looked on in awe.

"I, Thordan, seventh of my name, do swear to serve as an instrument of Halone's will. Embodying the spirit of King Thordan, our nation's revered founder, I shall preach the faith and protect the faithful, that together we might defeat the dragon menace and bring the Fury's blessing unto all men."

The archbishop's words stirred Artoirel to the core, reaffirming the lessons he had been taught since first he could remember. He was descended from the legendary knights twelve. His chest fairly bursting with pride, he made his own pledge.

Like my ancestors before me, I will become a knight brave and true. And I will serve Ishgard unto my dying breath.

At length, the ceremony came to a close, and the doors to the audience hall were thrown open to let in a flood of lesser peerage. Some wished to catch a glimpse of their newly anointed leader, while others sought to curry favor with the High Houses. Together with Emmanellain, Artoirel followed his father as he led them through the dance of nobility, keeping his eyes peeled in careful observance as he was taught. One day, he, too, would need to navigate these selfsame waters.

He noticed the members of Houses Durendaire and Dzemael take their leave early. Sharing fields of red on their crests, the two families tended to keep to their own, giving the impression that they were ever plotting some manner of intrigue. In contrast, Houses Fortemps and Haillenarte, which shared black fields and ancient ties, were hardly reclusive, and were in fact regular fixtures at social events. Even now, his father, Lord Edmont, had begun engaging in cordial conversation with Lord Baurendouin, his counterpart in the latter. Of the children of that house, all were present save Francel, who was yet too tender in years to attend formal functions. When the adults finally dispensed with the pleasantries and began discussing difficult matters, the sons and daughters took the opportunity to withdraw and speak among themselves.

Beaming his brightest smile, Emmanellain sidled over to where

Chlodebaimt and Laniaitte, the third- and fourth-born of House Haillenarte, were standing. Artoirel was not surprised to see a gaggle of younger children attending Chlodebaimt—he had a way with the little ones. Meanwhile, Artoirel turned to face Stephanivien and Aurvael, the first and second sons. Such noble children would one day become allies and rivals both, he knew, and it would behoove him to maintain friendly relations. *But not* too *friendly.*

"My lords," he said, sweeping them a well-rehearsed bow.

Stephanivien chuckled. "Oh, come now, let's not stand on ceremony. We are of an age, are we not?"

In a languid tone, Aurvael added, "Aye, and I've had my fill of the dry formalities. It's tiresome stuff, and I want to go home."

"Likewise, Brother. I am on the cusp of completing my latest invention. Shall we beg leave of Father?"

And as quick as that, the brothers bade Artoirel farewell, asked their father to be excused, and happily trotted off. As he watched them leave, Artoirel could not help but envy the carefree pair.

Finding himself bereft of company once more, he returned to observing the people around him. Ere long, he spied a dark-haired youth, slightly older perhaps than himself, regarding the archbishop's throne with what could only be described as a glare. Puzzled, he approached and asked, "Why do you frown so? Is this not a joyous occasion?"

The youth started at the question and turned to face Artoirel. His eyes widened in surprise, but soon narrowed as anger reclaimed his features.

"Clearly you have not heard the rumors of my birth. Not that it is any concern of yours."

Artoirel winced. In turn, the youth's expression softened in remorse.

"My apologies, that was ill done." Clearing his throat, he continued pleasantly. "My name is Aymeric. How was the ceremony, if I may ask? I did not have the pleasure of witnessing it."

The excitement of the event still fresh in his mind, Artoirel forgot his discomfort and held forth with unbridled admiration. "Oh, 'twas truly inspiring. I shan't soon forget His Eminence's oath. He swore that he would serve as an instrument of Halone's will and bless all men."

"Bless all men . . . Do you suppose he can do such a thing?"

Artoirel was about to reply when another stole the words right from his mouth.

"Absolutely! The archbishop is a great man!"

The two turned to find a golden-haired boy, garbed in common fashion, regarding them eagerly—the son of a knight, perhaps. Seeming to remember himself, the newcomer bowed deeply as one does to one's betters, before resuming his enthusiastic account.

"His Eminence graced our school with a visit last year. He prayed for us, that we would become strong, righteous knights. 'Tis my dream to serve him one day."

The boy's passion struck a chord with Artoirel, who nodded in approval. Aymeric, however, simply stared. He parted his lips as if to speak, but thinking better of it, said nothing.

Nary a moment later, a knight emerged from the throng and barked.

"Ah, there's Valhourdin's lad!" Placing a firm hand on their golden-haired counterpart's shoulder, he continued. "Come, your father's been looking for you."

Drawing himself up to his full height, the boy swept them another bow and departed with the knight.

"I too must be on my way," said Aymeric. "By your leave, Lord Artoirel."

By the time he had gathered his wits enough to wonder when he had given his name, his companion had already disappeared. Like himself, Aymeric too must have been taught to be observant, he concluded. *To listen and learn in preparation for the day you must join in the dance . . .*

"Lord Artoirel, are you well?"

A familiar voice plucked him from his reverie. He turned to see Aymeric standing a few steps away. Glancing about the chamber, he realized that it was empty save for him and his friend. *How far you have come since that day . . .*

After that meeting, Artoirel had discovered that Aymeric de Borel, the adopted son of a viscount, was rumored to be the illegitimate issue of Archbishop Thordan himself. Out of kindness, his parents had chosen not to speak of the matter to him, though it did nothing to shield him from the gossip of others. And so Aymeric had sought an audience with the archbishop to ascertain the truth—but as a child of a lesser house, such a wish was not to be fulfilled. In the end, he came to embrace his lot, and dedicated himself in service to his people. For his efforts, he was rewarded with command of the Temple Knights.

And now he held the highest office in the nation.

"Lord Artoirel?" Aymeric repeated, with a hint of concern.

"Forgive me, I was lost in reminiscence. The archbishop's coronation, when first we spoke . . ."

"I see," said Aymeric as he turned his gaze upon the throne, eyebrows furrowed not unlike that day. After a time, he continued. "It feels like another life, does it not?"

Artoirel sighed. *Once, I would have told you nothing.*

"I am torn to remember that day. To remember the child I was, who accepted all he was taught without question. The *lies*. The pride I had in my lineage—my very existence! Gods, what a fool I was."

"Our scars will not soon fade. Though we try to move forward, the pain lingers. A constant reminder of our fathers' betrayals and our traumas."

Aymeric had told him the tale during the campaign at Ghimlyt. How his friend had urged the archbishop to renounce the lies upon which Ishgard was built and was rebuffed as a naive child for wanting to tear down institutions that had endured for over a thousand years. And indeed, built upon a rotten foundation of deception though everything was, Aymeric had recognized the truth in his father's words, and they remained a thorn in his breast.

We cannot easily forget that which had defined us for so long. Thus do we struggle to rebuild our lives.

Just as Artoirel was making to speak, Aymeric picked up the thread as though he had been privy to his thoughts.

"So let us forget neither the past nor the pain. Let us acknowledge whence we came, and whence we now stand set forth anew."

As the setting sun shone through the window, Artoirel nodded. In silence, they contemplated the empty throne, and the deepening shadow it cast.

Act III

Witnesses to Calamity

A Friendship of Record

In a quiet corner of Amaurot, the bustling metropolis at the heart of civilization, sat a vault known as Anamnesis Anyder. Within its expansive walls, not only were creation concepts cataloged, but every known natural law and phenomenon was documented in exhausting detail. In short, it held the sum of mankind's accumulated wisdom.

As vast as this collection was, it required the oversight of no few curators, whose responsibility it was to categorize—and subsequently organize—the ever-increasing number of papers, crystals, and other recordkeeping mediums. Such duties demanded an unrivaled breadth and depth of knowledge, and thus for those who valued scholarly achievement, an appointment to Anyder archivist was considered an honor.

A great honor indeed.

While others poured their passion into new concepts and creations, the man remained fascinated by the study of extant reality. He would ponder what made a stone a stone—the properties which defined its existence. He was of the firm belief that one could solve the mysteries of one's surrounds—indeed, of the star itself—by understanding the fundamental building blocks from which they were formed.

When time permitted, the man would step away from his

meticulous archiving to peruse the works on the shelves, referencing their ideas to flesh out his own hypotheses. There was little he enjoyed more, likening the process to a tree gaining rings with age, or layers of sediment building up over the eons.

One fateful day, the man was summoned by the chief archivist to attend to the needs of a visiting academic. *A rather distinguished one at that.* Over the last few centuries, this influential figure had produced striking results in the field of organic research, and her assertion that organisms were simply another form of matter was one which intersected neatly with his personal theories. Thus it was that the bookish man, unable to deny his interest and finding no valid reason to refuse, agreed to assist the academic in her pursuit of reference materials.

At the appointed hour, he took himself to the anteroom which abutted the entrance hall. A woman's voice, vibrant and clear, answered his polite knock. Pushing open the heavy door, he beheld the scholar standing alone, garbed in the same black robes and white half-mask worn by the majority of the citizenry, himself included. As he entered the chamber, however, she swept back her hood and slipped off her mask with smooth, unhurried motions.

"I am Venat. A pleasure to make your acquaintance."

The archivist was stunned. With the exception of circumstances where identification was mandated, it was inappropriate to bare one's face to anyone save intimate friends. The custom was otherwise broken only when seeking earnest counsel, entreating a mentor for aid, or making a life-changing commitment. *None of which should apply to me . . .* Regardless, it signaled her intention to engage him with candor and respect.

With a deep breath, he reached for his own mask and returned the gesture.

And so began a friendship that would endure until the end of their days.

Venat was cheerful, well spoken, and undeniably brilliant. Her carefully crafted arguments drew sighs of admiration from her audience and concessions from her opponents. *A rounded gemstone, without edge or flaw—the refracted light rendered a soft glow.*

His perception would evolve years later.

Venat, having been writing furiously at one of Anyder's desks, at last put down her quill. Observing this, the archivist replaced the book he had taken from a shelf, and peered over her shoulder.

The argument was whole and free of contradiction. *No longer theory, but indisputable truth.* His heart swelled with elation and relief.

"It seems congratulations are in order."

Venat appeared not to have heard him.

Puzzled, the archivist shifted to the side of the desk and saw the scholar transfixed by her own work. For a time, she sat perfectly still. Then all of a sudden, she brought her hands to her mouth . . . and smiled. So broad and heartfelt that modesty could not conceal it. Unadulterated, unabashed joy—a jubilance that sparkled in her ocean-hued eyes. *I recall not when you removed your mask, but I am grateful that you did.*

"A miracle . . ." Venat muttered, as if in a trance. "Our existence is nothing short of a miracle."

"What an odd thing to say. Have you not just proven that life was the inevitable outcome of natural law?"

"Yes, but it is that inevitability which amazes me so. The sublime mechanism itself . . ."

The revelation yet commanded her full attention. As he watched Venat stare at the parchment, he felt his image of her fracture. Sharply cut facets now reflected the light with piercing intensity. *All the more dazzling in her radiance.*

He knew in his heart that this was the Venat she was meant to be.

Venat's perception of the world had changed, the archivist realized. As if for her the true shape of things had been brought into stark focus.

"I am leaving on a journey."

Her entrance was unexpected; her declaration abrupt. "Where will you go?"

"Nowhere," she replied. "Everywhere. This star has so much to share with us. Whispered wisdom to which I would hearken. Untold experiences I yearn to feel. Mysteries and wonders I must understand."

"Then you had best get started," he said, knowing full well that she needed no encouragement. "But do take care."

In lieu of a farewell, Venat graced him with another joyous smile. Her robe twirled about her feet as she turned and strode from the echoing vault. He watched, waiting until the distant door had swung closed behind her, then returned to his labors. Looking over the documents with a practiced eye, he quickly determined the first item's rightful place. He reached for another, and then another—carrying out his tasks with quiet efficiency.

Yet his mind wandered. *What will she seek when next she returns? I must be ready.* The time he had set aside for his own academic pursuits was gradually consumed by the study of subjects outside his field of expertise—a diversion he found strangely rewarding.

When Venat did interrupt her travels to return to Anyder, it was always without warning. Sometimes months would pass—and on occasion, years—before she appeared again, seeking to deepen her knowledge on this or that matter. As she enthusiastically regaled him with her adventures, he was struck by how different this Venat was from the brilliant yet rather more subdued scholar he had met once upon a time. *A crystal bathed in sunlight. So blinding in her delight she outshone the very stars.*

Her discoveries astonished him, as did her daring deeds that allowed her to make them. He, in turn, astonished her, producing the resources she required ere she had finished describing her query.

Venat's standing in society, too, began to change. In recognition of her work, she was elevated to a seat on the Convocation—to the office of Azem.

As well she should. The mantle of the Traveler suits her well.

Despite their history, her well-deserved new status demanded all the more respect—and distance. When next she appeared, however, the ceremony with which he presented her documents did not sit well with his esteemed visitor.

"Must I suffer this exhausting pomp from you as well?" she asked, her brow creasing in annoyance.

"Am I to speak to Azem as if she were my study partner?" he retorted. "You represent our highest authority now. You must accept the trappings with which it comes."

Venat went on to embrace her duties, accomplishing all manner of notable deeds in her time as Azem. When she caught word of a settlement beset by rampaging wildlife, she tracked the creatures to their lair and identified the cause of their hostility. When a citizen feared for a colleague yet to return from an expedition, she braved precipitous mountain peaks to find him. She toppled a towering creation born from a child's errant imagination, weeded out poisonous plants that had infested a farmer's crops, and when a matter required greater intervention, she brought it before the Convocation of Fourteen with a solution she herself provided. Astride her golden familiar, she journeyed without cease across land and sea and sky . . .

Thus when Venat announced her decision to relinquish her office, it was that much more unexpected. *A jest, surely.* Yet she spoke in glowing terms of her chosen successor, a "fascinating person" she had met on her travels.

"You would surrender the seat of Azem with so much left undone?" the archivist asked, still reeling at the implications.

"A true traveler has no need of a title," Venat said. "And my replacement would benefit greatly from the opportunities granted by the appointment."

"The journey is different for each who undertake it. Even following the same route, and visiting the same destinations, they will have different thoughts and experiences. They will make their own discoveries, and observe that which I failed to perceive."

Though she spoke of a successor, hers were not the words of one preparing to return to the star. *Not yet, please. Not yet.* Having attained the apex of their "personal truth," no small number of his Anyder colleagues had gone to their rest amidst a shower of praise and accolades.

But the archivist felt no pressing desire to join them—rather the opposite. For there was but one purpose he considered worthy of fulfillment: to keep watch as this incandescent jewel walked her path, and bear witness when she arrived at its terminus.

Venat stepped down from the seat of Azem to don the white robes of a neutral advisor. The man, meanwhile, stepped up to assume the role of chief archivist.

And so it was that when the Final Days were upon them, Anamnesis Anyder would serve as headquarters for Venat and her loyal followers.

The Final Days brought fire and ruin until Zodiark put an end to the calamity.

His devotees then resolved to sow new life—a bounty of souls to take the place of their sacrificed brethren. In time would they reap this crop, and by rendering it unto their god would the lost be returned, and the world restored to the paradise it was and ever should have been.

Venat, along with the archivist and their like-minded companions, objected to this undertaking. The future, they believed, must not bear the cost for saving the past. Only in accepting pain and loss—by learning from the mistakes of yesterday—could they greet the morrow. A power such as Zodiark possessed was anathema to the progress of man.

Venat's faction thus resolved to manifest an entity capable of shackling that power. To have any chance at defeating the nigh-omnipotent Zodiark, however, the sacrifice must be absolute. Not even their souls would remain.

In the evening after this consensus had been reached, the archivist approached his friend.

"Venat, please . . ." he wavered. "Why must it be you?"

Hydaelyn, as the entity would be known, required more than the collective's souls to manifest: She needed a heart. Venat was the obvious choice, though some believed that their leader should be spared—to carry on the cause in the event their efforts ended in failure. But as Venat explained her reasons, he knew that she would not be swayed.

"Rest assured, however: I shall not vanish from this world," she said. "The form I take shall ever remain my choice."

". . . Then I will press you no more. Only know this . . . you will be sorely missed."

She stood before him in silence, and he knew he would never forget how the light caught the tears in her eyes she dared not let fall.

"It is I who shall miss you."

He had thought only of her sacrifice, and naught of the pain his own passing might cause. *What is a candle to the sun?*

And yet . . .

Unable to find the words, the archivist retreated into ritual. He held out a crystal—as he had countless times before—upon which was stored the last chapter of cosmological wisdom Venat had sought. Though she had spoken of its importance, he suspected she withheld the entire truth. Of her glimpse into the future, she had offered precious little.

"What we anticipate and what comes to pass need not be the same," she had once said. "'Tis best we work towards the greatest good without foreknowledge which might cloud our judgment."

The rounded gemstone, before life and revelation shaped her into so much more.

"The change in you has been . . . miraculous," he began, choosing his words carefully. "The change in myself almost equally so. A small sample size, perhaps, but if all mankind can grow in similar fashion, then I fear not for our future. Prove my theory, Venat. Prove it was worth the sacrifice."

His challenge hung in the air between them for an age.

Venat sighed, a small smile playing about her lips as she accepted the crystal. The archivist grinned.

"I regret only that I cannot see it through at your side. If you are to be Her heart, then I would be Her eyes. I would watch, unblinking, until the very end."

If only. He would fade into oblivion, and that would be his end. But his challenge would endure.

May it bring you joy and solace on the long road ahead.

And at your journey's end, I pray you look upon our fellow man . . . and know they shall carry on in our stead.

A Question of Life

Few things in the world can be crueler than kind words. Than the presumption of understanding.

All will be well. Fret not. 'Tis passing weariness. I'm always willing to listen.

The empty platitudes echoed in his mind—polite dismissals wielded to render feelings insignificant. Smoothing over jagged grief, paring away thorns of anger, until what remained could be molded into a socially acceptable shape.

Sometimes he would resist, bristling at sympathetic colleagues. Claw at their consoling hands as they urged him to bury his demons. But they would only look down at him, pity plain in their eyes.

Tell them what they want to hear.

And every time, he was accepted once more, and the sacred pretense of harmony restored.

But this time—this time, I am surely beyond acceptance.

Hermes stood on the prime artifice, high in the skies of Ktisis Hyperboreia. From the lower levels, the emergency announcement echoed faintly. Dangerous creations may be on the loose, droned the pre-recorded voice, and the facility had been placed in a state of alert. A field of dampening magick hung over its dimensionally interconnected spaces, suppressing the abilities of all present save for authorized staff. *All this chaos at my whim . . .*

With a hand greatly enlarged by his transformation, Hermes reached out to the facility's aethernet. He commanded more enclosures be thrown open, and images etched in light confirmed the result.

The specimens thus released would fall upon his pursuers, whose priority was not their well-being. In their haste, they would slaughter rather than subdue, and the blood of those innocent creatures would be on his hands. *The choice is mine and mine alone, and so too the blame.* His heart wrenched with shame, but disadvantaged as he was in both strength and numbers, he had precious few options. Never before had he offered violent resistance to anyone—and merely "anyone" his pursuers were not.

When man is likened to the lifeblood of the star, it is not for the role he plays in nurturing it. In this collective duty, all must flow in a single direction, and disagreements seldom depart the realm of civilized debate. Hermes was not given to asserting his beliefs, but he was about to do so with force, and the prospect filled him with an indescribable dread.

The intruders were pressing ever nearer, leaving a trail of death in their wake. As he set free more hapless creations to bar their way, his thoughts drifted to one of them. Azem's familiar—or so it had been initially claimed. In truth, they were a traveler from the future, from a time long after civilization as Hermes knew it had ended. A person who, despite turning the Elpis flower a sorrowful hue, could continue to smile. What Hermes had glimpsed in their gentle countenance was neither kindness nor forbearance, but strength. And that strength had allowed them to overcome innumerable hardships.

I must be strong too—I will be. He would confront and accept these feelings. Even should they break him. Even should they drive him to do the unthinkable.

"No matter what, Meteion, I will not turn away from the answer."

He looked to his beloved creation, whose gaze took in everything and nothing. *Forever changed by the knowledge.* He tried to take solace from the fact that she heeded his request to wait, which suggested that her shared consciousness had stabilized.

According to Meteion's report, there was little joy to be found in the distant stars. Assuming there were beings out there who could share what gave their lives meaning, he feared the answer would be too bitter for his fellow man to swallow. That was why he needed time—the time to come to terms with the truth alone, his thoughts unclouded by well-meaning debate or pragmatic concerns for future implications.

With a heavy heart, Hermes opened a higher-clearance enclosure and unleashed the fearsome Ladon Lord in Concept Review. The creation was his last chance—if it failed to hold off his pursuers, he would have no choice but to confront them himself. There could be no justifying the crime. No turning back.

So be it. Better to be seen as an aberration than abide in the fiction for their sake.

"I sent you unto the stars. I won't let your efforts be in vain."

Hermes knelt low before Meteion, but in his transformed state, he towered over her still. With enormous hands made to tame unruly beasts, the gentlest touch could nevertheless do harm. And so he gazed into her eyes, the same striking blue as her wings, and recalled the days that had led them to this reckoning . . .

Hermes blinked as the blurry images became the room at Anagnorisis. *How long have I been asleep . . . ?* He sat himself up on the sofa and was still trying to shake off the haze when Euanthe walked in. With a pointed sigh, she explained how they had found Hermes collapsed in a corner of the garden and subsequently borne him here. He shrank in embarrassment as the memories came flooding back.

"Forgive me . . . I . . . may have been neglecting to take adequate rest. It's just . . . I'm so close now. I almost have the concept."

Many years had passed since Hermes first conceived of a starfaring creation—an entelechy possessed of free will. Due to an utter lack of precedent, however, satisfying the design criteria was a challenge indeed. Drawing upon the power of dynamis, it needed to be able to traverse the vast emptiness swiftly, and thence locate and communicate with other intelligent life-forms. In pursuit of his vision, Hermes had experienced countless cycles of excitement and disappointment. But at long last, the solution had begun to take shape.

Smiling wryly, Euanthe held out a basket of fruit—her not-so-subtle reminder of life's necessities.

"Does this mean you've finally managed to settle on an appearance?"

Hermes's hand halted halfway to the proffered basket. Unlike men, who were expected to conform to established fashions, it was believed that other living beings should look unique. Add color to the star. Alas, while some such as the incumbent Lahabrea, the foremost authority in the field of phantom creation, could produce beauteous concepts at will, Hermes was consistently at a loss. *Aesthetics were never my forte.*

"Its form should be as simple as its nature is complex," he began. "Birds I know well, of course, and their attributes would suit the abilities it will have. But to facilitate communication with other sentient beings, it should also have the features of a man."

"That's all well and good for a guiding principle, but what about the details? Its physical characteristics, personality, and so on and so forth?"

Hermes hadn't considered such things, hoping in vain that his subconscious would fill in the blanks. Since there was no way of knowing what qualities other life-forms would favor, he could rely only on his own sensibilities. Furrowing his brow, he began rummaging through the cluttered chambers of his mind in search of potential inspiration. The invisible spark of dynamis. *The universe and the stars. Birds soaring in the sky . . .*

". . . Blue. I want it to be blue, like the sky of Elpis. Our portal to the cosmos beyond."

The words tumbled out even as he thought them. Euanthe blinked a few times in consideration before favoring Hermes with an approving chuckle.

"A fine idea."

In the days that followed, Euanthe and other colleagues provided Hermes with design documents, and even held private lectures for his benefit, all of which helped him to form a clearer image of his creation. As was his wont, it took him more time to settle on its appearance than its more practical aspects, but at long last he succeeded in finalizing the concept.

He would never forget the first time he brought her forth. The nervous anticipation as he channeled his magicks. The gathering motes of light that coalesced into a brilliant storm. The moment of manifestation.

Hello.

The songbird was barely larger than his open palm. Her blue feathers tinged black at the tips. *The threshold to the universe as seen from the prime artifice.* Already he could imagine her long tail tracing a line in the sky, like unto a meteor.

"Meteion."

No name could be more fitting, for to speak it made his heart soar. So terrified he had been he could not do her justice. But beholding the creature before him now, he knew there was nothing more beautiful in all the world.

So began their exploration of the universe.

Hermes created Meteion's sisters, the Meteia—though their shared consciousness made them more akin to a single entity—and sent them on brief forays beyond the bounds of the star. Early results were mixed. Though Meteion did not lack the abilities she needed to fulfill her purpose, she encountered one problem after another out in the great expanse. *But we have come so far already—and we will go further still.*

Hermes was conducting further test flights in the Elpis twilight when Meteion, presently in the form of a girl in order to relay her sisters' messages, cried out. He turned to see her frozen in shock, eyes wide and mouth agape. Before he had the chance to speak, she reeled as if struck by a heavy blow, and it was all he could do to catch her.

For a painfully long while, she remained stiff as a corpse in his arms, and gave no indication that she heard his worried words. Then all of a sudden, she awoke with a gasp for air, her body relaxing as if time flowed again. By the way she trembled, feathers standing on end, it was clear that she felt an intense chill. He was rubbing her shoulders to offer comfort when she wailed in frustration.

"We've failed again . . . Lost another one . . ."

Though Hermes had expected as much, it didn't make the news any less bitter. As he struggled to console her, Meteion rose to her feet and dutifully delivered the report in her halting voice. Her sister had been caught in a raging torrent of dynamis, she explained, and was subsequently unmade. *Like so many others before . . .*

As a being of dynamis, Meteion could survive in most any environment by reducing her constituent aether to a bare minimum. A star may be wreathed in flame, frozen from pole to pole, or shrouded in toxic gas, but such hazards would not trouble her. Should lifeforms be present who found their environment excessively harsh, she would share in their sensations, but this was purely academic, for life would not flourish in such conditions in the first place.

Yet by the same token, being made of dynamis rendered Meteion vulnerable to its influence. Though its potential was suppressed on aether-rich Etheirys, it behaved in unexpected ways in the void beyond—ways that confused and confounded her. In one sector, there was a star that could manipulate dynamis. It was capable of harboring thoughts and feelings, if not in a manner man could comprehend. In another, dynamis raged as an endless tempest. At its heart lay a great pool of aether not unlike the aetherial sea, the intermingling of innumerable memories giving rise to the surrounding turbulence.

In her search for intelligent life, Meteion relied on dynamis. And so, like a moth to a flame, she was liable to be drawn to that which could destroy her.

"But don't worry! We learn more every time. What places are bad. We'll find stars with life, I'm sure of it!"

Despite her recent trauma, Meteion retained her enthusiasm. But Hermes's own seemed to have deserted him. How many more of her sisters would be sacrificed for his cause? How many times would he have to see her collapse, the life driven from her body? *Even if you suffer no lasting harm, I fear I do . . .*

"Perhaps we will. And yet . . ." he managed to say before falling silent and hanging his head in shame. He sighed and opened his eyes, only to see a pair of inquisitive blue ones peering up into his own. Scolding himself for failing to control his emotions, he took a deep breath to regain his composure . . . and felt a tiny hand on his head. Meteion was stroking his hair, the motions exaggerated and awkward.

"Have faith, Hermes. We'll get answers. Then everyone will be happy. You, me, everyone!"

The stroking continued for a good while before she withdrew her hand, leaving his dark hair an unkempt mess—and his soul somehow comforted. Hermes looked at her and smiled, and she returned the favor, giggling in her endearing way.

"You're right, Meteion. We will find the answers in the distant stars. And then we will bring change to our own."

He rose to his feet to behold the star-speckled sky once more, with hope in his heart for the future.

That hope did not last. One day, Meteion's shared consciousness became unstable. She and her sisters could not sustain their existence, and all dissipated with a burst. The resultant shockwave accidentally triggered Kairos, which erased several days of memories from those in the vicinity, including visiting observers.

He later learned that several enclosures had been opened in Ktisis Hyperboreia, and many creations perished fighting amongst themselves. After delivering this report, his underling suggested that, in his confusion, perhaps Hermes had sought to free them.

"It seems like something you would do, Chief," the man said with a pitying smile.

Does it? Knowing it was the likely outcome, would I have been so reckless? So cruel?

But it would not have been the first time.

Hermes cursed himself. For sending Meteion forth. For creating her. But most of all, for daring to have doubts. Had he simply thought like everyone else—had he made peace with their morality—he wouldn't have inflicted such pain upon himself and others.

Tell yourself what you need to believe.

And so they did not resent him, and instead gifted him their cruel acceptance.

All will be well. Fret not. 'Tis but a few days of memories. The creatures can always be remade.

The utilitarian logic assailed him. But this time, he offered no resistance. He internalized the lie and came to live as others did. When he was officially nominated to the Convocation of Fourteen, he rose to the occasion, and labored for the good of the star to the very end, to the moment reality itself was sundered.

Of his desperate struggles, nary a mark remained . . . or so it seemed. Yet be it in the ancient past or the distant future, the yearning for which he sacrificed so much would endure. The fire would rise in those who looked up at the heavens in defiance of oblivion—the desire to confront the answers for which Meteion journeyed . . . no matter how terrible the truth may be.

In Pursuit of Knowledge

"If you assist us, we shall share with you all we know."

So ended the letter which his fellow gleaner had delivered to him in snow-swept Ishgard. As Erenville regarded the signature of the petitioner, Krile Baldesion, he recalled the eclectic group that had greeted him in Labyrinthos. *What's your story?*

He was pondering the proposition in his lodgings when his linkpearl rang. It was the guild's administration officer, who launched into the shocking news before Erenville had the chance to speak.

"There's to be a great exodus! An exodus from the very star!"

In frantic tones, the man relayed the details of the Forum's announcement. The coming of the Final Days, as foretold by Hydaelyn, and the means by which they might escape: the moon. *I knew they were hiding something.* Even as he struggled to take it all in, he felt vindicated by the revelation.

"Time is of the essence! Do what you must and return to Sharlayan at once!"

Despite his best efforts, it took Erenville a full three days to return his animal charges to their natural habitats. Days during which he received unsettling reports of calamity and chaos in the Near East. Upon manifesting in the Sharlayan aetheryte plaza, he marched to the nearby Baldesion Annex, where he found Krile in the middle of a discussion with the receptionist.

"Tell me the details," he said, declaring himself and his purpose in one breath, as he thrust out the letter in front of him.

Krile stared at him, dumbstruck, but quickly gathered herself and obliged.

And what a fantastic tale it was. The Scions of the Seventh Dawn had uncovered not only the true history of the star, but the cause of the Final Days. And now they sought to forestall them, that all might be saved.

Erenville had always endeavored to cultivate a broader knowledge of the world, both for his work and for himself. He had, of course, heard about the Scions—their renowned champion not least of all. He had not, however, expected to send said champion on an errand to round up runaway marmots, nor to encounter them again shortly thereafter in the form of a toad. *So this is how "adventurers" amuse themselves.* But to now be privy to the Scions' knowledge and their purpose, he couldn't help but feel the smallness of his own.

Even within the limited scope of his experiences, there seemed to be no end to the star's mysteries. Krile's dizzying account made it plain that he hadn't even scratched the surface, and it pained him to imagine all those secrets left behind, never to see the light of day. *All those stories forever untold.*

"Tell me how I can help." The earnest plea tumbled from his mouth.

Krile's expression softened, and she proceeded to explain the role the Scions would have the gleaners' guildship play in the preparations for the maiden journey of Sharlayan's first starship.

The grand plan was swiftly set into motion. Employing their vast networks, Erenville and his fellow gleaners secured a large part of the manpower needed to enhance the vessel's aetherburner. Those who answered the call assembled at Scholar's Harbor before transporting supplies to the Central Circuit. There, they labored under the Forum's watchful eye to complete the massive ark that would fly to the very edge of the universe.

As the work entered the final stages, while the Loporrits' hyper-hopper was brought in, the specimens that had previously been loaded onto the ark needed to be removed. Aided by the staff of Labyrinthos and members of the Ilsabard contingent, the gleaners tended to the arduous task, bearing load after load from Thaumazein to the Archeion.

Though Erenville was no stranger to heavy lifting, the sheer quantity of cargo soon left his muscles and joints screaming in protest. He had delivered another crate to the lift, and was vainly trying to stretch out the kinks in his back, when a weary voice called out to him.

"Pardon me, old boy." The young Elezen was clad in Ishgardian mail, and the gold trim of his collar marked him as a member of House Fortemps. The smirk narrowed it down further. *He was bickering with that pirate at the harbor like they were old lovers.* "I'm supposed to take this package to Kokkol's Forge, but I fear I'm hopelessly lost. Would you be so kind as to direct me?"

"Kokkol's, you say? In that case, you need to—" Erenville began, before thinking better of it. "Actually, I'll just deliver it."

"Truly? You're too kind—a veritable *saint*! My heartfelt thanks!"

His face beaming, the lad surrendered the package to Erenville. No sooner were his hands free than he placed them on his waist and arched backwards, groaning in relief. Erenville felt a tinge of guilt when he gestured to the nearby mountain of crates. "While I see to your package, mind taking care of this in my stead?"

The color drained from the lad's face as the enormity of his fresh burden sank in. He slumped forward in defeat, groaning again for an altogether different reason.

"Fury take me . . . Had I known how hard this would be, I would have asked the dragons for help . . ."

That was an option? The war between man and dragon had ended,

Erenville knew, but had relations already become so amicable that they would labor side by side? He considered asking about it—out of a professional and personal interest—but ultimately bit his tongue. His aversion to overly familiar individuals aside, there would be no future opportunities to engage with Dravanians should they fail to complete the ark.

A brisk walk saw him to the forge, where enhancements were being carried out on the aetherburner. The air was thick with the clanging of hammers and the chatter of engineers, punctuated by the barked orders of Kokkol Dankkol. Erenville handed the package to the first person who spared him a glance. As he watched it borne away, his eyes fell upon a yellow, birdlike creature coming from the other direction.

In the course of recruiting collaborators for their great project, Erenville had learned that it was a member of Garlond Ironworks. *Whatever it is.* Though he had been curious to know more, he hadn't found the right moment to ask. *But if not now, then when?*

The creature was accompanied by a Lalafellin engineer. *Wedge, was it?* Erenville began by exchanging casual pleasantries.

"Taking a hard-earned break?"

"No rest for the righteous, as the chief would say. The three of us are off on an errand." Wedge turned to the feathered enigma. "Isn't that right, Alpha?"

So that's its name. But who makes three? The diminutive, beetle-like machina at Alpha's heel was an altogether different mystery. *Some manner of toy? Certainly doesn't appear designed for bearing cargo . . .*

"Forgive me, but I've been wondering: what is Alpha, exactly?"

"Why, he's a member of the Ironworks."

"Ah, what I meant was, what manner of creature is he?"

"A chocobo, of course. What else could he be?"

Chocobos were a common sight across the Three Great Continents, having been domesticated long ago. There existed several major breeds, and Erenville could readily identify all of them. *Apparently not . . .* In all his years, he had never encountered a variety like this, either in the wild or in a tome.

His brow furrowed, and in response Alpha gave Erenville an archetypal "kweh!"

"He does sound like a chocobo, I suppose . . ." Erenville conceded. He was trying to think of another question when the little machina suddenly rammed Wedge's leg, causing the engineer to jump with a start.

"Ack, the chief!" he blurted out, having been painfully reminded of his responsibilities. "We need to get going, I'm afraid, but it was nice talking to you."

And with that, Wedge hurried off, with Alpha flapping and the machina clanking along behind him, leaving the bewildered Erenville alone with his thoughts. As he watched the last of Alpha's plumage disappear from sight, he found himself unsatisfied. *There must be an incredible story there . . .*

It couldn't be ruled out that Alpha was an undescribed species; he himself had captured more than a few in his time. There were academics who were tasked with studying, classifying, and then naming such specimens, and they could doubtless do the same for Alpha.

But to what end . . . ?

The Scions' discoveries were a stark reminder that truth has never been the province of a select few. *Certainly not the Forum.* Nor was the future set in stone, as the end of the thousand-year war between man and dragon demonstrated. Elementary and obvious conclusions, perhaps, yet they conspired to make him wax philosophical: how does one identify the unknown, and at what point does it become the known?

Think. Keep thinking, and you will find your answers. Your tale.

A passing engineer brushed against his shoulder, pulling Erenville out of his reverie. As the faces of those around him came into focus, he felt a newfound appreciation for their individuality. The cryptic yet colorful snatches of overheard conversations, amidst a vivid landscape that suddenly stood out in sharp relief.

There's so little I know . . . So much I've yet to learn . . .

The Scions must triumph, and he would do his part to make it so. With one last stretch and a deep breath, he moved on. *The mountain isn't going to move itself.*

Work on the ark continued at a breakneck pace, as if the busiest months of the year had been condensed into a week.

The Loporrits scrambled to and fro, picking their way between porters as they imparted their knowledge to attentive Sharlayan scholars. Careful urgency was the order of the day, and even members of the Forum could be seen moving with uncharacteristic haste as they oversaw the efforts. Kokkol's Forge remained a source of boisterous commotion, with its master bellowing orders in an ever-hoarser voice. Ironworks engineers were present in Thaumazein at all hours, toiling beside Hannish alchemists.

Keeping this massive workforce fed were family members and servants and the staff of the Last Stand, who prepared meals in bulk with ingredients sourced from Meryall Agronomics and the mitato. Nary a moment passed when coffee, chai, and nutritional supplements weren't being distributed. Blankets were set aside for those who needed rest, and weary workers gently laid them over their slumbering peers.

Eventually, the downpour subsided to a drizzle, and the gleaners began finding themselves free. By the time Erenville had made his last delivery, more than half his colleagues were idle. Nevertheless, they remained in Labyrinthos, ready to answer the call at a moment's notice.

Until one day, when the ringing of a bell echoed throughout the artificial sky. When from the scattered amplification devices, a crackling voice began to speak.

"Attention, everyone. This is Fourchenault Leveilleur." Hands halted their work and feet froze in their tracks. As all listened intently, Fourchenault thanked them for their tireless labors and many sacrifices. The ark's systems were undergoing inspection, he continued, and the city held its breath, uncertain whether this announcement would be cause for celebration or disappointment.

". . . But the vessel itself stands completed. The stars are now within our reach."

Labyrinthos erupted into a chorus of cheers. Some laughed, some wept. Some shook hands, while others embraced. In their shared triumph, every soul rejoiced in their own way.

Erenville, for his part, only sighed in relief. To some, he may have even appeared indifferent, but the warmth that filled his breast was no less invigorating. *We did it.* With all his heart, he prayed that their hopes would reach the distant stars and deliver their own unto the morrow.

And sometimes, wishes come true.

The Final Days came and went, and peace returned to Sharlayan. On a morning much like any other, Erenville approached the Baldesion Annex. This time, however, he sought not to answer a petition, but to offer a proposal. In exchange for helping to rebuild the Students of Baldesion, he would request their assistance in restoring the archives to their proper order. While he was somewhat concerned he might be dragged into troublesome Scion business once more, deep down he almost *hoped* it would happen.

One day—perhaps when his part in their adventures is ended—he will lay to rest a long-deferred matter. That which had confronted him in his faraway home long before he took his new name, and chose to walk the gleaner's path.

With renewed purpose, he strode through the annex door to find Krile, who again received him with a surprised look.

Delight in their stories, but do not forget your own. For it is far from finished.

A Question of Death

Jullus awoke to near darkness.

He was but one of many soldiers, young and old, lying in Tertium. Every ilm of the carriage floor was covered in bedrolls, leaving no room for careless movement.

Taking care not to disturb the others, he sat up, straining to make out the hands of the old clock salvaged by who-knows-who that was hidden somewhere in the gloom. *The near edge of dawn* . . . Further down, beyond his sleeping fellows, was the wavering blue glow of the ceruleum stove.

It was not the cold that had roused him from his slumber. *We're old friends now.* Before accepting the Ilsabard contingent's proffered aid, his people had little materiel—and certainly no magic—to warm frozen fingers and toes. The exhaustion that often carried him to sleep still failed to prevent him from regularly stirring in the night.

Thinking he might pass the time with fresh air at least, he reached down to drag his boots and bag towards him. Conscious of every noise, he dressed stealthily, holding his breath when Publius rolled over next to him. Fortunately, there came no word of complaint, and Jullus was free to slip out and mull over the events of the previous night in peace.

They'd been huddled around a lamp in an out-of-the-way corner, the familiar scent of honey and spices wafting from their cradled mugs—one small comfort afforded by a surplus in rations. The conversation had again settled into a lull when Publius broke the silence.

"I may just leave for Sharlayan."

The grimacing youth—of an age with Jullus, though low in rank—had barely spoken a word all evening. Now that he had, none knew how to respond.

It wasn't surprising. *Inevitable, really.* Survive the Telophoroi and Final Days they had, but Garlemald was still in a sorry state. The Emperor was gone, the senate disbanded, and nations were hesitant to commit to any policy concerning the erstwhile empire.

There had been some hesitant steps towards forming an interim government, but neither Garlemald nor its neighbors had the means to establish one immediately. The provincial leaders were waiting to see which way the winds would blow, welcoming their countrymen home while making no moves to resurrect the Empire themselves. Rumors that this or that province was poised to formally declare independence, or had as good as seceded already, ran rampant.

It was only natural to give Garlemald up as a lost cause. Even as some returned to rebuild, others who had been tempered and taken to other nations for treatment petitioned to remain there, and these nations—Sharlayan among them—welcomed the refugees with open arms. Though Publius might be the first among present company, he would not be the last to make a new home far from the old.

Publius stared into his cup as the moment dragged on. In this nation of the fallen, what was left to say?

". . . You should speak with Alphinaud or Alisaie on the morrow. They'll put you in contact with someone you can trust," Jullus ventured. The ever-helpful pair was staying at Camp Broken Glass, and like as not had plenty to be doing already, but he would be remiss not to mention it.

"I'll do that."

With that small gesture, the atmosphere changed. Publius exhaled in relief, and the others were soon offering their own words of encouragement and vows to meet again. Though their drinks had long gone cold, their cheers gave them warmth enough.

"To our brothers and our homeland!"

The brisk winds carried away sleep's warm haze as Jullus climbed the slope that led out of the station. Beyond the shaft's angular portal, the weak morning light revealed the stark outline of his reality.

The remaining spire of the once-shining Palatium Novum stood alone in the city center, amongst homes reduced to steel skeletons and grey rubble. Beyond these unnatural hills loomed the Tower of Babil, grasping for the heavens.

Tertium's surrounds had been spared out-and-out obliteration, but were dead all the same. None remained to hurry to work or school, or stagger home after a night on the town. None remained to clear snow from a neighbor's path, or rove helplessly in their dog's wake. The people who had given this place life a few short months ago were gone. *How many even had the chance to say good-bye?*

Jullus breathed deep of the frozen air, but though its icy pinpricks grounded him in the present, it was powerless to dispel the long nightmare. The vision endured, implacable, without regard for the dreamers. To the shrewdest of minds and the purest of hearts, fate offered no justice nor justification.

"Yet you would ask me why."

That injury should have healed. Yet it itched at him now—a scab that bled and bled, threatening to hollow him out from within. Even as he picked at it, his feet carried him forward—*better to survey the surrounds for threats*—and into the silent city.

Unforgiving grey. Destruction and loss. All silent as the grave, as if even beasts preferred not to pick through these bones of an empire so early in the morn.

A flash of movement caught his eye—a scrap of old newsprint trapped in the tumbledown debris of a roadside ruin. *The last will and testament of someone's breakfast table.* He drew closer, mindful of the potential for further collapse.

"I remember this . . ."

A special edition, distributed on Unity Day several years past. The celebration commemorating Garlemald's founding and the heroes who had labored for the Empire was always a tremendous affair for residents of the capital, most of whom spent the day reveling. The eldest told stories of meager harvests and desperate clashes as choirs sang old marching songs. Hawkers along the avenues sold food, drinks, traditional adornments from the campi, and the latest magitek baubles.

Naught was more highly anticipated than the military parade—a show of strength and patriotism that never failed to inspire both awe and pride. Countless soldiers and magitek units moved in time through the city, beating a steady rhythm towards the imperial palace, where the Emperor's family stood assembled to receive them.

They led us to greatness. We who formed the vanguard of history's grand march forward. His city was the heart of the world, through which flowed blood stronger than steel—a bond between countrymen that would remain unbroken even should their every enemy join together to oppose them. *Glory be to Garlemald.*

The Unity Day described in this print had taken place while Jullus was in the Academy, and marked the last year that the ailing Solus had been in attendance. Though the lead article detailing the events and speeches of the day was in tatters, the accompanying portrait of the imperial family remained.

At its center, naturally, was the stern visage of Solus zos Galvus. Though still dignified in his old age, the gaze which he fixed upon the reader was more melancholic than proud. *Never saw the man smile once.* To the Emperor's right stood Titus, second of Solus's sons, along with his wife Arrecina and son Nerva. Both Titus and his son had a strained look about them, not dissimilar to the younger Solus found in the history books.

On His Radiance's left was his grandson Varis, the only legacy of the deceased crown prince Lucius. A proud one, too—Varis was tall and broad of shoulder, and his comportment marked him a prime candidate for high legatus even then. His wife and right hand,

Carosa, had passed away in her prime, and so he was flanked instead by his mother, Hypatia. Though she departed to join Carosa a mere year after this portrait was taken, she supported Varis's claim to the throne until the very end. And then there was the young man with a faraway look in his eyes and an air of detachment . . .

"Would you be 'happier' had I a 'good reason'?"

Zenos yae Galvus. Though his anger had cooled since their encounter on the Eblan Rime, Jullus nevertheless found himself wrenched back to the present with no little displeasure.

His homeland was gone. That much was plain, even as he clung to the ragged scrap of remembrance. He hadn't known then whence the fervor of that day would lead, but knew well now that it would never be reborn. Even should Garlemald rise from the ashes, its age had ended.

And what of us? A new day had dawned, and Jullus would not suffer his people to remain in the dark. Yet what star were they to follow?

Jullus shook out the paper, folded it neatly, and tucked it in his pocket before leaving the ruin behind.

The streets were still and silent, his crunching footsteps the only sound. Playing his role of watchman, he investigated the semi-intact structures he came across, but found little of note. No food or supplies remained, only the detritus of peaceful lives—naught worth saving then or now. A fine layer of ash covered splintered furniture and forgotten trinkets, forming cairns in the gloom.

After a time, he arrived at a house he had never explored in his prior wanderings. With the roof torn off and the walls half-crumbled, it seemed unlikely to hold anything of value, but he nevertheless picked his way through the frosted rubble that would have once formed the lintel. Once inside, he dusted himself off and took in his surroundings—and drew a startled breath.

Jullus had seen enough death by now to recognize it at a glance. He approached the soldier and knelt to examine his corpse. Though the cold had prevented significant decay, it was clear he had died some time ago. Had it been during the war, the body would have been removed, so he could only be one of the tempered or their victims. The bite and scratch marks suggested the latter. *Like the scars my family gave me.*

He removed the man's helmet carefully—not a face he recognized, so probably not a member of the Ist Legion. Just another poor soul who had escaped the tempering, exhausted the last of his strength, and died anyway.

Jullus would offer no gods-bound prayers as an Eorzean might, but nevertheless set the helmet aside to pay his respects. Though the sentiment rang hollow, he silently encouraged the deceased to find peace with his ancestors and watch over his kin.

Alphinaud and Alisaie claimed that the Scions had visited the aetherial sea, where all souls returned. There, they were healed of their traumas and washed clean of memories—even should not a single prayer be offered on their behalf. Their deeds in life had no bearing on their place within the relentless machinery of death and rebirth—made no more difference than Garlemald's vaunted unity had to its ultimate fate.

If the twins spoke true, then what meaning was there in any of it? What was life, if not another pointless parade?

It occurred to him that this was probably not the most respectful place to ruminate on life's worth. *My new friend here would certainly have an opinion.* He had no tools for a proper burial, but if he could at least make note of the man's name . . .

Alas, there was no identification to be found. *Understandably not a priority for you at the time.* His armaments were standard-issue, and provided no hint either. Although . . .

"What have we here?"

Gently prising open the corpse's fist revealed the empty case for a magitek armor identification key. Had it been stolen after his death? That didn't make sense—a thief wouldn't have repositioned the dead man's hand, which had been clutching the thing so desperately. *As if in prayer.* But if he had reason to hope that a comrade might escape, or that rescue was on the way, then maybe . . .

"You gave it away," Jullus muttered, as another memory surfaced in his mind.

It was summer—of the same year as the newsprint he'd found earlier. A friend had insisted he read some poetry collection, and in the spirit of camaraderie Jullus obliged. He had little interest in elegies, often finding them difficult to parse, but one inscrutable passage had stayed with him:

"Let this be my final gift to you. In death, my love."

In death we have the power to bequeath the life we might have had—the possibilities and potential—to others. To grant them what they need to go on . . . or so the poet said.

Was your key one such gift?

Would my mother, my brother, my sister—would they tell me to accept theirs?

Lord Quintus, with his suicide? My comrades, whom I failed? My countrymen, gone without a word?

Did you leave your lives, and your love, to me?

The dead do not answer, yet the wound within ceases its bleeding for a time.

If that is our truth . . .

"Then let it be our meaning. Let it be the chain which binds us through generations. Live on in me, as I would have in you."

And perhaps . . .

"Perhaps we may yet live on in others."

The dead do not answer, but light shines through the broken ceiling, and Jullus follows it to behold a brightened sky. His comrades at Tertium will be waking soon. In apology and gratitude, he offers one last silent prayer to his kinsman ere departing.

Be at peace—and know that you are with me.

Jullus stands, and forges ahead into the dawn.

Act IV

Dénouement and Complication

As Azure Fades

Estinien Varlineau was quickly discovering the potency of Hannish spirits.

Back when the hunting of dragons consumed his every waking moment, he had seldom partaken of drink. Indeed, he might well have abstained completely were it not for the cajoling of a persistent friend. But having cast off the mantle of Azure Dragoon and taken to the road at the end of the Dragonsong War, he had been surprised to find that he rather looked forward to the reward of a drink in the evening. And this evening, he had met his match in a new variety of liquor. *More fire than water, this . . . Trust an alchemist to concoct such stuff.*

He followed his first sip with a strip of dried squid. Supplied by a local fisherman, the savory morsel was the equal of any he had tasted in the Far East. It served to settle the palate, and he dared to drain his cup of the rest of the fiery liquor, its warmth spreading through his body as he reclined in his lavish chamber in Radz-at-Han.

After the exertions of his quest to the very edge of existence, life in the city as the satrap's honored guest suited Estinien well enough. Yet despite the lack of an impending threat, he continued to train as diligently as ever. He had taken up the lance that he might avenge himself upon Nidhogg for the murder of his family, and even having done so, found that a habit formed over a lifetime was not so easily shed.

Thus did an old custom meet a new one, and after Estinien had trained to his satisfaction each day, he permitted himself the indulgence of a drink or two. But given the enthusiasm of the Hannish alchemists, only one was required on this occasion. He had scarcely savored a second strip of dried squid when exhaustion and liquor swept over him like a tide, gentle yet insistent, bearing him away to the land of slumber.

Beyond the veil of consciousness, in the depths of dream, he was fighting a dragon.

The beast roared, and he felt its unbridled rancor as plainly as the stirrings of his own heart thanks to the Eye, the source of the Azure Dragoon's might. He leapt high to avoid his opponent's snapping maw, twisting in midair as he channeled the dread orb's power into his lance. Then, like a blazing meteor hurtling from the heavens, he plummeted back down to the earth.

The lance found its mark, piercing the seam of scales along the dragon's neck and sinking deep into flesh, where it released its energy in a fiery explosion that shattered bone with a telltale crack. *Be still.*

The great beast howled in agony, thrashing desperately to throw him off, but it could not long sustain the effort. With a final shudder, it collapsed and moved no more.

Another victory, he thought, though he felt neither joy nor relief. *Now let us count the cost . . .*

No sooner had he set foot on the ground than the searing pain racked his chest, bringing him to his knees. *Worse than expected . . .* While the Eye lent him strength, in harboring Nidhogg's undying malice, it was also slowly corrupting his being. Ere long it would finally consume him, leaving naught but a vessel for the beast's dark will—an untaught truth he knew to his very core.

"Silence, wyrm."

Though little more than a whisper, his voiced defiance served to staunch the pain. But words could not halt the Eye's growing influence. The fits grew more frequent by the day, and more intense. *The hour is nigh . . .*

He slumped against the body of his fallen foe and closed his eyes. *Just a moment's rest . . .*

He awoke on the floor of an unfamiliar room. Furs laid under him tickled his cheek. Struggling to his elbows, he blinked his surroundings into focus. Battered stools crowded around sturdy tables, and a counter spanned the length of one wall. The lingering scent of charred meat and mulled wine completed the story—this was a tavern.

"Father!" a maiden's voice rang out. "He has awakened!"

The call was answered by pounding footsteps, and a brawny man well into his middle years burst into the room.

"Halone be praised," he said, relief plain in his voice. "How do you feel, Lord Haldrath?"

Estinien's mind reeled for a moment. *Oh.* This was a dream of the past, and he was experiencing events as Haldrath, one of Ishgard's founding fathers. Together with his sire, King Thordan, he had slain the great wyrm Ratatoskr and later gouged out her brother Nidhogg's eyes, whose power he had harnessed to become the first Azure Dragoon. As these memories rose up, he found he could remember the man regarding him with such worry.

"Ser Aureniquart . . . ?"

"I'm no ser, my lord. Haven't been for a good while," Aureniquart replied with a grin. "Just the keeper of a tavern now, as you can see."

Twenty long years ago, Haldrath had sworn to live out his days in exile as a solitary hunter of dragons. In the course of stopping for supplies in nearby settlements, however, he had learned of Ser Aureniquart de Cordillelot's retirement from service and subsequent purchase of the establishment in which he now found himself. The news that one of their number had chosen a quiet life had come as something of a shock, but to behold his old comrade in his new home, he could not help but feel assured.

"And neither am I a lord, my friend—be it yours or anyone else's. But tell me—how did I come to be here?"

"Berteline, my daughter," Aureniquart replied, gesturing at the dark-haired maiden beside him. "She found you lying next to a dead dragon."

"Father has regaled me with tales of your deeds ever since I was little," said Berteline, her words tumbling out with ill-concealed excitement. "You are an inspiration to me, my lord. Like you, I wish to protect our people from the Dravanian menace."

"She's bent on joining the Temple Knights," Aureniquart interjected with a grunt, "and nothing we say or do will dissuade her. As a matter of fact, she was out training with her lance when she stumbled upon you."

As he gazed at Berteline, Haldrath knew a twinge of sorrow, for in her determined eyes he saw the fire that had once burned in his own. *Long since extinguished . . .*

"My first thought was to seek the Temple Knights' aid," Berteline continued, "but you spoke my father's name in your sleep, so I brought you here instead."

"Well, now," Haldrath grinned, "what good fortune to be found by the daughter of an old friend, and not a friend of my fallen foe."

Berteline did not return his smile.

"Begging your pardon, my lord . . . 'twas more than good fortune. A voice led me to you."

"A voice? Whose?"

"I . . . I do not know," she conceded, frowning in the act of recollection. "But I heard them in my mind, and they sounded like storm winds."

More than good fortune indeed. Haldrath looked to the heavens, thanking the goddess Halone for ordaining this meeting. At long last, he had found the one to whom he might entrust all.

"What you heard," Haldrath began, "was the will of Nidhogg."

So speaking, he laid a hand upon his silver breastplate, where a grotesque object had fused itself: one of the great wyrm's eyes, pulsing with baleful light.

"His eye calls to those who seek power. To corrupt and conquer their minds, that it might be free once more."

"Then . . . mayhap we should take you to the Temple Knights after all!" Berteline exclaimed, taking a step forward. "The chirurgeons might be able to help you—"

Haldrath stayed her with a raised hand. "'Tis no use, child," he said gently. "It is already joined to my body, armor and all. When Nidhogg could not claim my mind, he turned his attention to my flesh, and he will not be denied. Soon, I will be his puppet."

The revelation stunned both father and daughter into silence. Haldrath allowed them a moment before turning to look his old friend squarely in the eye.

"Ere I cease to be myself, I want you to end it."

Anger flashed across Aureniquart's face. "You've lost your bloody wits if you think I'm going to kill you!" he spat. "Damn you for even asking!"

The erstwhile knight had been wont to betray his lowborn roots in moments of passion, and Haldrath couldn't help but smile to see that the years had done little to change him.

"It is no small thing I ask of you, I know," he continued. "But were I left to become Nidhogg's thrall, I would deliver his prize unto him. And I need not say what would befall should that come to pass."

Shorn though the great wyrm was of his full strength, he and his horde remained a dire threat to Ishgard. Thus did the nation's new ruler, the archbishop, establish the Temple Knights to lead the fight against dragonkind. Bolstered by the noble houses, the order had managed to hold the walls so far, but only barely. If Nidhogg were to reclaim his eyes, he would visit untold devastation upon the Holy See.

"Damn it all . . . I swore an oath, Haldrath. To you and you alone."

"That you did. And then we made our choice together, when we learned Nidhogg's mind—that he believed mankind weak and unworthy. In order to preserve our sovereignty, we committed the grave sin of betrayal. We chose a path of blood, for ourselves and our children both, and we cannot now turn back. Lo—though you have laid down the sword, your daughter has taken up the lance."

To that, Aureniquart could offer no reply, and so he stood there, jaw clenched, staring at the floor.

Haldrath turned his gaze to Berteline. "To you who would hunt dragons—who did answer Nidhogg's call—I entrust his eyes. As custodian of their power, I charge you with the protection of our people."

Berteline's eyes widened, her lips parting as if to speak, but Haldrath pressed on. Time was running out.

"So long as justice burns in your heart, Nidhogg will never claim your mind—yet your flesh will eventually succumb. Ere it does, you must find another to take up the burden and carry on the fight in your stead. Lest you forget, our enemy is nigh immortal. This war will rage on long after we have returned to dust . . ."

This much he managed before the pain seized him once more, doubling him over. Somewhere beyond his stifled scream, he heard the cries of father and daughter, desperate to help but with no means to do so—save one.

"Do it, Aureniquart," Haldrath rasped. "If your oath to me was true, I bid you end it now!"

Through the haze of agony, Haldrath saw his old friend take up his faithful lance with trembling hands. The deadly point came to rest at the seam of his breastplate.

But there it stayed, and as Haldrath beheld his old comrade, torment writ plain upon his face, he was struck by the true enormity of his request. He had extended the hand of fellowship to Aureniquart, raising him up from ruffian to knight, and Aureniquart had never forgotten the debt. He had rewarded Haldrath's faith with absolute loyalty, and could no more harm him than he could his own kin.

Cursing himself, Haldrath sought for the words to compel his friend to do that which his heart forbade when Berteline's voice rang out.

"Let me help, Father." And without waiting for an answer, she wrapped her hands around the shaft of the lance, just below her sire's. "The burden of this sin, I shall bear with you."

The pair shared a solemn glance, and Aureniquart nodded with a look that was equal parts sadness and pride. Haldrath managed a smile, in spite of the pain.

"Thank you, my friend, my successor—and farewell. May the bloodshed come to an end one day, and our progeny know peace once more . . ."

With that, the mighty lance that had slain countless dragons plunged into his chest, impaling his heart and bringing an end to the dream.

Estinien woke with a start. A film of sweat had formed on his brow, and as he wiped it away, his eyes wandered to the fearsome halberd propped in the corner of his chamber—a weapon which bore the name of his nemesis.

Of all the things to show me . . .

Once upon a time, he had taken both of Nidhogg's eyes in hand and been possessed by the wyrm's vengeful spirit for his trouble. Could it have been the Eye's twin, once embedded in Haldrath's ageless corpse, which had given rise to the vision?

Estinien shook his head. Why waste time wondering when the few who might feasibly know were long dead.

Besides, it's over now. Rising to his feet, he walked to the window and opened it to let in the breeze. *It took a thousand years, but we have peace again. Rest well, Haldrath.*

Outside, beneath the veil of night, Radz-at-Han shone resplendently at him in all its many colors.

Bringer of Shadow, Bringer of Light

North of the central mountain range lay the seat of the Garlean Empire, where the snow lay thick upon the earth, hiding its features beneath a nondescript veil of white. A tense silence pervaded the region, as if the land itself knew that its suffering had not ended with the Final Days. Even in this modest city, more than four hundred malms west of the ruined capital, the people shuffled about with sullen expressions. What brief snatches of conversation could be heard on the streets were hushed and hurried, serving only to punctuate the oppressive quiet.

A man walked down the main avenue, clad in the standard-issue overcoat and cap of the imperial army. He cast his gaze about with the same hard look worn by the other patrolling soldiers, none questioning his purpose. After a quick glance over his shoulder, he slipped around a corner, proceeding down a succession of narrow, shadow-filled alleyways until he reached the city's outskirts. When the paved path gave way to a field of snow, the man's gait became more languid—whereupon he stopped dead, as if struck by a sudden thought.

A solitary creak of leather served as a prelude to the attack. In one fluid motion, he turned and drew his sword, deflecting the slash which would otherwise have opened him from stem to stern, and dove forward into his opponent, jerking his elbow sharply upwards as he did so. The sound of crunching teeth was his reward. His assailant staggered backwards, dropped his scythe, and fell mutely into the waiting snow.

"Let's call this one a draw and go our separate ways, shall we?" Thancred had come only to observe.

Although the Scions of the Seventh Dawn had officially disbanded, he maintained a lone vigil. It was all he could do to honor the memory of the woman he had loved like a sister—the woman who had given her life to save what she held dear. For the time being, a tentative peace had settled upon the world, it was true, but whispers of unrest within Garlemald had lured him from his leisure. Thancred regarded the motionless form of his would-be assassin. Clothed entirely in black, only his eyes were exposed to the elements. The deep creases in their corners marked the man as a seasoned veteran—doubtless he belonged to the Reapers, agents of the empire who culled its enemies before the advent of magitek. Clinging to the tattered glory of his nation, this lone survivor had likely identified him as an outsider, and thus a target for elimination. *Bad luck.*

Even as his gaze drifted back to the blanket of white stretching off before him, Thancred found his mind's eye turning to the past. The sight of the old soldier and his scythe lying in the snow had stirred memories of another. One who had dwelled in a world filled with light as blinding as this frigid waste. Within that brilliance the man fought, and within that brilliance he died.

General Ran'jit had been an implacable foe.

Thancred had made it a priority to delve into the general's past as he prepared to rescue Minfilia from her prison in Eulmore. His search had led him to records which mentioned a group of assassins that operated within the shadows of the First before the Flood of Light. The contracts they accepted were few, but they had never known failure. What scant details Thancred could uncover of their inner workings beggared belief. Purportedly a brotherhood bound by blood, they obscured their origins by rearing offspring of every conceivable race and instructing them in the ways of their bloody art. Even the forbidden magicks of foreign lands were at their beck and call, but such mastery came at great cost: the training they endured was said to be tantamount to torture. The wellspring of their devotion and the beliefs which drove them had been lost to history, but what stories remained indicated a zeal that bordered on obsession.

A century before, Zal'bard, leader of this secretive group, had visited Eulmore for an audience with its mayor. It required little imagination to deduce the purpose of their meeting, but even Thancred had been taken aback by the twist of fate which was to follow. For the Flood of Light had poured over the First even as the mayor and Zal'bard parleyed. Consequently, Zal'bard and his followers had little choice but to remain in Eulmore as the mayor's guests. Whether out of gratitude for the hospitality they duly received or simple necessity in the face of the world's seemingly imminent destruction, the assassins drilled Eulmore's unblooded soldiers in the art of warfare. And thus did Zal'bard come to lead the defense against the sin eaters surging forth from the Empty, driving them back and buying a precious reprieve for the beleaguered city . . .

After twelve years in Eulmore, Zal'bard sired a son. Considering the dearth of information pertaining to the child's mother, it was plain that his main concern had been to procure an heir to whom he might pass down his skills. Records told that the boy began training in earnest before he could form a sentence, and that his father named him Ran'jit.

The world had been driven to desperation by the relentless onslaught of the sin eaters. Voeburt teetered on the brink of collapse, and would surely have tumbled over the precipice had it not been for a miraculous occurrence. Among the populace, a girl was discovered who could not be turned by the sin eaters' corrupting influence. Two years later, she came to be sheltered in Eulmore and was given the name Minfilia, after a figure of legend said to have stemmed the Flood of Light.

Knowing that Minfilia's unique talents would prove invaluable on the front line, Zal'bard resolved to train her himself, though she was then a girl of but twelve summers. Young, perhaps, yet older than Ran'jit who had only recently turned five. Together the two children studied under Zal'bard, one the world's would-be beacon of hope and the other the heir to its darkest arts. The path each followed would ultimately lead them to different destinations, but for now they walked side by side. Whether they viewed each other as friend or rival, comrade or competitor, was never recorded. Yet one account from the period described Minfilia during her days in Eulmore as "a bright and cheerful girl who has taken to life in the city as if she were Eulmoran born and bred. Despite her singular gifts, she remains humble and devoted to her mission, displaying an appetite for training equal to that of her master's firstborn son."

In time, Minfilia grew into her role, and after years of secrecy her existence was revealed to the world. She would, it was announced, take her place in a newly formed elite battalion known as the Sinbound, commanded by Zal'bard himself, and they would lead Eulmore's counteroffensive.

Every drop of blood shed in battle afforded the Sinbound a deeper understanding of their foe, and it was thanks to this hard-earned knowledge that they finally succeeded in tracking down a most elusive quarry—the region's Lightwarden, hidden in the Duergar Mountains. Could they but defeat it, the theory went, all of Kholusia might be liberated. Though the battle that followed was long and brutal, victory came at last when Zal'bard landed the killing blow. Yet the Sinbound's joy was to prove short-lived—their cheers replaced all too soon by cries of horror—for even as the Lightwarden perished, the corrupting radiance stored within its body poured forth, engulfing its vanquisher body and soul. The great general let out an inhuman howl before transforming into that which he most despised. It was then that a terrible truth was laid bare—those who slayed a Lightwarden were doomed to become one.

The Sinbound had no choice but to retreat. Upon their return to Eulmore, they declared that Zal'bard had given his life to put down the Lightwarden, his heroic sacrifice paving the way to ultimate salvation. A half-truth at best, but one the people could tolerate better than the bitter reality. And so the First grieved the death of a leader, while celebrating a historic victory, and Minfilia dutifully smiled and waved. Later, far from the public eye, it fell to her to disabuse the realm's leaders of their false hope, and to propose a solution. If she were the one to slay the Lightwarden, then perhaps her natural immunity to the enemy's baleful influence might prevent victory from spelling defeat.

And so, the Sinbound continued their hunt, with Ran'jit, still scarcely more than a boy, assuming his father's command. While it was unclear how far his training as an assassin had progressed, he was every bit as ferocious as his forebear on the light-drowned battlefields. The loss of father and teacher did not deter him; rather, it seemed to lend the youth an as-yet unseen steel.

While Ran'jit's prowess was beyond doubt, military records showed that Minfilia was in fact the mastermind behind the Sinbound's stratagems, and the general's equal on the field of battle. For every sin eater slain by Ran'jit, Minfilia would slay another, and he would answer in turn. On and on this cycle continued, until the land was littered with their foes.

But all good things must come to an end. Ten years after the Sinbound's founding, Minfilia was dealt a grievous wound. Though immune to the sin eaters' influence, she bled like any other, and this time no chirurgeon could save her. Fading fast, she summoned her comrades to her side and delivered a prophecy: that Minfilia would come again. The Oracle of Light spoke through her, she assured them, and they saw from her undimmed smile that she told the truth. Her duty thus fulfilled, she requested a final moment alone with Ran'jit.

What words were then exchanged only two would ever know—a bringer of shadow and bringer of light. Did the dying Minfilia falter at the last? Or did she depart this world with her familiar smile, undaunted? Ran'jit never told.

State records spoke of a grand funeral, where all whose lives were uplifted by Minfilia's presence mourned her passing. She was interred in Eulmore's crypts, her mortal remains carried there by Ran'jit himself.

It took nigh on three years of searching to find Minfilia's prophesied reincarnation. The girl delivered to Eulmore had the same flaxen hair, the same bright eyes, and—it was duly confirmed—the same resistance to the sway of the enemy. But that was where the similarity ended. She was young and almost painfully shy, greeting the approach of a stranger as most would greet a sin eater. Regardless, she was destined to bear the people's hope, and just as Zal'bard had taken the previous Minfilia as a pupil, Ran'jit resolved to do the same with her successor.

In the end, she lasted but a dozen summers, and did not live to see her tenth battle. While the world awaited her rebirth, scholars worked feverishly to discern the true nature of the sin eaters, hoping to discover some hitherto unnoticed weakness—one which even a child might exploit. Yet their findings dashed any such hopes. Though the sin eaters looked like living beings, the truth was quite otherwise. There were no vital organs to pierce, no arteries to open. Like dolls, the loss of a part served only to diminish the whole, and not destroy it. Only brute force could stop their advance.

Ran'jit continued to train Minfilia after Minfilia, as she was born and reborn, some taking to his methods while others did not. A few begged him to end their lives, that they might make way for a more suitable student. One way or another, to save all that was left, they gave all they had.

Who would break this merciless wheel? Eighty years after the Flood of Light, Eulmore came under the rule of Vauthry, a man who could bend the sin eaters to his will. And thus were the Sinbound rendered surplus to requirements and disbanded. Yet Minfilias were still born into the world, and after having a dream that he would someday meet his end at one's hands, Vauthry ordered that the Oracle's current incarnation be put to death. From that day forth,

Ran'jit was tasked with a new mission: to seek out the next Minfilia and confine her, that she might never rise against Vauthry or the sin eaters under his thrall.

None can say for sure what the aging general thought of this sad duty, but his words to the Warrior of Darkness and their companions, who aided in Minfilia's rescue, were recorded for posterity:

> "Defiance only begets more suffering. It is through acceptance alone that one may find solace in this godsforsaken world.
>
> "Man is an inherently flawed creature. In his vain pursuit of righteousness, he but sows the seeds of future conflict. Thus have I chosen to place my hopes upon he who has transcended men. Upon he who is unbound by the vagaries of conscience."

Ran'jit died in battle at the age of eighty-eight. His body was found lying before the graves of his former pupils, all taken before their time.

In Storm's Wake

"You have a letter, Raha."

It had been some time since the turmoil of the Final Days, and G'raha Tia was making the most of a rare moment of quiet with a leisurely lunch out in the midday sun. Duty would eventually call him back to the Baldesion Annex, however, and he had barely arrived when Krile emerged from the office to greet him. In her hand was an envelope marked for his personal attention—a rare occurrence, as nearly all missives the Students received were addressed to the collective. He examined the envelope and the elegant Eorzean script in which his name had been written, noting that the sender's name was curiously absent. Availing himself of a letter opener from Ojika's desk, he quickly extracted the missive, and had barely begun to pore over its contents when a sudden, sharp gasp escaped his lips, drawing quizzical glances from Krile and Ojika. In disbelief, he read the message again to confirm his eyes were not deceiving him, before turning to his companions in bewilderment.

"I've been invited to Doma . . . for a private audience with Lord Hien."

"Lord Hien?" Krile repeated, doubtfully. "What business does he have with you?"

"I should very much like to know that myself. Had he bade me bring our adventuring friend, I could understand it, but I haven't the faintest idea what he could possibly want with me . . ."

G'raha flipped the letter over and held it up to the light, searching for a clue—some hidden cipher or sign that might explain this unusual correspondence. Yet none was to be found. Conceding that there was no secret subtext, he began to contemplate how best to proceed when the Warrior of Light's stories of Doma sprang to mind.

"Well, I can hardly reject an invitation from the great Lord Hien," he pondered aloud, hoping the words might convince his colleagues that duty and obligation were foremost in his thoughts. But the smiles playing on their lips quickly gave the lie to that. Donning what he hoped was a neutral expression, he ignored their knowing looks, and the burning of his cheeks, and set about making preparations to depart forthwith.

Passing through Kugane, G'raha made for the small fishing village of Isari in the Ruby Sea, where a chartered skiff awaited him. From there, a gentle tide bore him along the One River, all the way to the Doman Enclave. No sooner had he disembarked than a towering Lupin welcomed him with a graceful bow, introducing himself as Hakuro, a retainer of Lord Hien. In keeping pace with the wolfman's giant strides, G'raha scarcely had time to take in the distinctive architecture of the enclave. Ornate stone walls with round gates and fan-shaped windows lined either side of the street. He caught glimpses of craftsmen hard at work within, but quickly averted his gaze, lest he be distracted from the purpose of his visit. *Duty first!*

At the end of the road stood a manor nigh as grand as the mountains behind it. According to Hakuro, the structure had once been the residence of the enclave's magistrate, but had since been renamed the Kienkan—roughly translated as "the Swallow's Homecoming"—and had served as Lord Hien's domicile since the end of the imperial occupation. Hakuro ushered him inside and swiftly guided him through a labyrinthine series of halls. There was a uniquely floral fragrance in the air, though it was unclear if the aroma was inherent to the aged wood or if the halls were purposefully scented. In any case, the serene surroundings did little to settle his nerves. As G'raha struggled to recall what he knew of Far Eastern customs, he made a point to be mindful of his posture. He was no envoy, nor less an emissary come on stately business. But even so, his time as the Exarch had taught him the importance of appearances. *I remember that much, at least.*

At last, he reached the center of the maze, and there, sitting cross-legged in a massive chamber, was the man he had come to see.

"Well met, friend. Pray accept my apologies for bringing you all this way," Hien said with a warm smile.

They had met once before, when the leaders of the Eorzean Alliance held council on the matter of the Telophoroi. G'raha had been thrilled to meet the man he'd only read about. *A hero from an altogether different book of history.* It was a tale that would thankfully never come to pass, and he knew all too well it served no purpose to entertain stories from its tattered pages. Thus he endeavored to separate the man from the myth, electing simply to introduce himself as the newest member of the Scions.

Since their first meeting, G'raha had known the Doman lord to be every bit as impressive as the heads of the other city-states. Yet seeing him there in the Kienkan, framed by the imposing ink painting of Yanxia, the man seemed somehow larger than life. Blinking, G'raha reminded himself that Hien had been born the year after the annexation of Doma, which would make them the same age. But his demeanor betrayed no hint of youth. G'raha could only imagine the hardships he must have endured in his childhood to foster such presence of mind.

"It was no trouble at all. I am most grateful for the invitation, though I am not sure what I could have done to deserve such an honor. Is it truly me you wished to see?"

"But of course! There is a matter upon which only your counsel will suffice."

The young lord gestured for G'raha to sit, and he gratefully obliged, curious to hear what his host had to say. As Hien explained it, the seeds of change had begun to quicken in Garlemald, and Radz-at-Han, having reopened trade with the ravaged nation, was now organizing a summit between the leaders of the resurgent Garlean community and the dignitaries of various surrounding countries. And, lest he further strain relations between Doma and Garlemald, Hien wished to gain insight into the Empire's present state. The acting viceroy of Locus Amoenus—or Corvos, as it had formerly been known—would be in attendance, and intelligence regarding the province was therefore of particular interest.

Recalling that Thancred had infiltrated Locus Amoenus during the Final Days, and trusting none more than the Scions to keep an accurate account of events in the midst of such chaos, Hien had reached out to the grizzled rogue for any information he might care to disclose.

"Imagine my surprise when he told me there was another Scion better suited to the task—one who not only joined him on the mission, but hailed from Corvos besides."

G'raha nodded slowly. "Be that as it may, I was brought to Sharlayan as a child, and have had little contact with Corvos since. I fear what knowledge I can provide may not prove as useful as you hope."

"'Tis not uncommon for those of us born in the provinces to become estranged from the land of our birth," Hien replied with a knowing smile. "But I am eager to hear whatever you are able to share."

To this, G'raha gave a self-deprecating shrug, and after a moment's thought, resolved to start with what he knew best—the province's history.

If one were to ask who the land belonged to in the very beginning, both Corvosi and Garlean would surely claim it was their own. Yet from the perspective of a scholar of Allagan history, the facts were clear to see: it was the site of a provincial city founded by the Allagan

Empire more than five thousand years ago, when the Allagans sent scores of Miqo'te slaves to till the fertile lands south of the continent of Ilsabard. After numerous Umbral Calamities and centuries of war over territory and resources, however, only the Garleans and Corvosi had remained, and it was the latter who had subsequently driven the Garleans into the frigid northern wastes, where they would live in obscurity for eight hundred years.

This lengthy exile had lasted until roughly sixty years prior to the present day, when legatus and future emperor Solus zos Galvus harnessed the power of magitek to revolutionize the Garlean military. In the name of reclaiming their ancestral homeland, he marched Garlemald's great armies south to crush their former nemeses, who could find no answer to the might of the Empire's machina. After brutally subjugating the Corvosi, the Garleans wiped the name of Corvos from all records, retitling it Locus Amoenus. As the only province in the history of Garlemald to have its name entirely erased, it was clear the Garleans were not above holding a grudge.

"To think it has been more than fifty years since the name Corvos became all but a footnote in the annals of history . . ." Hien murmured, no doubt imagining what might have become of Doma had it met a similar fate.

G'raha nodded. "Thankfully, its legacy lives on in the city that remains, and the culture that survives there to this day. Yet it should not be forgotten that those who have taken the helm of governance were born during the period of imperial rule."

G'raha remembered vividly the Corvosi response when the Final Days had arrived. Even allowing for the fact that it was a calamity without precedent, they had been slow to act compared to neighboring Radz-at-Han. Not that this was entirely surprising. After Garlemald's destruction, a Corvosi youth—one notably not of Garlean descent—reported that the chain of command had quickly disintegrated once contact with the "homeland" had been lost.

Hien closed his eyes and exhaled slowly as he considered G'raha's words. "When at last we won our liberty from the Garleans, Doma had been an imperial province for twenty-five summers, Ala Mhigo for twenty. But had either nation borne the Empire's yoke for another ten—or even *one*—who's to say we would have prevailed?"

He paused for a moment, staring at the polished hardwood floor.

"'Tis difficult, after all, to find the strength to fight for a way of life few still remember."

"Aye," Hien continued, "I can think of no force more formidable than time and its inexorable flow. Had it not been for my parents and the guidance of my mentor, Gosetsu, I cannot say with any certainty that my conviction would have held through the years. It may well have been washed away by the tides of time, my imperial education molding me into an altogether different man. I doubt there is a Doman in this world who has lived a life free of the wages of imperial rule."

Hien's face darkened as he recalled the suffering visited on him and the other children born during the imperial occupation. Without imperial citizenship, Domans and Ala Mhigans alike had become foreigners in their own land, branded "savages" by their subjugators. The only reprieve to be had from their mistreatment came from citizenship, which could only be obtained through distinguished service in the military. Yet to gain the favor of their oppressors was to invite the contempt of kith and kin, to be labeled a loyal hound of the Empire. And so, from their earliest years, they struggled amidst a maelstrom of anger and resentment to discover who they were—Doman, Ala Mhigan, or Garlean? Their elders might speak of halcyon days, but how were they to understand that which they had never known? There was only the Empire.

A dreary silence fell upon the room. G'raha breathed deep of the calming, floral aroma in the air, wondering how he might lighten the mood. After a moment of searching, an answer came to him.

"Historians and archaeologists like myself attempt to identify the turning points of civilizations. Where one era ends, and another begins. Yet the reality is not so black and white. Rulers come and go, as may a country's name—but the people remain. Life goes on. When the winds of change blow, they set their sails accordingly, becoming the pioneers of a new generation, their course leading them ever onward, be it unto joy or sorrow. And when, centuries later, we scholars look back upon their journey, we see the history not of a nation, but of a people."

Hien gave G'raha a look of faint surprise before bursting into laughter.

"Forgive me, my friend, 'twas not my intention to sour the mood—and yet I do not regret it, for I have been rewarded with some unexpected morsels of wisdom!"

G'raha shrank back, his face reddening. "Mayhap I spoke too freely."

"Not at all! You but spoke your mind. 'Tis little wonder the Scions welcomed you with open arms. Though, for a moment, I could have sworn I was listening to the words of a wizened sage!"

G'raha's ears drooped in embarrassment as Hien erupted into laughter once more. At length, the young lord gestured apologetically, and fixed G'raha with a grin.

"'Tis as you say. We must not fear change, but accept it as a part of life. The Doma beloved by our ancestors, like our own, and that of our progeny, shall all become part of a single shared history."

His grin fading, Hien gazed past G'raha as if peering into the future. It was a look G'raha knew well. He had seen it on the faces of other brave souls who, no matter the hardship or danger, never strayed from their course. Brave souls who had saved the very star. Recalling them, G'raha pictured the Doma of tomorrow. Whatever lay in store for this liberated land in the era Hien and his people would help to shape, he looked forward to seeing it.

"Well," Hien said at last, "I suppose there's nothing for it but to make the most of this summit, and *set our sails accordingly*. Come, tell me more of Corvos. I would know of its delicacies—there is no better way to find common ground with another than through his belly."

Hien stood as he spoke, pausing when he saw the look of confusion on G'raha's face. He chuckled softly.

"Surely you do not think me so heartless as to make you speak of such delights on an empty stomach? You have traveled far to answer my questions, and as my honored guest, you shall taste the best Doma has to offer."

G'raha's stomach growled in response. His confusion quelled, and appetite duly whetted, he stood up and, together with Hien, exited the Kienkan. Across the One River, he could see the ruined remnants of what once stood as the very center and symbol of the land—Doma Castle. Yet the enclave was bustling with people determined to restore and rebuild.

Even after the storm of blood, the people remained to usher in the dawn of a new era. *And life goes on.*

A Legacy of Hope

Rearranging even a single chamber in the grand Leveilleur estate was a monumental task, yet Ameliance welcomed the challenge all the same.

Having volunteered to host an exchange student from Thavnair, she had seized the opportunity to repurpose the dusty old meeting room. Gone were the conference tables and stiff-backed chairs, replaced by a plush feather bed and a carefully curated handful of cheerful knickknacks. With each new furnishing the attendants delivered, the space had grown cozier, until the air of cold bureaucracy was quite dispelled.

Once everything was in place, Ameliance paused to survey her work, a satisfied smile beginning to form on her lips . . . until a jutting desk drawer caught her eye. A single discordant note spoiling the harmony. *Well, that won't do.* She gave the offending item a hearty shove, but the drawer remained stubbornly open.

That's the trouble with these old antiques. Always in need of attention . . .

Indeed, with its faded wood and old-fashioned decoration, the desk more than qualified. *This must have been in the family for two—nay, three generations?* Her husband's father had likely purchased it when he was but a young man, after which it would have been passed down to Fourchenault when he came of age, before he in turn entrusted it to Alphinaud. *Little wonder it won't budge an ilm.*

Subsequent attempts to close the drawer proved fruitless. With a sigh, she pulled it open instead, and the source of her troubles became clear. Towards the back, the cover of what appeared to be a concealed compartment had worked itself loose, obstructing the drawer's closure. Louisoix had been rather rebellious in his prime, and had doubtless acquired the desk to serve as a home for his secrets.

As Ameliance had raised two rebels of her own, she had stumbled upon more than a few contraband-filled nooks and crannies in her time. Naturally, she could not help but take a look, and inside found a leather-bound notebook. *An old journal, perhaps?* A moment later it was open in her hands, and a grin crept across her face as she recognized the confident curves of Alphinaud's letters on the faded parchment.

It was 1572—a year that would go down in history as the last of the Sixth Astral Era. The first sun of the Third Astral Moon had risen, and spring winds from the south had finally reached Old Sharlayan's shores. A crisp, refreshing morning like this held boundless possibilities . . . yet Alphinaud Leveilleur was insufferably bored.

Though he had been accepted into the Studium—at the remarkably early age of eleven, no less—it would be some time before he walked through its hallowed gates as a student. His day's schooling already concluded, he drifted about the manor, aimless and anxious. He had hoped to pass a few hours with his grandfather, but Alisaie had set off with the Archon at dawn to browse the markets—and while his sister had taken their dog Angelo with her, she had conveniently forgotten to invite her own brother. *Hmph.* Still, he did not blame Alisaie for wanting to spend as much time with their grandfather as she could. Louisoix would soon depart for the benighted realm of Eorzea across the sea, for it was not in his nature to ignore the plight of those in need.

Alphinaud eventually resigned himself to an afternoon of reading in the gardens and made for the estate's great hall. The chambers stood dark and empty when he entered, save for a figure standing tall in the doorway.

"Have you business to attend to, Father?"

"An inspection."

Fourchenault addressed his own flesh and blood with the selfsame terseness he would a junior colleague. Not that Alphinaud was deterred. It had ever been thus.

"How very industrious. But was this not to be a day of rest?"

"I do this of my own accord, not at the Forum's behest."

"In that case . . . might I join you?"

The young prodigy attempted to hide his excitement, but his wide eyes betrayed him. Fourchenault regarded him thoughtfully. After what felt like an age, he answered with a nod. So it was that the boy escaped the stifling walls of the estate and followed his father unto destinations unknown.

Alphinaud breathed deep of the crisp air as he basked in the pale sunlight. Their path afforded them a view of the Agora—and unexpectedly of Alisaie. Curious yet cautious, he took care not to be spotted as they passed, his gaze flitting back and forth between the path ahead and the distant plaza. Alisaie was unattended, kneeling as she played with Angelo. Nearby, Louisoix was surrounded by a small crowd of academics. Scholarch Montichaigne stood tall in their midst, flanked by the rather more diminutive Professors Rurusha and Nenelymo Totolymo. *An impassioned discussion, no doubt.* Alphinaud suspected it would go on for quite a while.

As the bustle of the city grew distant and the path steeper, Alphinaud realized they were bound for the Rostra. The proud hill had once been an open forum, where all were welcome to take part in grand debates. Now, however, only the ninety-nine members of the Forum—his father included—were granted that privilege, and they conducted their deliberations behind closed doors. *What manner of personal matter would necessitate a visit here, of all places?*

"Stay close."

They entered through a small doorway on the building's left, where a dimly lit stairwell awaited them, extending deeper and deeper until it finally gave way to a sizable chamber.

Alphinaud's eyes were drawn to a set of two metal gates under heavy surveillance. From somewhere below he could hear the quiet chatter of scholars, though he was more acutely aware of the sentries' questioning gazes. There were few in Sharlayan who did not know his father, however, and they visibly relaxed as Fourchenault identified himself. After fielding the relevant procedural inquiries and paperwork, the Leveilleurs stepped through the gates and entered a circular room. Moments later, the floor shuddered and sank beneath them, a metallic hum accompanying its descent. They had, Alphinaud belatedly realized, boarded a lift. As his mind raced with possibilities, the cold marble walls of the Forum suddenly vanished, and a beautiful horizon stretched out beneath him.

"Father, what is all this?"

"You must surely have heard the rumors surrounding Labyrinthos?"

Sharlayan had been built over a dormant volcano, and some whispered of an artificial ecosystem hidden in the hollow caldera. A vault to house flora and fauna from every corner of the star. *But never in my wildest dreams . . .* Alphinaud gaped in awe at the artificial sky, brilliant blue in the light of a man-made sun. The lift screeched to a halt as they reached the ground, and he caught his father smirking as they strolled into a stone courtyard.

"A marvel, is it not? The wind generators were but recently completed. After initial testing, I was not convinced they would function as required . . . but it appears my concerns were unwarranted."

Artificial though it was, the breeze was no less pleasant than the one they had enjoyed on the surface. Strands of Alphinaud's hair danced in the wind while the false sun warmed his shoulders. He approached the parapet, admiring the rising and falling of the verdant hills.

"It's as if we've left Sharlayan entirely," he uttered in quiet wonder.

His father was but a few steps behind, ready with an answer.

"We sought to recreate the milder climes of Corvos in southern Ilsabard. The Garleans call that region Locus Amoenus—their utopia. Seeing this . . . one can understand why."

It was rare for his father to speak at such length. *Or with such passion.* The scenery was idyllic, but Alphinaud suspected this "utopia" had not been created without substantial difficulty.

Later, Fourchenault took him to Logistikon Alpha, where Alphinaud listened intently to lectures on the weather systems. It was a veritable feast of knowledge. To be surrounded by the latest in Sharlayan technology made his heart soar, and he wished for nothing more than to learn all he could about the inner workings of Labyrinthos.

They had joined a tour to see more, and once it had ended, Alphinaud motioned towards a wooded road to the north.

"Might we venture further in?"

His father shook his head. "Our business here is concluded. It's time I took you home."

Alphinaud's heart sank like a stone, as he felt the magic of this wonderful world begin to fade. But he knew from his father's tone that the matter was settled. *I must be reasonable. Mature.* The boy took a breath and nodded, his calm countenance befitting that of a Leveilleur.

And then he felt the spark of childish hope flicker once more.

"But Fourchenault, dearest, 'tis the perfect weather for a picnic!"

As if by divine providence, Alphinaud's mother had materialized behind them, bearing a hefty woven basket and the promise of delicious respite. Alisaie and Louisoix waited not far beyond, laughing as Angelo frolicked in their midst.

"You've all been having such lovely adventures without me. I think we're overdue a proper family outing, don't you?" Ameliance's voice was gentle as sunshine, but neither Alphinaud nor his father were so naive as to presume this was a suggestion. *Not even the Forum united could deny her.*

Thus did the Leveilleurs proceed to picnic on the grassy hills of the Medial Circuit. At the base of Pneuma they unfurled their blanket, and from Ameliance's basket withdrew sumptuous sweets from the Last Stand, all packed neatly in rows, that would be paired with equally fragrant teas. Naturally, the gathering garnered attention, and those who recognized the family could not resist stopping for a chat.

The wise old Galuf Baldesion spotted them first. He excused himself after brief pleasantries and returned with his adoptive granddaughter, whom he was eager to introduce to Alphinaud and Alisaie. Knowing that Krile would be their senior at the Studium, Ameliance was delighted to share a cup of tea with the young Lalafell. Krile accepted with a smile and assured the Leveilleur matriarch that she would keep a close eye on the twins.

Not long after the Baldesions had taken their first sips of tea, Alphinaud espied his grandfather's stalwart disciples. Moenbryda Wilfsunnwyn announced her arrival with a full-throated greeting, before dragging Urianger Augurelt in the direction of the picnic blanket. Urianger, for his part, expressed a reluctance to intrude upon the Leveilleurs' leisure, but Moenbryda simply stated, "the more, the merrier" and pressed down upon his shoulders until he was seated, whereupon a warm cup was thrust into his hand. To Moenbryda's delight, it was not long before her straitlaced companion was drawn into a vigorous discussion of prophecy with their mentor.

As the afternoon wore on, the Leveilleurs' impromptu picnic continued to grow. Archon Rammbroes arrived to captivate Urianger and Louisoix with his insight into the cultures of ancient Allag, while Dickon of the Last Stand answered Ameliance's summons with a fresh batch of confections to prove his hotly debated theories on baking the perfect sweetmeats.

Conversation flowed as freely as the tea they shared—every back and forth, every peal of laughter warm and comforting—until azure skies blushed crimson, and the pale sun faded, making way for the shadowed moon.

Ameliance gingerly closed the journal, then shut her eyes to recall the journey home that fateful evening. In the fading twilight, Louisoix, Fourchenault, and Alphinaud had each made a solemn vow.

"The flames of hope yet burn bright, and I shall not see them smothered."

Louisoix knew only too well that his efforts to forestall the Seventh Umbral Calamity would place him in mortal danger. Yet on that day, surrounded by family and friends, he had been the picture of contentment. *And our hope burns brighter still for your legacy.*

"Mine is a difficult path, but I shall walk it gladly. For our children and their children."

Fourchenault's meaning was clearer in retrospect, with knowledge of the exodus. Though he had not seen eye to eye with his father on matters of politics, Louisoix had never pressed. He simply listened and nodded—aware perhaps of the secrets his son had sworn to keep. *But you need keep them no longer, my darling. Our children live, and these burdens are not yours to bear alone.*

"I shall study, learn, and grow, that I might become a man worthy to follow in my father and grandfather's footsteps."

Young Alphinaud's aspirations had been pure and selfless meanwhile. A child's promise. *But not an empty one.* He and Alisaie had done so much for so many. They had defied their father, and in so doing rekindled his hope. And together with countless allies they had met on their journeys, they had spread peace far and wide.

Against all odds, you each remained true to your word, and will each remain forever in my heart.

Private Reflections

The hearts of men are mysterious things, eluding even the understanding of those to whom they belong. In seeking to assess the emotions that churn within one's breast, it is known that committing one's experiences to parchment can be an enlightening exercise. Thus do I take up the quill to impose order upon the maelstrom of my thoughts.

It was shortly after my return from the edge of existence that I learned of the sudden passing of my father, Y'rhul Nunh. He had been in Nagxia, gathering literature in his capacity as a gleaner, when he contracted and succumbed to a local disease. As he had been the picture of health despite his some threescore years, his demise came as a shock to us, his twelve daughters.

None took it harder than his tenth-born, Nazqha, who had been accompanying him as his apprentice. After witnessing him draw his last breath, she was forced to mourn him alone in a foreign land, for his body was not permitted to be repatriated lest the contagion that claimed him spread. At the physician's urging, she tearfully acquiesced to cremation and subsequently scattered his ashes over the Ruby Sea, that he might roam the world once more before the tides bore him home. She then returned to Sharlayan and revealed the tragedy to our eldest sister, Adebh, who, in accordance with our father's wishes, bade all his daughters convene.

Here it would be meet to note that our family structure is unlike most Seeker of the Sun tribes. Traditionally, our people gather around a "nunh," a breeding male, and half-siblings abide together as part of a large but close-knit community. As a gleaner, however, our father had mates in those places he visited, and they and their children did not have occasion to dwell with their counterparts elsewhere. The result being that, despite sharing a sire, my half-sisters have always felt more akin to distant relatives.

The fact that I was taken from my mother at the age of seven only contributed to this perception. The difficult births of my younger twin sisters left her frail, and she struggled to care for me. With the Forum's intervention, I was apprenticed to Master Matoya, whose dimly lit cave in the Dravanian hinterlands I called home until the age of seventeen. I then journeyed to Sharlayan to pursue my Archon's mark, but as my full-blooded sisters, sixth-born Mallibo and seventh-born Mhitra, remained at the colony, I never had the opportunity to live with them.

Such an upbringing led to uncertainty as to how I should interact with my kin. While I have since grown close to Mhitra, it is only because we have academic common ground—she with an interest in Allagan magicks, and I with my studies of the arcane arts. In contrast, her elder twin, Mallibo, and I have had next to no contact with each other.

So it was that, for the very first time, our "family" came together, and in the Rostra of all places. It occurred to me that Adebh was perhaps abusing her privilege as a member of the Forum, but I cast aside the thought as she called to order her eleven siblings, who sat sparsely in a chamber designed to hold ninety-nine with ease.

"Ere he passed away, our father conveyed his final wishes to Nazqha. I summoned all of you here to see them carried out."

Nazqha stepped forward, hefting her enormous gleaner's knapsack, and addressed the gathered sisters.

"As he attended his duties," she began, "Father privately collected literature. It was his desire to bequeath to each of us an item from his library." At those words, Nazqha reached into the bag and produced twelve tomes selected by our late sire.

"To Adebh, a first edition of *The Philosophers' Pledge.*"

Even if Adebh's eyes, ordinarily impassive and impenetrable, had not widened at mention of the work, its worth was known to all. It was here, in the very space the Rostra now occupied, that the founding fathers engaged in debate to codify the ideals of their new nation, and the tome contained a detailed account of that defining event. The first edition held tremendous historical value, and no gift could be more fitting for a Forum member.

"To Sumbla, *Into the Water's Flow.*"

The work was unknown to me, but as second-born Sumbla took it in hand, she explained that the Nymian treatise documented an attempt to develop a perpetual engine by drawing upon gravity and the flow of water. To an engineer who had sequestered herself in Labyrinthos to facilitate the ark's construction, such a tome was more precious than its weight in gold.

The gift for third-born Ranmaia, a navigator whose time at sea dwarfed her brief stints on land, were the voyage logs of the fabled explorer Ketenramm. The Eorzean was her inspiration, the very reason she had taken up her calling, and her delight was plain to see.

Ranmaia's full sister, fifth-born Talhdi, was presented a collection of sketches compiled by an art dealer. This single volume contained the works of famous artists such as the wandering pictomancer Janquetilaque, and Talhdi, a painter by trade, trembled with elation to receive it.

My full sisters Mallibo and Mhitra were both given ancient Allagan tomes—items suitable for archaeologists who delved into aetherochemistry as Sons of Saint Coinach. In keeping with their respective specializations, Mallibo's volume had a scientific focus, and Mhitra's arcane.

Next came eighth-born Raigoh, who was artistically inclined like her full sister, Talhdi, and made her living as a musician. To her, our father left a book of compositions penned by the legendary minstrel Santhelme. How he came to possess such a prize was a mystery in and of itself.

Ninth-born Sohnjin is my sister and cousin both, on account of her mother being younger sister to mine. The proprietor of an armor shop in the Agora, she was an unusual character even among this unusual company. Her attire alone marked her as different, clad head to toe in plate despite the formal occasion. To Sohnjin, our father bestowed an Ishgardian workshop's tome that detailed furite manufacturing techniques—a jealously guarded secret of the Holy See. One could only hope that it was not acquired through illicit means.

This brought us to Nazqha, who inherited a most singular tome: a book of Corvosi folklore predating Garlean rule. It was not simply an antique, however. The elaborate arcane patterns it contained—the handiwork of a skilled copyist—had the power to immerse the reader in the worlds described in the fanciful tales. Nary a finer item could grace the shelf of one who so loved rare books.

Prior to taking to the road as an adventurer, eleventh-born Jhimei had trained in arcanima in Vylbrand. She had caused friends and family great distress when she went missing in an Ixali attack, and left them equally confused when she reappeared as though nothing had happened. For one who delighted in danger, our father bequeathed the imposing leather-bound memoirs of Count Edmont de Fortemps, *Heavensward*. If the intent was to encourage her to follow the example of the Warrior of Light, then she had her work cut out for her indeed.

Napa, the twelfth and youngest, was still in the midst of her studies at the Studium. To her, our father left a book constructed in the Far Eastern fashion: a Hingan treatise on the art of suiseki, wherein stones resembling mountains are displayed on basins. Napa had developed a fondness for the practice and pursued it with her peers at the cost of many a missed lecture. While a fine hobby, one would be hard-pressed to make a living with it, and I remain concerned for her future.

So, what manner of tome was it that my father had left me, his fourth-born? When my turn came, Nazqha held up an ancient volume shrouded in a sinister aura owing to its cover, which was skin harvested from a voidsent.

"For Y'shtola . . . *Gateway to the Void*."

No sooner was the title uttered than Adebh's eyes narrowed in disapproval. The Mhachi grimoire bore the secrets to opening a gate large enough to beckon lords among voidsent. While the contents were obscured beneath layers of magical encryption, such knowledge had the potential to wreak unspeakable destruction upon the world, and thus had the tome earned its forbidden designation.

Having been mentioned in several respected works, the mythical grimoire's existence was not in question, but never had I dreamed that it would one day come into my possession. I could see from Adebh's frown that she was tempted to confiscate it here and now, that it might be placed under lock and key in Noumenon. Before she could do so, I snatched the tome from Nazqha and, cradling it in my arms, spun on my heels and returned to my seat.

Our father's knowledge of our passions was as comprehensive as it was impressive. He knew what inspired each of his daughters, and acquired those books that would help us on our respective paths.

The road had been his preferred companion, and for long years I assumed he thought only of his own interests. But in his way, he had loved us—believed in us. I have lived my life feeling no strong bond with him, nor with my mother or sisters, yet it cannot be denied that we are family. So I now ask myself, what could I bequeath to them?

The answer, of course, is obvious: cross-rift travel. For as disparate as my sisters may be, the prospect of visiting other worlds could not fail to interest them.

Adebh would contemplate the diplomatic implications. Sumbla would jump at the chance to study unfamiliar sciences. Ranmaia would dream of crossing new oceans. Talhdi would seek out unknown painting techniques, and Raigoh unheard melodies. Mallibo and Mhitra would compare Allagan and otherworldly technologies.

Sohnjin would obsess over exotic armor. Nazqha would embark on a search for rare books, for which she may well accompany Jhimei on her adventures. And together with like-minded peers, Napa would find joy in collecting rocks and stones from entirely new realms.

As my quill races upon the page, it becomes clear what abides in my heart. There is no sadness, but not for want of attachment. For through my father's gift, as weighty and terrible as it is, I feel the hopes he harbored for me.

I will make it reality. I will find a way to traverse worlds. Then I will go and see he who waits for me and tell him of my travels and hardships. And of the father whom I hold in the highest esteem.

Footprints of a Traveler

The song of oblivion, which had wrought untold ruin upon Etheirys, had been silenced once and for all.

In the wake of this joyous event, the traveler and his brethren had convened at the heart of their realm to discuss the future of the star for the last time. At length, the proceedings came to an end, with the inseparable siblings who chaired the assembly directing their closing words at Oschon.

“May your final journey be fulfilling,” Nymeia said with a smile gentle as starlight.

To this, her brother Althyk added, his voice tinged with hope, “We look forward to receiving the adventurer here in the Omphalos.”

Oschon said naught in answer, choosing only to nod. In that moment, he was overcome by emotion, and he knew that it was the same for the others. Thaliak was as relieved that man’s history would endure as he was proud of those who had fought to preserve it. Azeyma’s breast swelled with the elation that, after so very long, Venat’s plan had succeeded. Halone and Menphina, meanwhile, shared in their ardent admiration of their children’s courage, and fondly spoke of the day the starship *Ragnarok* had set sail for the edge of existence.

How they had hoped then that mankind would triumph. And how they hoped now that their long-held wish would be fulfilled.

The wish that their aether, accumulated over millennia of prayer, would be restored to the star as a blessing both for those who lived and those yet unborn; and that their cores, forged from the souls of Venat's stalwart allies, would return to the aetherial sea to arise as new life. With the Final Days averted, they had concluded that the time was right to take the necessary step—to face and be felled by their beloved children.

Byregot and Rhalgr promptly set about preparing the stage for what would be the first and only battle. Llymlaen transformed into a seabird and took wing for Limsa Lominsa, that she might gaze upon the deeds of her faithful one more time. And assuming his guise as the mortal Deryk, Oschon set forth from the Omphalos to enlist the aid of the hero central to their plan.

Although accorded dominion over mountains, Oschon was better known as the deity of travel—He who roamed the star and shared in men's solitude. In his role as the Wanderer, he had spent more time without the gods' domain than within, and was careful ever to reenter the world of men where he had left it. This precaution he took lest rumors spread of a peculiar traveler capable of vanishing and manifesting at will, unlike the realm's many aetheryte-bound adventurers.

So it was that he first teleported to a quiet corner of Treespeak in the Twelveswood. The nearby fauna scattered in shock at his sudden appearance, but no other eyes were present to bear witness. He took a deep breath, then set off westward with the nonchalance of a traveler carrying on after a rest. It was not long before he heard the rushing of Murmur Rills, the river that marked the start of Alder Springs.

Prior to the gathering in the Omphalos, Deryk had sojourned nearby in Hyrstmill, and had been able to enjoy several relaxing days in the area unremarked, despite the hamlet's relative seclusion, thanks to the steady stream of adventurers who passed by it. During that time, he had become acquainted with the local Wood Wailers, and was thus favored with warm smiles by those standing guard when he crossed over the bridge.

As he proceeded along the forest trail, his eyes narrowing against the descending sun, Deryk pondered the route ahead. It was but a short distance to Coerthas, and thence to Mor Dhona, where, posing as an explorer, he would approach the Sons of Saint Coinach with the claim that he had discovered the entrance to the mythical phantom realm.

"Far too brief a journey . . ."

The words rose unbidden to his lips, and he knew a pang of melancholy. To ensure that his quarry undertook the request, their meeting needed to seem natural; he could not simply seek out the now-disbanded Scions of the Seventh Dawn, much less their champion directly. Given said individual's keen intuition, Deryk knew his true identity was not like to remain hidden for long, but it would not do to arouse suspicion from the outset.

Thus would he contrive to have the petition reach the Students of Baldesion by way of a closely connected organization. Such was the plan that Thaliak and Nald'thal had conceived, and the reason Deryk was now bound for Mor Dhona. *Would that it could have been somewhere farther away . . .*

He looked down at the trail upon which he walked. The passage of innumerable feet had trodden the earth into a hard-packed path, much as the weight of momentous events, one layered upon the other, had defined the course of mankind's history. As a god, he yearned to become one with all the souls in the aetherial sea. But as a traveler, he could not deny that a part of him still yearned to continue exploring the star and observing men as they made their way.

As such thoughts tugged at his mind, Deryk passed through the gates of Fallgourd Float. Built upon a lake lest any trees be felled, this village was famed for the hospitality of its inn. Its location made it a popular waypoint for travelers and merchants en route to Coerthas, and even now a group of adventurers could be seen at the aetheryte on the central isle. He could not help but smile as he skirted the crowd, close enough to regard them, but far enough to escape their notice. And it was then that someone called out to him.

"Here, you're not headin' out *now*, are you?"

He turned towards the voice to see a man sitting on a bench, likely a resident of the Float.

"Only, it gets dangerous after dark. You'd be better off stayin' the night at the Bobbin' Cork, if you ask me."

Somewhat bemused, Deryk glanced up to see that night had indeed begun to fall, and that the lampposts were already aglow throughout the village.

"Thank you for your concern," he replied, eventually finding his words, "but I must press on. I am in some haste, you see."

It was true enough. Deryk's brethren had bid him find the adventurer as soon as possible. But quite apart from that, he could not bring himself to deprive another of a bed. As one of the Twelve, it was only natural that he place the needs of mortals before his own.

The kindly resident's gaze drifted down to Deryk's feet, and it appeared as if he had something else to say. But after a moment's silence, he seemed to think better of it and bade Deryk safe travels. He thanked the man once more before taking his leave.

The scenery changed dramatically the instant he stepped out of Fallgourd Float. This area had once been home to a lush and towering forest like the rest of the Twelveswood, but large swaths of it had since been laid waste by the fragments of Dalamud, which had rained down during the Seventh Umbral Calamity. What met his gaze was a scarred land whose bowels lay exposed, with naught remaining of its ancient residents save jagged stumps and gnarled roots. For the benefit of the Twelveswood's surviving inhabitants, however, the roads were still maintained and patrolled, and taking advantage of the rent earth, industrious souls now gathered here in droves in hopes of striking rich mineral veins. *Truly, the children of man are nothing if not resilient.*

Determined to reach Coerthas before the last light faded, Deryk made to quicken his steps, only to be stopped in his tracks by a familiar voice.

"Ere you go any further, there is something you may wish to know."

He spun on his heels to spy a hovering seedling with a pair of handlike vines raised to its chin, and recognized it at once as Nophica's avatar.

"That you should call to me out here," he began, his brow darkening. "What is it?"

"Pray look down," Nophica instructed, her tone amused.

Deryk did as he was bidden . . . and immediately noticed a baby opo-opo by his feet. Trembling faintly, it grasped the corner of his cloak with a tiny hand and, looking squarely up at him, let out a pleading whimper.

His eyes widened in surprise. "Have you been following me, little one? Since when?"

"Since before Fallgourd Float," Nophica answered in the creature's stead. "Its pack fell prey to a beast of the forest, leaving it orphaned and wounded. And when it saw you passing by, it decided to follow you."

As the patron deity of Gridania, Nophica had no doubt come to watch her faithful while their brethren made their preparations. And in the course of her observations, she must have caught sight of him—along with his unexpected companion.

"Since you seemed entirely oblivious to its existence, I thought it best to bring it to your attention before you went too far. That's all. I shall be on my way now."

Without another word, Nophica transformed into an orb of light and vanished into the darkening wood.

Deryk regarded the opo-opo, his face the picture of consternation. The creature returned his gaze unflinchingly, trust and expectation plain in its large, innocent eyes. Alone and wounded as it was, it could not long survive in the forest, and to turn it away would be to betray its faith in him.

Very well. With the time I have left as a man, I can at least keep you company.

Thus resolved, Deryk resumed walking, using the light of a nearby lamppost to guide his steps. The frontier guard tower soon came into view. He ascended the rise that led to it, the opo-opo scampering after him, and announced himself to a Wood Wailer warming himself by a campfire.

"Might a traveler share the fire awhile? My little companion here has come to some harm, and I would tend to its hurts," he said, gesturing to his charge.

The sentry assented with a chuckle, and waved for Deryk to sit on one of the tree stumps that served as seats. This he duly did and, taking the opo-opo into his arms, quickly located a deep gash on its hip. When injured, he knew, wild animals were wont to move normally so as not to appear vulnerable to would-be predators, but such a wound must have been painful to conceal.

Deryk rummaged in his knapsack and produced a pot of healing ointment, a gift from a merchant who had worried that he traveled too lightly. He applied a generous amount to the wound, glad of the chance to make use of it, and noted with satisfaction how the opo-opo ceased trembling and settled on his lap.

"It certainly trusts you," the sentry observed, grinning. "Now, assuming you intend to head through the pass, I would let your companion rest a spell. You might yet return to Fallgourd, but if you do not mind the lack of comforts, you are welcome to stay at the spire. We always enjoy hearing the tales of travelers."

Deryk took in the sky as he considered his options. Night had well and truly set in, and the stars glinted like jewels scattered upon a veil of black. To press on to Coerthas now would be punishing on the baby opo-opo. This time, it would be wise to heed his host's suggestion, he concluded.

A tale in repayment for their kindness, then. The one he had overheard at a tavern in Ul'dah, perhaps, about those individuals known as inspectors who dealt with all manner of mysteries. Or of his visit to Ala Mhigo in the days following its liberation. Or . . .

As he gazed into the flickering flames, searching the well of recollection, fragments of a distant memory came rising up, of a woman with whom he had shared a campfire in the wilderness. She too had gazed into the flames as she passionately spoke of the joys of roaming free—of seeing new lands and meeting new souls as she journeyed the star in search of problems to solve.

He cast his mind to past, present, and future. To that woman who so loved the world, to the loyal comrades who shared her dreams, and to the adventurer in whom she had entrusted her hopes. Would they forgive him this indulgence, and let him enjoy his final journey just a little while longer?

The opo-opo shifted in his lap and began to snore. *Well, that settles it.*

With glinting eyes, he looked around at the gathered Wailers, and cleared his throat.

An Abiding Aspiration

In a nameless domain floating beneath an endless night sky walked a figure clad in ivory armor—Zero, half-mortal, half-voidsent. Around her, inexplicable structures piled haphazardly one atop another bespoke a simple truth: that the master of this place was lost to reason. Indeed, the horde of voidsent lurching towards her from the shadows seemed incapable of mortal speech, driven only by an insatiable hunger for aether.

I had hoped for an exchange of words . . . but if it is to be blows, so be it.

Centuries wielding the reaper's scythe had not served to dull her swordplay, and with graceful strokes she felled the encroaching creatures one by one. The last was larger than the rest, but dispatched in a similarly effortless flourish of steel. Zero sheathed her blade.

Our host, no doubt.

Having watched the battle to its conclusion, an incongruous creature drifted forth—a nixie summoned by Zero's friends from another world. In this realm ravaged by Darkness, it made for a precious companion. One well worth the regular morsels of aether required to maintain its presence.

But as she lifted her hand to stroke the familiar's head, a stygian pool of aether welled up beneath its floating form, from which a shadow reared, bent on devouring it.

"Damn it all!"

Even as Zero clasped the hilt of her blade, she heard a peal of thunder, and looked on bemused as the dark denizen was unmade by a timely bolt of lightning.

"Careless to let your guard down, Zero."

Vestiges of the levin spell crackled along the gauntleted fingers of a massive figure encased in heavy black armor. Another companion of Zero's. Or, rather, a "comrade."

"Much obliged, Golbez."

He nodded. That the two of them could share such a nonchalant exchange was still bizarre to her.

"'Twould seem our hopes for this domain have come to naught," he began. "None here possessed even a modicum of intelligence."

Casually, he stretched out an arm to absorb the misty residual aether of the vanquished. Though he wore the armor of a mortal, Golbez had long since joined the ranks of the voidsent, and thus was bound by the rule which united them all—devour or be devoured. The natural law of the void.

Yet in the act of feeding, Zero saw him hesitate, and he turned to face her.

"Aether is here for the taking."

"I desire it not," she replied with a slight shake of the head. "Ambient aether is enough to sustain me."

Golbez regarded her in silence for a moment.

"If that is true, then you possess a strength unlike any other in this world—and a temperance to match. Wherefore do you deny yourself that which we all crave?"

"I dislike the feeling. Of merging one's soul with another."

"So you have fed before."

Zero turned away, wishing she still had the brim of her hat to hide behind. But Golbez's words hung stubbornly in the air. At length, her lips parted, and she began to speak of things long past . . .

Zero's mother was a memoriate—a warrior who sealed away the power of eidolons, creatures of great malefic power. In a battle against one such fiend, she had been bathed in a surge of Darkness, which had tainted the kindling life in her womb, condemning her child to be born a daughter both of man and the abyss.

All Zero remembered of her mother was a single bedtime story. The story of Zeromus, a hero who had appeared when the world was at its darkest to restore the boon of Light. And though Zero knew the tale to be little more than a fantasy, it was burned within her breast.

Even as time passed, even after her mother was slain in battle, even after Zero could no longer remember the lines of her face or the color of her eyes, the tale remained etched in her heart. But reality is not as merciful as tales. For when the final eidolon was at long last laid low, it did not herald an era of peace for mankind, but one of new conflict.

Seduced by the very power they had once sought to vanquish, many former heroes turned their gaze upon their fellow man, their hunger for strength beyond sating. And thus the memoriates who yet clung to the Light, like Zero and her mother, set forth to defeat these traitors, not for the glory it might bring, but for hope.

Alas, the memoriates of Darkness were strong, brutal, and above all else, numerous. Only alongside stalwart allies could the likes of Zero hope to prevail against the corrupt. Yet how could she place any faith in fellowship? She who had been ostracized as an aberration from birth, a child half-mortal and half-voidsent. She could not. And when at last a pair of knights bid her join them, she *would not*, her heart having long since become closed to the dream of companionship.

If only I had given them a chance . . . If only I'd been stronger . . .

Her defeat was not long in coming, the sheer number of her adversaries having rendered it inevitable. And it was in the very hour of her defeat, as she lay stricken on the battlefield, that it happened—the stars were blotted out in the heavens as a pall black as pitch enveloped creation, and the world broke.

Yet her tale would not end there. For when the Flood of Darkness came crashing down, she was swept through a tear in reality unto the rift, in what would prove a peculiar mercy. That place beyond time served to preserve her as she was, and saved her from the calamity which befell her home, whose fate she would discover when she found her way back through the faintest of fissures.

What greeted her then was unrecognizable: a scene of destruction absolute. The earth had rotted away, and in its place distorted isles of substant Darkness now floated in a starless sky. No familiar forms of life remained, only corrupted monstrosities, hostile to man.

Her body weak from an eternity in stasis, she trudged along, scanning this unknown territory. Yet the more she looked, the heavier resignation weighed upon her. She would not find any living in this wasteland. Everyone was already dead.

It was then that she heard a sound—a familiar sound. A *voice.*

"Someone . . . please . . . *Help me*!"

She flew. With a strength she didn't know she possessed, Zero flung herself towards the cry. No sword, no shield, no plan of attack—but if someone yet lived, if someone yet called out for succor, she could not abandon them. There was yet hope.

"Where are you? Tell me!"

". . . Me?" the voice whispered. "I'm *here*."

Only by a hair's breadth did she manage to evade the descending claw. Rolling, she whirled to meet her attacker.

A gruesome face leered back at her. Nay—not a face. For the abomination had neither eyes nor nose, only a grinning jaw filled with razor-sharp teeth.

"How strange . . . A meal that chose to keep its mortal shape."

These sinister words spoke all. Zero's heart sank as she understood what had become of mankind.

". . . Then I am the last."

"Yet hardly the least," came the smirking reply. "For in devouring you, your strength will do *much* to greaten mine!"

The beast howled and drew back one of its great claws, primed to finish its prey. Yet the thought of fleeing never crossed Zero's mind, defenseless though she was.

Even if this world has ended . . . No, because it has ended, I cannot!

As if in answer to her determination, the ambient Darkness began to stir. Swirling, bending, lengthening . . . until Zero felt the weight of a great scythe within her grasp. Surprise seized her for only a moment before she clenched her hand and swung reflexively at the horror above her, cleaving the wailing creature in twain.

Foe vanquished and strength spent, she fell to the ground.

"Aether . . ."

Instinct guided her trembling hand as she reached out, gathering the creature's dissolving essence and absorbing it. An instant later, she felt her body begin to heal, a strange new energy imbuing her limbs. *Power. More power.* This was what the beast had spoken of, then. This was what it meant to "devour."

A wave of disgust washed over her. Dizziness and pain scattered her thoughts, her body convulsing as if fighting to expel something vile.

A second voice echoed in her head.

"More, damn you. More! Only once I have been devoured will I—will we be complete!"

"What . . . ? No . . ."

The voice of her vanquished foe now harrowed her consciousness, as if boring into her very being. Death itself, then, had also become distorted—no longer did souls return to their source, to be cleansed before rebirth. They were simply bottled by those who devoured them. And thus began a battle of wills, during which the stronger would bring the weaker to heel. She had to fight.

A chuckle reverberated behind Zero's eyes. *"Stubborn one, aren't you? And pure . . . So intact in self and purpose . . . Let's see what's in you, hm?"*

The creature pressed further into her mind, freeing memories she had long since locked away. Of the lonely child pale as snow. Of her mother's face. Of . . .

"A statue? Of whom? Why would you treasure such a pitiful, ugly thing?"

Zero fought. Yet try as she might to resist the fiend, she and it were now one and the same. She could no sooner stop her own thoughts than she could keep it from knowing her innermost secrets.

Zeromus. I wanted to save the world like Zeromus did.

The creature howled with laughter. She could see the faceless monstrosity again, its grinning jaw filled with razor-sharp teeth.

"Simple fool . . . You really don't know how the story ends, do you?"

But now that the thoughts of that vile voice permeated her mind, she found that she knew only too well. Zeromus did indeed save the star . . . only for his fellow man to cast him out in fear of his all-conquering strength. A hero turned pariah.

Perhaps her mother hadn't known the tale's end. Or perhaps she withheld the truth to protect her voidsent daughter. Whatever the case, knowing it now did nothing to shake Zero's conviction.

If the Light to save mankind makes me an outcast, then gladly shall I become one!

Thus, with clear resolve did she purge the lingering rancor from her thoughts. Her mind grew quiet, as though it had never been host to another, nor did she ever hear that dreadful voice again. Brought to heel, it would seem.

But being forced to face her innermost thoughts left Zero disconsolate.

How am I to save mankind, when no one is left to save?

Thus did her aimless journey begin. Countless times others came to claim her soul, and countless times she tore them asunder—but never again would she consume their aether, even if it meant starving to death. Rebirth was but a small inconvenience, after all. And so it went on. For thousands of years she traveled, losing herself piece by piece, until one day . . .

". . . I'd completely forgotten," Zero concluded. "But I remember now—thanks to you, Golbez."

Having listened to her tale, her comrade responded in his ever-dispassionate tone.

"So long as one possesses sufficient strength and fixed resolve, one need not fear dissolution, even should one be consumed. I would never lose my sense of self. You must have harbored some lingering doubt."

Zero shook her head.

"Not doubt, exactly. More . . . an unreadiness to accept myself. To accept that someone as weak and alone as me could dream of becoming a hero."

She raised her head and gazed upon the endless sky.

"I always wondered about that statue in the center of my domain. Now I finally understand. Broken and timeworn though it is—feared and ostracized though he was—Zeromus ever lived within my heart as a hero who wished to save the world. As I do."

The armored figure appeared to consider this for a while.

"Then I, too, shall devour others no more. I do not believe the practice contradicts my desire to save our home . . . but mayhap in forswearing it, I will come to know who I truly am as well."

Zero's eyes widened at his words, and she felt the beginning of a smile tug at the corner of her lips.

"Then let us move on. We may find allies in this vast world yet."

And so the pair set off again, trailing a nixie forged by bonds of the past, with hopes for the future and for a world made whole once more.

The First of Many Festivals

Wuk Lamat, Vow of Resolve and Dawnservant of Tuliyollal, looked upon the splendor that was the nation's capital, a many-hued tapestry of lives and cultures that unfurled before her. In the evening light, the colors grew even more vibrant, as all manner of people flowed through the city streets. *The lifeblood of our nation.*

And in recent days, their community had grown even larger, as returnees from Yyasulani gradually made their way back home, finally free of the mysterious dome which had severed them from the outside world's temporal flow. For thirty years, they had abided in the realm of Alexandria and grown accustomed to its radically different way of life, only to emerge and find Tural exactly as it had been when they left—and themselves thirty years older than their kin.

Though the returnees were in many ways strangers to Tural, Wuk Lamat was wholly committed to helping them retake their place in Turali society, and she had devised several plans to facilitate this process with the aid of her brother. One involved the staging of a hunting festival in the city. The previous Dawnservant, Gulool Ja Ja, had been especially fond of such events, and it would provide an excellent opportunity for the people to enjoy themselves and each other's company.

How old was I when I first took part? Sixteen? Ah . . . but there was that one time I snuck out as a cub, with Papa none the wiser . . .

She chuckled to herself as she closed her eyes and cast her mind back to that day's misadventure. Had it been fourteen years already?

The several dozen participants milling about the Winged Walk wore expressions that bespoke nervousness and eagerness in equal measure. The tension broke when the Dawnservant at last appeared upon the balcony, addressing them with a booming voice that all knew at once belonged to the Head of Resolve.

"I salute you, brave warriors, and thank you for coming! But before the festivities commence, I must remind you that this is not *just* a celebration of martial prowess. This day we hunt not to take the life of our prey, but to acknowledge our place within nature's design, and give thanks for the bounty of Tural!"

Their hearts swelled with passion and pride as they listened to the Dawnservant's words, and each and every one stood a little bit straighter. The Head of Reason proceeded to outline the rules of the competition, his measured tones ensuring no part was misunderstood.

Beasts would be released into the city from the Arch of the Dawn, and participants would be tasked with slaying them within the allotted time. The one who laid low the largest specimen would be crowned the victor and granted a boon of their own choosing. So great was this honor that one would surely be proclaimed a hero to their people—like the Xbr'aal Hunmu Rruk, a former champion who had returned to his village with a priceless greatbow from the palace's own treasure vault.

As Gulool Ja Ja concluded his opening remarks, the drummers began to play, and the participants raised their voices in approval, surging forward and flowing out into the streets. A wave breaking upon the rocks, their joy and energy revitalizing the city.

The Head of Resolve grunted in approval.

"Many villages sent their best for this one. Will our son acquit himself well against such formidable competition, I wonder?"

The Head of Reason seemed bemused by his brother's question.

"You needn't worry about Zoraal Ja. Thirteen he may be, but a warrior grown he has proven himself already. If he hadn't, you would never have consented to his taking part."

Those unfamiliar with blessed siblings might have been confused to witness their exchange. But despite sharing the same body, each head was a separate and distinct individual. The Head of Resolve listened to the words of the one he trusted more than any other and nodded in concession.

At that moment, a breathless man of the Landsguard came running, his face a picture of panic.

"Apologies, Dawnservant, but the Third Promise, Wuk Lamat, has escaped from her room and is nowhere to be found! The door was locked and sentries posted, just as you instructed, Head of Reason, but even with these precautions, she somehow—"

The Head of Resolve's boisterous laughter cut short the man's report.

"Bwahaha! So eager to see the festival that she couldn't abide her confinement, no doubt! With such an insatiable curiosity, she is sure to surprise us in the years to come!"

At this, the Head of Reason could only sigh, though he knew his brother spoke true.

And indeed, Wuk Lamat would not be denied a front-row view of the festivities. *I had to be there, in the thick of it.* She soon made her way to Bayside Bevy, darting from shop to shop to avoid discovery, before pausing briefly in the shadow of a pile of cargo, straining to listen to the sounds of nearby activity. Forbidden from taking part, she had nevertheless yearned to experience the excitement firsthand. Overcome with anticipation of the battles she imagined she would shortly witness, her pulse quickened in time with the beat of the distant drums.

"This is no place for kids like you."

The disapproving Yyasulani drawl was so close she could feel the breath on her neck.

Wuk Lamat leapt out of hiding and whirled to find a figure

shrouded in a large cloak, with dark, wavy hair that shimmered like the sea at dusk. The tall ears and glittering almond eyes were striking to behold. It was the first time she had ever seen a Shetona girl in the flesh.

"Hey, you're a kid too! If you're so scared, then you should go hide in Sunperch!"

She was disappointed to find the older girl wholly unmoved by her words.

"That I can't do. I came all the way from Yyasulani for the festival. The palace is too far from the action. I wanna see it up close—be in the thick of it."

Hearing her own sentiments echoed, Wuk Lamat couldn't help but grin.

"Me too! Say, why don't we—"

But before she could extend her invitation, they were interrupted by the arrival of one of the beasts set loose for the festival. An avian creature that approached them slowly with uncertain intent. Wuk Lamat gestured to it with her head.

"What is *that*?"

Coolly eyeing the beast, the Shetona girl replied, "A toucalibri. Fond of fragrant flowers, normally harmless—but keep your distance. If we antagonize it, it'll use that huge beak to defend itself, attacking anything and everything it sees."

The young Wuk Lamat didn't catch everything the older girl was saying, but she understood that this was a formidable foe, and her heart began to beat faster. Just then, the toucalibri let out a shrill—and distinctly antagonized—cry. Spying a small hand axe that was leaning against a nearby crate, Wuk Lamat seized the weapon and raised it aloft.

"Don't worry! I'll protect you!"

Heroic proclamation thus issued, she charged the beast. Hers was not a martial technique honed with years of physical and mental training, but the sum total of a child's unbridled ferocity. Thus did Wuk Lamat bring the axe crashing down, channeling her tremendous might into a single devastating blow.

Sparks flew from the blade as it clanged against the cobbles, a hair's breadth shy of the beast's head. While utterly ineffective as an attack, the sound and fury was enough to startle the toucalibri, which promptly took wing and fled.

Victory, she thought . . . before falling to her knees, spent. Her heart was pounding louder than the Dawnherald, her whole body shaking from the thrill of her first battle. And then the fear she had somehow beaten back returned in full force. *That could've ended very, very badly . . .*

She looked up to see the Shetona girl beside her, holding out her hand.

"Not bad for a kid your size. Still, we shouldn't stick around. Let's head to the palace before something worse shows up."

Once she had helped Wuk Lamat to her feet, the two began walking in silence. The shadows lengthened as the sun sank low on the horizon, and they remained vigilant for the faintest sign of movement as they trudged up the steep path. A short while later, the stairs leading to Sunperch came into view, and they both breathed a sigh of relief.

A brief reprieve that was shattered by the sound of thunderous footfalls.

The Shetona girl looked back, her eyes widening in apparent disbelief.

"A mane like a Far Eastern horse, tusks like spears . . . That's a zaghnal! What were they thinking?!"

Even if Wuk Lamat hadn't heard the fear in the older girl's voice, it was plain that this beast was a far greater threat than the bird had been. She brandished her axe reflexively, gripping the handle tightly with both hands.

"Don't be stupid," her companion hissed, "this isn't a toucalibri. Even a party of hunters would struggle to kill it. Our only chance is to run!"

But Wuk Lamat would not be deterred. Placing herself between the Shetona girl and the gargantuan monstrosity, she barked her reply, "I know! I'll keep it busy! Buy you some time!"

They had only just met, yet she would risk her life to save the older girl. Though others might question the logic of her choice, to Wuk Lamat it was no choice at all. *Why wouldn't I?*

By the same token, the Shetona girl did not waver in her own decision, even as her trembling legs betrayed her crippling fear.

"No. My mother taught me that naturalists heed their instincts. And she would never forgive me if I left you—even if you *are* too heroic for your own good."

Alas, the zaghnal could not comprehend such noble sentiments, nor cared to try. Scraping its hooves and crouching slightly, it readied itself to charge—when a stone came whistling through the air and struck it squarely between the eyes.

"Run, Lamaty'i! Run!"

The zaghnal cast about for the source of the offending object. Its gaze fell upon the Hhetsarro youth atop the stairs, and the leather slingshot in his hand.

"Koana!"

Wuk Lamat seized the Shetona girl's hand and sprinted to join her brother. Koana loosed a second and third stone, peppering the beast with well-placed but meaningless blows. Shrugging off this distraction, the zaghnal bellowed in rage and barreled towards the two girls.

"It's going to catch us!"

The Shetona girl's panicked cry was enough to rekindle Wuk Lamat's courage. Once more, she resolved to ensure that at least one of them survived. Slowing her steps just shy of the stairs, the child pivoted and broke away—and the zaghnal followed. She heard the older girl's angry, pleading voice, but ran on, sparing her not so much as a glance. *I had to give her as much time as I could.*

As it turned out, however, Wuk Lamat's valiant attempt would amount to little, for she tripped before she had taken half a dozen steps and landed in a heap on the ground.

Knowing the zaghnal was nearly upon her, Wuk Lamat shut her eyes and braced for the end. Yet as the long moments passed, she realized she was still breathing. Opening her eyes a crack, she spied a hulking, motionless mass through the legs of a towering Mamool Ja, who stood with his blue-scaled back to her, bloodied sword in hand.

Only one man had ever inherited both the stout frame of the Hoobigo and the blue scales of the Boonewa: the First Promise of Tuliyollal, Zoraal Ja. *The trueborn son of Gulool Ja Ja. A bond Koana and I could only dream of*. . . On this day, he had earned yet another accolade as the youngest ever to participate in a hunting festival, and in felling the zaghnal with a single thrust had demonstrated his worthiness of the honor, saving his stepsiblings and their friend in so doing.

"So this is where you ran off to. Koana—take your sister home. *Now*."

And thus did Wuk Lamat's adventure come to an end, as did the hunting festival not long after. Zoraal Ja was the undisputed victor, and for his prize he claimed a second sword, that he might follow in their father's footsteps and master the viper's art.

To not only participate in the hunting festival at the age of thirteen but also win it was a scarce credible feat. Zoraal Ja's legend was born, as Turali far and wide declared him the Resilient Son—a testament to his miraculous conception and birth—who would surely succeed his father as Dawnservant when the time came.

But Zoraal Ja did not become a hero only to the common man that day. Wuk Lamat and Koana cheered for their brother as loudly as any, and never forgot how he had come to their rescue.

". . . Did you even hear a word I said?"

The spell broken, Wuk Lamat opened her eyes and saw Erenville giving her the quizzical look she had seen more times than she could count.

"Remind me. Who asked that I come and select the beasts for your hunting festival?"

That old, familiar grumbling.

"Sorry, sorry—I was just thinking back to the one where we met. The one Zoraal Ja won."

"Oh . . ."

He looked away, eyes narrowing as he reflected on the memory. *On a promise broken—or perhaps kept?—to his mother, and their shared misadventure.*

"You were so beautiful, I mistook you for a girl!"

"Well . . . technically speaking, you weren't wrong."

It was not widely known that male and female Shetona were indistinguishable from one another until the age of thirteen. As they were long-lived and few in number, outsiders rarely chanced to encounter a Shetona adolescent.

"Still, you really surprised me! And not for the last time, either. Truly, I couldn't have asked for a better *childhood friend*."

She felt the smirk creep across her lips before she spoke the dreaded words. And sure enough, Erenville rolled his eyes in response . . . but failed to conceal a faint smile of his own. *That old, familiar exchange.*

"Long-standing acquaintance, thank you very much. Now then, I believe we have a festival to arrange."

The time for old memories had passed, as thoughts turned to the making of new ones.

Together, the pair made their way along the cobbled streets through which they had once run, side by side.

A Precious Gift

Removed from the busy streets of Tuliyollal, Krile was enjoying a moment of calm and quiet on the Arterial Climb. She sat on a bench and idly considered the city's new diversity of garb, the juxtaposition of Solution Nine and Turali styles making for a heartwarming sight.

The harmony was welcome after all she had witnessed in Alexandria, now bereft of its former king and queen. Only a few days had passed since their return to the capital, but Vow of Resolve Wuk Lamat and Vow of Reason Koana were already hard at work seeking solutions to the myriad problems facing the two nations. The integration of returnees to Tuliyollal was of particular importance, and Wuk Lamat was eagerly planning a hunting festival to facilitate their transition. Indeed, mere moments before, Krile had spied her energetic friend rushing to the palace, doubtless deeply embroiled in her duties as Dawnservant.

Thankfully, there were no pressing matters that demanded swift action on her own behalf. If anything, Krile had come here seeking a reprieve from the cartwheeling thoughts she had yet to commit to writing, concerning all that had transpired since her arrival in Tural. Never did she imagine that a single letter to Galuf Baldesion would ultimately lead her to another reflection. Now, having faithfully retraced the steps of her beloved grandfather, Krile hardly knew how to commit the epic tale to parchment.

A small shadow caught her eye, and she turned to see a bird

perched upon the rail by the cliff, its jade and scarlet plumage bright in the warm sunlight.

"Come to rest your wings with me?"

As she spoke, Krile could not help but remember another bird she had watched, together with her grandfather, back when she was a girl. The day Galuf had gifted her a hood . . .

"A seedkin . . . Well known for its noxious breath—"

"I know! A morbol!"

The young voice rang brightly over the steady tone of her instructor, who narrowed his eyes.

"Very good," he said, his lips briefly curling into a faint smile. "Now, if we were to combine one of its vines with mandrake and quicksilver, what alchemical agent would we create?"

The difficulty of this supplementary question tempered the girl's enthusiasm. Her brow furrowed.

"That's not fair, Grandad! You said it was a *biology* quiz, not alchemy!"

"And what is one without the other?" Galuf grinned down at her. "Knowledge must be considered from every angle if we are truly to expand our horizons."

Krile puffed out her cheeks and turned away. In the near distance, the statue of Sharlayan's guardian deity, Thaliak, towered over the curved, almost shell-like walls of Scholar's Harbor. Their small ship was fast approaching Old Sharlayan, where awaited an end to these tranquil hours. Krile sighed.

Galuf and his colleagues constituted the renowned Students of Baldesion, an organization dedicated to the research of unexplained arcane phenomena. Their base of operations was an island off the coast of Sharlayan, and it was to this place—known as the Isle of Val—that Krile had moved, after a dozen summers in Galuf's orphanage.

It would be an exaggeration to say they lived together. The only time Krile saw her tirelessly diligent grandfather was during meals, or before bed, when she would discuss the books she'd read during the day. Even so, life on the island afforded her peace. A quiet reprieve from the constant whisper of her gift.

For as long as she could remember, Krile had been exceedingly sensitive to the intentions of others. Indeed, she could instinctively discern the innermost thoughts and feelings of those she interacted with. Unspoken apathy, intolerance, or hatred could overwhelm her in an instant, reducing her to tears. Concerned by her sudden emotional shifts, Galuf had conducted a series of tests to better understand her abilities.

He duly discovered that Krile was blessed with the Echo. More specifically, she possessed the ability to transcend speech and access the truths concealed within people's hearts. Unfortunately, controlling her power was easier said than done, for which reason Krile had gradually withdrawn from those around her. Little wonder, then, that she found life on the Isle of Val, where people were few and familiar, far more bearable.

But Galuf could not remain with her on the island all the time. Apart from anything else, each moon saw him depart for Old Sharlayan to present research findings to the Forum and order supplies.

And thus Krile had insisted on accompanying him on one such visit. Doing so meant spending more time together, aboard the ship and otherwise, which is how she found herself traveling to the mainland after several months away.

Once they had arrived, Krile decided to take a walk about the harbor while Galuf met with his colleagues at the Studium. She did not wish to interfere with his work. *With luck, I'll see a puffin like the ones in my bestiary!*

Sadly, her plans were dashed when she came face-to-face with a group of youths, seemingly in the throes of a hotly contested game of tag. Among them was at least one Krile recognized from her brief attendance at the Studium's academy for children. Instinctively, she turned to flee, but a girl's accusatory voice stopped her in her tracks.

"Hey! What are *you* doing here?"

Krile knew she should keep moving, but her feet would not obey. In an instant, the claws of unspoken malice seized her heart, enveloping her in darkness. *Hostility. Rejection. Disgust* . . . Tears welled in her eyes, but she blinked them back, willing her lip to stop trembling. She needed to leave. *If I can just find Grandfather, everything will be fine.* But a Lalafellin boy with long hair blocked her path, his arms crossed. *Another one?* Krile flinched as he stepped forward, but to her amazement he passed straight by her and addressed the opposing group of children with outrage.

"Have you no shame?!"

Krile stared, dumbstruck like the other children. The boy continued his tirade.

"Singling out one of our own and bullying her to tears?! How dare you call yourselves Sharlayans! We seek enlightenment through knowledge and reason, not power through persecution!" He carried himself with a composure well beyond his years, but as Krile looked closer, she noticed his ears were flushed a bright red.

Heat kindled in her own chest as the boy's feelings intruded upon her thoughts: concealed trepidation about confronting a group alone alongside earnest indignation. Without a doubt, his anger was on Krile's behalf.

But why? He doesn't even know me. Krile's own bafflement was mirrored in the children who confronted her.

"What's it to you, Ejika?" one of them snapped. "You know nothing about it. She's an aberration!"

The air grew tense as fists clenched and the children regarded the boy named Ejika with unconcealed hostility. He recoiled, but spluttered a retort, nonetheless.

"S-So, what? Are we to resolve this like dull-witted brutes, then?"

Krile had to do something—and fast. But just as she opened her mouth to speak, another voice rang out from behind her.

"Those quick to anger are quicker still to err. With clouded judgment, we forsake any wisdom we might otherwise stand to gain."

The familiar timbre immediately put Krile's heart at ease; Galuf must have finished with his Studium business early and come to find her. The other children stiffened at the unexpected presence of an adult, Ejika most of all. Galuf continued with no little disappointment.

"People fear what they do not know. But it is our study of just such unknowns that defines us as Sharlayans. Through our acquisition of knowledge, we beget understanding."

The children shifted awkwardly, none willing to meet his gaze.

"My granddaughter is indeed possessed of a unique ability. She treads a path unknown. But being true to herself is no cause for condemnation."

The children had little recourse against his gentle-yet-forceful words, so they mumbled their apologies and scattered—all save one. Suddenly aware of his slack-jawed stare, a flustered Ejika clamped his mouth shut as Galuf turned to him.

"Our righteousness," said Galuf, "may be wielded like a blade, 'tis true. But to do so without first procuring a shield is like to invite injury." Galuf's brow softened, a small smile nestled in the corner of his mouth. "For rising in defense of my Krile, however, you have my sincerest thanks."

Ejika nodded gravely. Krile turned to thank him as well, but he spoke over her.

"You probably don't know who I am, but I know all about you." He fixed Krile with the same grave look he had given Galuf. "To be frank, I couldn't care less about your ability, or how it makes you different. What galls me is your position. Walking beside Master Galuf and answering his questions . . . when I could answer *twice* as many, and twice as *difficult*, come to that!"

Krile's eyes widened as she considered the surprising source of his vexation. Both the look in his eye and the thrum of his emotions spoke only a single truth.

"My name is Ejika Tsunjika, and I will surpass you to become Galuf Baldesion's greatest disciple! Mark my words!" Having bombarded her with his one-sided declarations, the aspiring scholar turned on his heel and scampered off, leaving no room for rebuttal or even a word of gratitude.

"My disciple, eh?" Galuf murmured. "It seems you've found yourself a rival, Krile."

He placed a hand on her head, stirring the tears she'd fought to hold back.

"I don't want a rival," Krile's voice wavered. "His jealousy will turn to hatred, I know it will." And for a moment, she imagined listening to the whispers of his heart growing ever more bitter, powerless to stop his poisonous resentment. *Better to be alone.*

Galuf's hand left her head, and something soft replaced it.

Krile reached up, and her fingers found light fabric covering her hair and ears.

"I'm sorry to have kept you waiting. And with such company besides." He smiled awkwardly before gesturing in her direction. "I commissioned that from a friend at the Studium, you see, and only thought to pick it up."

Krile removed the garment atop her head, and saw that it was a hood, accented with catlike ears. Clearly it had been made for a Lalafell, but even so, it was slightly oversized.

"Must it have such large ears?" Krile sighed. "People already worry that I hear too much."

She made to return the hood, but Galuf gently pressed it into her hands.

"Remember what I said, Krile." He looked out towards the harbor, and Krile followed his gaze. "There is no shame in being who you are, and to tread an unknown path only ensures that your feet will carry you to new knowledge. To spurn your gift is to risk having it turned against you. Learn to accept it, and others will follow suit. When that day comes, I daresay the ears on that hood will represent you perfectly."

Off in the distance, Krile's coveted puffin bobbed in the water. Galuf smiled. "A cloudkin . . . Well suited for life in the water, and indeed is a faster swimmer than flier . . . Now tell me—what does it feel?"

Krile focused on the puffin with quiet intensity. After a few moments, she knew.

"Like its soul is soaring on the wind, even as its body basks in the warmth of the sun." A gentle smile found its way to her lips. "It feels joy."

Galuf beamed at her. "A wonderful discovery," he said. "One only your power can glean. You need never fear it, Krile. It is yours—a precious gift."

A gentle tapping on her boot roused Krile from her reminiscing. The red and green shorebird looked up at her hopefully.

"I'm sorry, little one, but I haven't any food for you."

The bird chirped as if in reply before taking flight, leaving behind the memory of Galuf's words. It had been some time before she could truly believe them, but she knew that the journey to accepting her abilities, and herself, had begun that day.

With her grandfather's guidance, Krile began studying the Echo in earnest. In understanding its nature, she found less reason to fear it, and as her fear waned, so too did the unbidden whispers of others' thoughts. Those halcyon days spent by Galuf's side stayed with her even now, as a full-fledged member of the Students of Baldesion.

Krile watched the bird fly away, its silhouette framed against the setting sun. Her grandfather must have admired this same, picturesque sky once—a sky now hers to walk beneath, as she continued along the path he had left behind. *Perhaps this, too, was a gift from Grandfather.* She pulled her hood a little closer and rose from the bench.

Encore

Days Gone By, Days Yet to Come

"Oh my, how careless of our Azem."

Thus spoke Hythlodaeus, having ambled into his office at the Bureau of the Architect to find a crystal sitting rather conspicuously on a chair reserved for guests. *Slipped from a singularly adventurous pocket, no doubt.* He marveled at the way the light played on its facets, like the surface of a tranquil lake, and recalled the first visitor he had received that morning.

Azem had sought the chief's assistance with the refinement of the Fourteenth in their series of concepts to help ease the burdens of travel, which was contained within the palm-sized crystal. But as was so often the case, the conversation concerning the escapades that inspired said concept's creation had spiraled into a full-blown recounting, leaving Hythlodaeus insufficient time to evaluate it before Azem had to hasten to a meeting with the Convocation. Hythlodaeus was not without his own pressing obligations—the formal evaluation of a massive living-being concept, for one—and had only just returned to the bureau a moment before.

"And absent such comforts, how unbearable your wanderings will surely be," he mused aloud as he collected his friend's crystal.

Turning to the nearby window, Hythlodaeus cast his gaze over the great Capitol where the Convocation gathered and, with a practiced act of will, viewed the world in a different light. While many could feel the flow of aether, only those with experience could perceive its currents with their eyes. Rarer still were those born with the ability to do so as keenly as Hythlodaeus—Emet-Selch being another such natural talent.

So it was that Hythlodaeus effortlessly descried Azem's strand amidst the weave. Though he could not be certain of his quarry's exact position at such a distance, he was confident it lay somewhere within the Capitol.

Blinking, he beheld the world as others did once more. Far beyond the panes, the sun was poised to kiss the horizon, and in its ardor bathed the city streets in rose and gold. The Convocation's business would be concluded shortly, making this an ideal moment to deliver the forgotten crystal. His course decided, Hythlodaeus departed the bureau, taking only the briefest of moments to mention his plans to the senior secretary. While the industrious soul was accustomed to his superior's carefree nature, he nevertheless attempted to detain him, only to be defeated by the tried and trusted tactic of politely nodding and pretending not to hear.

Outside the bureau doors, Amaurot basked in the evening light.

Never was a city more magnificent.

From the humblest streets to the highest spires . . .

Hythlodaeus's feet carried him up the gentle rise leading to the institution's grand doors, past which he spied two women he recognized, their cheerful banter a familiar duet.

"Mitron, Loghrif. A pleasure as always. I gather the meeting is concluded?"

"Well met, Hythlodaeus. It ended but a moment ago, yes," replied Mitron, before flashing a knowing smile. "I believe they're both still inside."

I am indeed a creature of habit. "Azem left a concept crystal in my office."

With a chuckle and a shrug, Mitron turned to make for the

Macarenses Angle. Loghrif offered some parting pleasantries before jogging to catch up.

"So, Mitron. What shall we do this evening?"

"Exactly what we discussed earlier—at length. Ever the forgetful one, aren't you . . ."

Hythlodaeus could not help but chuckle to himself as he heard their voices fade into the general hubbub. *Unchanging in their dynamic, be it in labor or leisure.* Mitron created life to thrive in the sea, and Loghrif life to thrive upon terra firma. Neighboring realms inextricably linked, and as the waves were forever drawn to the shore, so too were the pair inseparable. Hythlodaeus enjoyed their warmth, listening until he could hear them no longer, before returning to his task.

Not a single speck of dust marred the Capitol's vast and elegant foyer. Deeper within were two figures engaged in what appeared to be a rather serious discussion. As it was customary for the Convocation to debate matters of grave import with neither mask nor hood to obscure their features, it was plain from their unconcealed faces that the meeting had only recently ended—and that some points had not been settled to the satisfaction of all. *Or mayhap cousins know better than to try and hide their intentions from their own kin.*

Taking care not to disturb Lahabrea and Igeyorhm, Hythlodaeus passed through a nearby set of doors and stepped softly as he proceeded down the hall. Shifting his perception of the world, he picked up Azem's trail once more. *Closer now—the garden, most like. Which means I'll need to take the long way around.*

He recognized another strand of aether. *Well, since there's no need to rush . . .*

Clasping his hands behind his back, Hythlodaeus began to stroll, humming softly as he imagined his next encounter.

A short while later, he arrived at the entrance to the Convocation's meeting chambers. With impeccable timing, the heavy doors groaned and began to open, allowing a young man of modest stature to emerge. Affixed to his white robe was a red mask like no other.

"Good Elidibus, I thank and commend you for your service on this fine day."

"Oh. Hythlodaeus. As ever, you are too kind. If you're looking for Azem and Emet-Selch, they left not long ago . . ."

Truly, our proclivities are known to one and all. Elidibus and Mitron were no exception—indeed, when Azem or Emet-Selch visited the Bureau of the Architect, the staff usually refrained from asking their business and led them straight to Hythlodaeus. Only the redoubtable senior secretary and those not long in employment followed protocol to the letter.

After informing Elidibus that he had already deduced Azem's location, Hythlodaeus's curiosity compelled him to ask about the cousins' earlier conversation.

"Were the matters brought before the Convocation today particularly thorny? Lahabrea and Igeyorhm seemed to be at loggerheads."

"No, no . . . I would say that the situation is more or less resolved. However, it has been of great concern to Lahabrea, contributing to his intermittent attendance of late. I expect Igeyorhm is merely worried for his well-being."

"I see. What I witnessed was not an argument but a scolding, then. Even so, I cannot fathom what dreadful crisis could warrant the constant attention of the esteemed Lahabrea."

Elidibus's pained expression came as a surprise. *For one so brilliant to struggle to put his thoughts into words . . . It must be a delicate situation indeed.*

"I confess . . . the danger is not . . . inconsiderable, and there are aspects I have yet to fully comprehend," he mumbled, averting his gaze.

For a long moment they stood in silence, until Elidibus took a breath and stood a little straighter.

"But we have gained much from this episode, too. And I, new friendship." A wisp of a smile played on his lips. "Other blessings as well, descending from the heavens to aid us . . . A veritable guiding star . . ." There was a faraway look in his eyes, as if reflecting on a half-remembered dream.

"It sounds as if you have fond memories of the affair."

Elidibus blinked. "Yes . . . yes, I believe I do. And I shall cherish them for as long as I live."

Resolved to speak no further on the matter, Elidibus put up his hood and excused himself. Hythlodaeus thanked him for his time and watched as the emissary strode away, regaining a little more of his composure with every step, until an altogether different man left the Capitol behind. *Curious.*

With a small shake of the head, Hythlodaeus resumed his relaxed pursuit, sauntering towards the next bend. In that instant, a sable soul came barreling around the corner, and it was all Hythlodaeus could do to avoid a collision. Regaining his balance, he turned to ascertain the harried individual's identity and found himself looking into a pair of jade eyes.

"I'm so sorry. That was thoughtless and rude and inconsiderate of me . . ."

Our new Fandaniel. Having known the man quite well prior to his recent appointment, Hythlodaeus still thought of him as Hermes. Like the other Convocation members, he had neglected to raise his hood and don his mask following their meeting, and so his deathly pallor and the bags beneath his eyes were impossible to ignore.

"No need to apologize, my friend, I am quite unharmed. Yet if I may be blunt—you look all but spent. Have you been neglecting your sleep?"

"I . . . I have responsibilities. Things that must be understood. That *I* must understand."

Vague though the reply was, Hermes's reluctance to meet his gaze spoke volumes. *Burying himself in his work, just as Emet-Selch said.* Such behavior was not unheard of for the man, but this episode was notable for its intensity and duration. *Though perhaps that is to be expected . . .*

Hythlodaeus and Emet-Selch had been dispatched to Elpis to assess the then-chief overseer's fitness for a seat on the Convocation, but their visit had coincided with an accident. Seemingly without warning, a collective of familiars into which Hermes had poured years of effort had grown unstable and spontaneously dissipated, producing a shockwave that in turn triggered the activation of a memory reconfiguration system. In the aftermath, Hythlodaeus and Emet-Selch found they had no recollection of the period following their arrival in Elpis, while Hermes possessed only fragments with which he pieced together the circumstances.

While undoubtedly inconvenient, Hythlodaeus had taken the episode in his stride, and it soon became a topic for amusing anecdotes among the staff. But not Hermes. "I killed her—*murdered* her," he lamented—a passing strange sentiment Hythlodaeus had never heard anyone utter of a familiar—and as if he had been stripped of the wings he so often conferred upon his concepts, he could never again bring himself to make another flying creation.

Ever since, embracing his duties as Fandaniel, Hermes had spent his every waking moment conducting observation and study of extant phenomena.

"Far be it from me to deter you from your chosen pursuit, but might you consider taking a moment to rest—or eat, even? I'd be happy to bring you a snack. Do you have any particular preferences? A favorite fruit, perhaps? Something you might enjoy?"

"Fruit . . . ?"

Hermes shrank, his eyes quivering, as he stared through Hythlodaeus. *Lost and searching . . .*

"I don't . . . I don't know."

"Then I fear your fatigue has reached an alarming level. Then again, I don't have any strong preferences myself, for it is the pleasure of good company from which I derive the most nourishment. If it would move the implacable Emet-Selch to chortle, I might just devour my own mask!"

The corner of the dispirited man's mouth twitched ever so slightly. *Progress!* Hythlodaeus pressed the attack, this time more directly.

"My friend, what moves you to devote yourself so wholly to your work? I should like to think there is no problem so impenetrable that one of your considerable talents would need to sacrifice his health to solve it."

His question was met with silence, as Hermes again withdrew into himself to search for an answer. *Adrift in a starless sea, grappling with a dilemma all his own. Alone.* Emerging at last, he whispered.

"We can but go on."

Hythlodaeus regarded him carefully. "May I ask what you mean?"

"I can't explain it, but . . . I know not what awaits, or what will become of us . . . yet we live. We are here and *alive*, and . . . and because of that, I know—I *feel* that we must . . . keep moving . . ."

Adrift in a starless sea, gasping for air as the currents threaten to pull him under. There is a truth here, but he does not see it. He senses its presence and flails desperately to understand even as the words tumble from his mouth.

As Emet-Selch was the keeper of the aetherial realm, Fandaniel was his counterpart for the physical. The affairs of the living were naturally of primary concern to him. *But are these mere philosophical musings, or something more . . . ?*

Hythlodaeus held his tongue while he pondered the curious words. With a start, Hermes realized his outpouring had elicited no response and mumbled a reflexive apology.

"Sorry, that was . . . Ahem. Your concern is much appreciated, Hythlodaeus. I think I shall heed your advice and retire to my quarters for some rest."

"A wise decision. Emet-Selch said the other day—and I quote—'If he's determined to keel over where he stands, he might at least carry a cushion.'"

Failing to fight back an embarrassed grimace, Hermes thanked him again and went on his way. Though he appeared to slow his steps to mitigate the risk of crashing into unexpected passersby,

Hythlodaeus noted that he nevertheless brushed against the walls several times as he stumbled out of sight. *May your nap be a long one.*

The hunt recommenced, Hythlodaeus walked on, drawing ever closer to the garden. Just to be certain, he adjusted his perspective once more. "Hah!" Azem's thread endured, dancing in the air before his eyes. His pace quickened as he strode into the garden.

Much like the larger spaces of Anagnorisis, the humble sanctuary was plainly the beneficiary of constant care and affection. While surrounded by corridors, it offered an unobstructed view of the sky, meaning a traveler eager to get underway could call upon a familiar to carry them heavensward in a trice . . .

I suppose I should not be surprised. Azem was gone. A second familiar thread of aether terminated at a loitering Emet-Selch, who was craning his neck and gazing into the distance. In the privacy of this moment, his oft-furrowed brow was relaxed, and oft-downturned lips threatened to curl into something disconcertingly genuine.

"I daresay your smile is never so sincere as when you see Azem off."

No sooner had the words been spoken than the dour curtain fell. *So precious and ephemeral, your unguarded expressions.*

"Save for that one exception, you are rarely to be seen without your customary scowl—unless there are fools to mock."

"I presume you did not seek me out solely to etch new lines upon my forehead."

Sure enough, the skin above Emet-Selch's eyes was forming impressive canyons of annoyance. Hythlodaeus glided to his side and attempted to retrace the path of his earlier gaze. A heartbeat before it vanished, he managed to make out the shape of Azem.

There was nothing left to see, yet he kept watch. "It's a compliment. I find your smile quite charming, and only wish that you would grace us with it more often."

"Now who's mocking who? But I will admit, I find these occasions . . . rousing. Invigorating, even. To be present as our friend embarks on another journey with no destination and say, 'Go forth and seek discovery,' or some such."

"Yes, yes. And . . . ?"

So formidable was Emet-Selch's glower that it could compel almighty gods to cower in shame. Hythlodaeus, however, was unperturbed, having consorted with the indomitable figure since childhood. *Two troublemaking brats born with aethersight.* It was their long-standing association that guaranteed Emet-Selch knew his playful jests were simply that—and that Hythlodaeus need only wait patiently for honesty to triumph over pride.

". . . *And* I take comfort in the knowledge that whatever tribulations they may face, they will overcome. That whatever the future may hold, it will be livelier for their part in it."

Hythlodaeus could not contain his laughter. *Our friend the force of nature!* "Well said, well said!" he sputtered before succumbing to amusement once more. Emet-Selch sighed in exasperation and muttered a few words of reproach, but they were as leaves in the wind, a musical rustling that warmed the cockles of his heart.

And now, in that boundless sky where our friend sought infinite possibilities, I see only death.

There were no lands untouched by the Final Days. Not even Amaurot, over which the heavens now burned.

"Hythlodaeus, *please.*"

Emet-Selch had found him—after some effort, judging from his breathless, disheveled state.

"You mustn't . . . With your wisdom and skill, surely you could do more for our people if you remained . . ."

"I was wise enough to recruit others who surpass me in every respect. Enough will survive me to ensure our work can continue."

It hadn't been a concern voiced on behalf of the Amaurotines. *Better to pretend otherwise, though.*

To forestall the Final Days, the will of the star would be given shape and form. An offering of life unprecedented in scale would be required. The Convocation themselves had called for willing participants, and so Emet-Selch was in no position to deny any the right to volunteer. He could but dance around the unspeakable request and clench his fists in frustration when refused.

Hythlodaeus was not a fighter. It was the pragmatic choice to sacrifice himself. To be reduced to aether and serve as fuel for the great summoning—Hythlodaeus did not fear this. He understood death, and the terror which had come to grip many when it drew near, but that understanding only emboldened him to embrace it. Once, he would have died to perpetuate the cycle. Now he would die to preserve a myriad lives that might yet be saved.

Even so, it pained him deeply to see Emet-Selch reduced to such a state. Though he knew full well he was not the sole cause of his distress.

"Azem has not forsaken us. They follow their heart, as they ever have, and seek to defy this fate in their own way."

"Don't you think I know that?! There is no *time*, Hythlodaeus! We need solutions *now*. We have a *duty* to this star!"

The words were as a guttural howl, so terrible was his fury. *He who held out hope for Azem's return longer than any. He whose anger and frustration and pain I see writ plain in his pleading eyes. He who has ever been constant and true and who I am proud to call my dearest friend.*

"You are right, Emet-Selch. You are right, and that is why I must place my faith in the Convocation's plan."

The hour of Zodiark's summoning was at hand.

He speaks again, but there is nothing left to say.
I raise my hand in apology and farewell, and I leave him behind.
I do not turn to look. I remember a garden, and a sky, and a man, and it is enough.
It is enough.

It ends.
It ends . . . and yet it goes on . . .

How capricious fate—and tenacious Venat—to see two souls, at the edge of the universe, called to the stage once more. Thus did Hythlodaeus and Emet-Selch find themselves in the presence of the inheritor of Azem's legacy. Thus did mankind issue its answer to the question borne on the wings of oblivion.

And thus did we wield the power to create.

Duty at last fulfilled, Emet-Selch took a bow, departing not with hackneyed platitudes but a challenge to the traveler to go forth and seek discovery, adding with that most precious and ephemeral of expressions, "*I* certainly did."

I remember a garden, and a sky, and a man.

The excitement and expectation in his eyes. The pride in his breast. The unwavering faith in his heart. The joy on his lips as he wished Azem well on their journey.

Thus ends the encore. The players exit to take their place among the dead, and the living board their marble ship that they may be ferried back to where they belong. *We surrender to the gentle currents that call us home.*

Long awaited, yet sudden and surprising still.
From shimmering waters beyond the beyond, the multitude raise their voices in song.
Welcome, welcome—in unison, in celebration. The day is won.
It ends and it goes on.

Beside me, his eyes are closed, his ears bent to the distant gaiety. In the privacy of this moment, he smiles, for all that we had and all that they will.

I do not know the shape of his pain, nor how it shaped him into the man he became. But I know that when man first tasted loneliness and fear, bitterness and despair, he shared in their torment.

And now, as we are called to sleep, he beams. And I know—I know it is because of you.

Thank you.

He lifts his head to gaze into the waters.

He gifts me a final grin and a kind word, and he closes his eyes.

O star, two weary travelers are returning
We are thee, and thou art us
Flesh and soul and memory to unravel and entwine
with thy flow
To weave anew and cast upon the shore
One day

I imagine that day, and my pulse quickens.

As does yours, does it not, Hades?

Thus does life return to life.

And beneath dreaming eyelids, our final fantasy goes on.

Thus did the curtain fall, and all lay amidst deepest dream.

We are already dead—already free. We require neither patronage nor approval. If our gift was to your satisfaction, then we wish you the soundest of slumbers.

After all, it is but a brief respite. Ere long you will return to the stage, with new roles to assume, new costumes to don, and new travelers to engage. Yet cast your gaze to the floorboards at your feet, and you shall see old marks. Familiar or no, you left them yourself in a life since passed.

Such is the way of it in the world of men. No matter how often we take to the stage, we know not the plays in which we perform. Plays whose endings are dictated not by notions of righteousness, but by the will of the determined—the "wicked" and "inconsequential" among them. As we wait in the wings, we can but pin our hopes upon those who tread the boards.

Thus does our time come to an end. These rambling words, too, shall sink into the depths and give way to silence. Full honored am I to have been afforded this, your final moment. If fate is kind, somewhere beyond the shimmering waters, mayhap after a few score thousand turns of the star, we shall meet again—as friends old, in lives new.

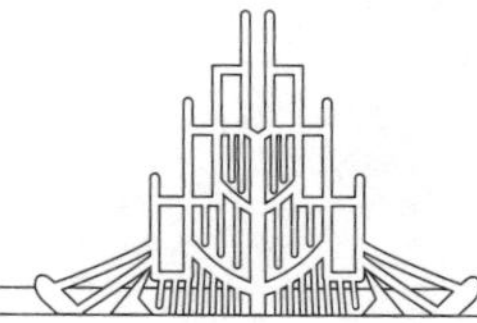